Black Bat Mystery

AIRSHIP 27 PRODUCTIONS

AN AIRSHIP 27 PRODUCTION

Black Bat Mystery-Volume 3

None So Blind © 2015 Greg Hatcher
Death on the Rails © 2015 Gene Moyers
The Magnificent Anderson © 2015 Gordon Dymowski
The Dark Magician © 2015 Erik Franklin

Published by Airship 27 Productions
www.airship27.com
www.airship27hangar.com

Interior illustrations © 2015 Marco Santiago
Cover illustration © 2015 Graham Hill

Editor: Ron Fortier
Associate Editor: Fred Adams
Production and design by Rob Davis
Promotions Manager: Michael Vance

ISBN-13: 978-0692562208 (Airship 27)
ISBN-10: 0692562206

Printed in the United States of America

10 9 8 7 6 5 4 3 2 1

CONTENTS
VOLUME 3

NONE SO BLIND

A Tale of the Black Bat's Early Days

by
Greg Hatcher

"The nerve of that son of a bitch," muttered Police Commissioner Jerome Warner. "Showing his face here at the Deputy Mayor's garden party of all places."

Tony Quinn knew perfectly well to whom the commissioner was referring. From behind his dark glasses, he had noted Sal Costello's arrival from the moment he appeared on the lawn. The mob kingpin appeared completely at ease, despite his impending arraignment.

But the world had to believe that Quinn was blind. So he carefully avoided looking in Costello's direction as he inquired mildly, "Which son of a bitch is that, Commissioner?"

"Costello." Warner shook his head. "Thirty-six hours to go. After that he's going inside no matter how many fast-talking lawyers he has on his payroll."

"No trouble with the witness, then?"

"Safely under wraps," Warner said. "Sorry, Tony, that's all I can tell you. You understand."

"Of course I do. I was a district attorney myself not too long ago, you know."

"You could be again," Warner offered. "A man as gifted as you are should be back in the game. You have one of the best heads for detective work I've ever seen, and blind people manage very well in all sorts of professions. After all, justice herself is said to be blind. You've come so far already."

Quinn's mouth curled up in a thin smile. "You have no idea."

It had been a little less than a year since the accident...*no,* Quinn amended, *the attack, it was no accident...*when a gangster had splashed Quinn's face with acid, blinding him. That had set off the chain of circumstances that had led to the creation of Tony Quinn's new identity.

After months of learning to function as a blind man, honing his other senses to extraordinary keenness, an experimental operation had restored his sight. More than restored it; upon recovering, Tony Quinn discovered that not only was he able to see, but his vision now reached well into the infrared wavelengths. Quinn could see in the dark, he could sense heat sources from behind solid walls dozens of feet away, and the months of blindness had also given him almost preternatural hearing. He was a creature of the night now, preferring to avoid daylight. And he had found a new way to use his gifts in the cause of justice as the masked vigilante, the Black Bat.

Commissioner Warner knew none of this, though sometimes Quinn thought his friend suspected. He felt a little guilty at Warner's obvious pleasure over Quinn's acceptance of the invitation to this Saturday afternoon gathering. Quinn had rarely socialized even before the acid and had withdrawn almost completely from the Manhattan party circuit afterwards. The commissioner probably thought that bringing Quinn to this lawn party was part of helping his old friend readjust to a normal life.

The fact was that Quinn had only accepted the invitation because he was worried about the commissioner and wanted to be on hand. His other operatives Silk Kirby and Butch O'Leary were nearby as well, unbeknownst to the guests, patrolling the edges of the property. The Black Bat had heard the word on the street; Sal Costello wasn't going down without a fight, witness or no witness. Costello owned at least half the judges and most of the other city officials in town. Warner was one of the few who hadn't been bought. And that made him a target.

That was why Tony Quinn was making this rare daylight appearance. Truthfully, Quinn's hypersensitive eyes were having a little difficulty with the afternoon August sunshine, but the dark glasses alleviated most of it. Anyway, it helped with his cover. For the Black Bat to function without interference, Tony Quinn must continue to be a harmless blind man, an object of pity and sympathy.

Costello was shaking hands with the Deputy Mayor now, and Quinn could see the Deputy Mayor looked uncomfortable. Costello leaned forward, his manner growing intense. Quinn strained his ears, but even the Black Bat's legendary hearing could not pick up what the men were saying over the clink of glasses and the conversation of the other guests. Quinn didn't think that the mobster and the politician were in collusion, but he knew the Deputy Mayor to be a man who hedged his bets; the politician wouldn't take a chance on getting on the wrong side of Costello until it was certain Costello was going to trial.

"Freshen your drink, sir?" It was one of the lovely young women who were roaming the lawn with a drink tray.

"No, thank you, miss." *The man doesn't skimp, I'll give him that,* Quinn reflected. *Hope this isn't being billed to the taxpayers.*

The blonde caterer turned to the commissioner, but he ignored her, so she bobbed her head and moved on. Warner was still fuming. "Look at Brewster. That glad-handing hypocrite," he muttered. "Shaking hands with that mob killer just like he would any other big-money supporter. I swear, Tony…"

"I can't really 'look' at much these days, Commissioner."

Suddenly Warner realized what he'd said. "Oh, hell. I'm sorry, Tony. I didn't mean…it's just a figure of speech. I keep forgetting. This must be hard for you."

Quinn smiled. "Spending my afternoon at Brewster's lawn-party barbecue sipping a cold drink isn't hard, even for a blind man. Forget it, Commissioner. You don't need to walk on eggshells. It's all part of the rehabilitative experience."

"Well, then," Warner said, "why not come back to work at the D.A.'s office? I can talk to Robbins. I know they can use you."

"It's very kind of you, really, but…" Quinn's voice trailed off. Something odd was happening. The sky had darkened. But his senses told him that despite the gathering clouds, the heat had increased. Quinn's enhanced eyesight could pick up a shimmer of…*something* coming from several of the other partygoers. *I have no idea what that is,* he realized. *Are some of the guests… glowing? Can anyone else even see this?*

One of the city councilmen, Alderson, suddenly tugged at his collar. "Hard to breathe," he wheezed. "So hot…"

Then he screamed.

There was a sharp crack of thunder and a bright flash from the sky. Councilman Alderson burst into flame. He barely got out one hoarse cough before his body collapsed into a smoldering heap of ash and bone. Another flash and one of the waitresses near the Deputy Mayor was instantly charred into a blackened skeleton, with its smoking claw of a right hand still holding the warped remnant of a drinks tray.

Now screams were coming from every direction. "It's lightning!" roared Warner. "Everyone inside! Now!"

There were three more thunderflashes and each one left a smoking corpse behind it. The guests broke and ran for the house.

It can't be lightning. No lightning I've ever heard of, anyway. This is targeted. Quinn let himself be helped along, but he gritted his teeth in frustration. He had been so worried about an attack on the commissioner, but not even the Black Bat could have anticipated something like this. Sal Costello had a lot of power but he couldn't summon lightning from the skies to do his bidding.

So who *could* do such a thing?

Tony Quinn had no idea. But he would find out.

"Seven dead," Tony Quinn said. "And we have no idea why."

He looked up at his two aides, Silk Kirby and Butch O'Leary. The three men were seated around the counter in the center of Quinn's hidden laboratory, a white-tiled room secreted behind the shelves of the law library in Quinn's study.

Silk was a slender, rakish-looking man with a sharp expression and a taste for expensive clothing, one of the few traits he retained from his days as a professional grifter. Butch was a broad-shouldered, beefy man, as one would expect a former professional boxer to be. Both men were fiercely loyal to Quinn and had proven invaluable to Quinn's work as the Black Bat.

"Uh... you *sure* it wasn't just a freak lightning storm, boss? I mean... Silk and me had the place covered. We didn't see anyone around. I don't see how it coulda been anything else." Butch looked a little embarrassed to be expressing such doubts to his employer, but he went on nevertheless. "Isn't the important thing making sure Costello goes away?"

Quinn nodded. "You're not wrong, Butch," he admitted. "But I can't shake the feeling that this is somehow linked to the Costello case. The timing of it bothers me. Costello shouldn't have even been there. For him to show up at a gathering like yesterday's...he had an agenda. I know it. I could see Costello talking to Deputy Mayor Brewster just before it happened, it was as if Costello was warning him."

"Warning him about the lightning storm?" Butch looked confused.

"No. I think he was warning him, or threatening him, but... it wasn't a storm. It was... honestly, I don't know what it was. I could see a sort of shimmer over the victims before they caught fire." Quinn winced at the memory. He went on, "And there was...I don't know, it was a flash from the clouds like lightning, true enough, but it didn't look random, or jagged. It wasn't an electrical discharge, I know that much." He sighed. "The trouble is, I can't tell anyone about these facts because there's no way blind Tony Quinn could know any of that. Even if that wasn't a consideration I don't know what good it would do. I've been over it and over it. I don't think anyone else at the party could even see the flash clearly. It may have been just me." Quinn raised a hand and rubbed at the old acid scarring around his eyes. "The difficulty with these new eyes is that I'm still figuring out which visual capabilities are uniquely mine. There's a certain amount of trial and error involved. But I'm certain that what happened out on the lawn yesterday was somehow man-made."

"But what kind of weapon can do that?" Silk asked. "You're talking like it was some kind of mad scientist's death ray, or something. This is the real world, here."

A wall slid open and Carol Baldwin entered. Carol was the only other person besides Butch and Silk that knew Tony Quinn was the Black Bat. In fact, it was her father's sacrifice of his own eyes that had made it possible for Quinn to see again. He owed her everything. As always when he saw Carol, this history flickered across Quinn's mind, coupled with the idle wish that their lives could someday be different. That there could be more between them than mere comradeship in their common war. He wondered if Carol ever felt the same.

At the moment, her feelings were obvious. Beneath the sweep of her blonde curls, Carol's pixie face was screwed into a scowl. "Have you seen this morning's paper? This is disgusting. I don't know how they can print this stuff." She slapped a folded newspaper on to the countertop.

The headline read, LIGHTNING TRAGEDY COULD HAVE BEEN PREVENTED, SAYS PSYCHIC. Below that was a grainy photo of a bearded man in a turban, with a stunning brunette hanging on his left arm.

"It's that Doctor Durga," Carol said. "You know, the fellow that claims to have magic powers. He's been all over the society pages the last few weeks. And now he's trying to get personal publicity off this tragedy!"

Silk snorted. "That's what guys like him *do*, kiddo. Take it from me, the spiritualist grift is the easiest action there is. People will trample each other to hand you money. All you need is cheesecloth, some white paint and a flashlight, most of the time. And a guy who's got the right kind of voice. It's the vocal work that sells it." He noticed the others looking at him and harrumphed. "Not that I would ever do that," he added. "Weepy old ladies who'd lost their sons in the War, parents with missing kids; those are the ones that go for the séance thing… I couldn't do it. Even when I was in the game, I had *standards*."

"Well, this Doctor Durga doesn't," Carol said. "He's saying there was a way to stop what happened yesterday."

"And all we gotta do is pay him," Silk finished. "Sure. Let me give you the rest of it. For a hefty chunk of dough, he offers to do some kinda anti-rain dance or something and then presto, everyone's lightning-proof."

While the others had been talking, Quinn had been reading the newspaper article. "No money, Silk," he said. "It says here that he's offered his services for free to the city. He hopes to cleanse the 'negative energy' that currently surrounds City Hall."

Butch blinked. "Negative what?"

"That's just a new name for the curse removal scam," Silk said. "The way they used to work it was you'd arrange a bunch of accidents to happen to the mark, and then your roper tells him that all the bad luck goes away if you get the curse removed. Take the mark to a séance or some other hooey, say some words, bump some chairs around and flash a couple of weird lights, and collect your fee. Still goes pretty good, even today when folks know about movie projectors and stuff like that. The best ones don't have to charge. They just let the true believers make an offer. If the money's a gift to the swami guy, it's even legal."

Quinn put the paper down. "There are other gifts than money," he said. "What if our mysterious Doctor Durga is somehow…"

The telephone rang. Silk picked up the receiver. "Tony Quinn's residence." He listened a moment, then handed it to Quinn. "Warner," he said.

Quinn took the phone. "Yes, Commissioner?"

The commissioner's voice was strained. "Tony, I know yesterday's outing ended badly, and I wouldn't blame you for saying no, but I'd appreciate it very much if you would join me down here later today. Have you heard of this Doctor Durga?"

"Yes, actually, we were just talking about him." Quinn smiled at the others. "Carol saw something in the papers."

"Well, he just left my office," Warner said. "It's insane. He just spent forty minutes telling me that Costello was innocent and it was putting our moral energies out of balance, or some damn thing."

"And you didn't just throw him out of your office? He sounds like a crank."

Warner's voice was vibrating with frustration. "I couldn't. He had the Deputy Mayor with him. And Brewster is apparently a believer. The two of them are scheduled to give a press conference at City Hall in an hour. Tony, I was hoping…"

"We'll be there," Quinn said. He hung up, then turned crisply to his aides. "Butch, bring the car around, you're with me. Carol, Silk, I need you to dig up anything you can on this Doctor Durga. Maybe some of your society friends can tell you something, Carol. You might nose around some of your old contacts, Silk. Maybe our turbaned friend has worked this scam in other cities. And be careful," Quinn added. "This Durga may just be an opportunist trying to capitalize on a tragedy, but if he's actually responsible for what happened yesterday, he's a ruthless killer."

Silk nodded as the others rose to go. He pulled the paper towards him and glanced at the picture. Then he stiffened.

Carol and Butch were already out, but Quinn saw the reaction and paused. "Recognize him?"

"Not him," Silk replied after a moment. "Her."

Quinn would have pressed it, but something in the other man's face stopped him. "All right, Silk," he said finally. "Let us know what you find out."

Silk nodded, hardly listening. He kept staring at the newspaper photo.

Quinn opened his mouth to say something else, thought better of it, and left.

A crowd had already gathered at the stairs in front of the entrance to City Hall, and a police cordon was working to keep the area clear around the podium at the head of the steps. Leaving Butch to stay with the car, Quinn put on his dark glasses and, tapping his white cane, walked slowly towards where Commissioner Warner was standing with a group of other officers.

Warner saw him approaching and said loudly, "Over here, Tony, follow my voice. Evans, go give him a hand." One of the younger officers hastened over to Quinn. Hiding a smile at these charades, Quinn let himself be helped to where the other policemen were standing.

Lieutenant McGrath of Homicide was there as well. He scowled at Quinn. "It figures. Lately it seems like every time something hinky happens in this town, it turns out you're around somewhere," he said. "You or your friend in the cape."

"The commissioner called *me*," Quinn replied, amiably. "Really, McGrath, do you check under your bed for the Black Bat before turning in at night? It makes about as much sense as these constant insinuations about me. It's becoming an obsession."

"Never mind the Bat," Commissioner Warner put in. "I did call him, McGrath. I want Tony to hear this. I'm thinking we might need some kind of… legal help," he finished after an awkward pause.

"Legal help?" Behind his dark glasses, Quinn blinked in surprise.

Warner glanced around, then pulled Quinn to one side. "This is not for publication," he muttered. "But I think Brewster's lost his mind. It's as though he's completely in thrall to this Durga. And the things that turbaned lunatic was trying to tell me this afternoon…"

Warner was cut off by a commotion at the head of the steps. "Never mind, they're coming out," he said. "But just listen to them, Tony. Tell me if there are any legal grounds for us to put a stop to... whatever this is going to be."

"Let's wait and see what they have to say before we panic," Quinn said.

Deputy Mayor Brewster took the podium. The gathering of press and onlookers shifted uncomfortably where they stood. Despite the heat of the afternoon sun, Quinn felt a sudden chill at the base of his spine.

"Thank you all for coming," Brewster said. "I have several items and I'd appreciate it if you all could hold your questions until the end." He took a breath. "First of all, I would like to extend my condolences to the families of those that we lost in yesterday's tragedy. Nature's wrath is a terrible thing, and too often we city dwellers forget how terrible it can be. There is…" Suddenly Brewster winced. Trained politician that he was, he cleared his throat and tried to recover. "There is…."

At that same instant, Tony Quinn felt pain such as he never had felt before. It started at the base of his spine and rocketed up his backbone, exploding out between his ears in a searing red wave. He grasped his cane to steady himself, but it slid out of his nerveless hands as he fell to his knees.

"Tony!" Warner was instantly at his side. "Are you all right?"

Quinn couldn't speak; he could barely think. In that moment, there was only the pain. Around him, others in the crowd were wincing, clearly affected by something, but there didn't seem to be anyone hit as badly as Quinn. He struggled to stand.

And then came the dogs.

From every direction, pouring out of alleys, tearing down the sidewalks, packs of snarling, barking dogs. Some were trailing leashes that they had clearly yanked from an owner's hand. All shapes and sizes. It was as though every canine in Manhattan, pets, strays, even a couple of police dogs, was converging on the podium atop the City Hall steps.

The barking and growling, combined with the screams of the crowd, created a hellish cacophony … a wall of sound that was making it even more difficult for Tony Quinn to get himself under control. Through the haze of agony that was paralyzing him, he thought he heard Warner ordering his officers to fire on the savage dog pack converging on the crowd.

There was a shout. *"Hold! No farther!"*

The pain abated and Quinn slowly got to his feet. A man in a white business suit stood next to the podium, holding out both hands, palms out. He was tall, with a thin face and high cheekbones, and a black goatee trimmed to a sharp point. Atop his head was a white turban with a red stone in the center. *Doctor Durga,* Quinn realized. Had to be.

"I banish you all!" Doctor Durga roared. "Begone from this place!"

And, incredibly, the dogs all obeyed him. As Durga spoke, Quinn thought he could feel something, a sort of prickly cold feeling that swept over him, but it was gone in an instant. The dogs fled.

He realized that Warner was anxiously gripping his shoulder, shaking him. "Tony! Are you all right? What the hell was that?"

Quinn looked up at Durga, still standing at the podium next to Brewster. The turbaned mystic was speaking softly to the deputy mayor, and got a brief nod in return.

Quinn shook his head slowly. "I don't know, Commissioner. Maybe it really *is* magic."

The scene was slowly recovering from the chaos of a few moments before. One of the uniformed officers was at the podium, telling everyone that the press conference would be rescheduled and asking the crowd to disperse. Another came trotting up to where Warner and Quinn were standing. "Sirs," the young officer said. "Deputy Mayor Brewster is asking you to join him and Doctor Durga in his office." He indicated Warner and McGrath.

"Come on, Tony," Warner said. "Sit in on this meeting. I'd like your input."

And I'd like a closer look at this Doctor Durga, Quinn thought. Aloud he said, "Happy to be of service," and let the helpful young patrolman guide him up the stone steps to City Hall.

Deputy Mayor Arnold Brewster was clearly upset…. *Even a blind man can see it,* Tony Quinn thought, amused at his private joke. The politician was seated behind his mahogany desk, with Doctor Durga, McGrath, and Warner seated in chairs facing him. Quinn was hanging back, perched on the cushioned armrest of a leather couch that was against the back wall.

Durga was speaking, his voice clipped and urgent. "I would think the truth of what I am saying would be readily apparent after the events of an hour ago," he said. "I certainly did not offer my services just to be harangued and ridiculed by this man." He nodded at Lieutenant McGrath, who was glaring at the self-styled magician.

"Shut up, swami." McGrath's voice was a graveled rumble of contempt. "Commish, you seriously can't think of turning loose of our witness because Doctor Doohickey here shows up with his magic dog whistle? That's crazy."

Doctor Durga rose to his feet. "The fact that you think I somehow caused these paranormal events is offensive. I *stopped* this one. I could have stopped yesterday's had I been there. I am trying to *help* you." He sighed. "Yet such is always the way of the unbelievers. Only when it is too late do you consider explanations that lie outside of your experience. Deputy Brewster, you know where to reach me." He turned to go, but Quinn's voice stopped him.

"Doctor Durga, please wait." Then, addressing the others, Quinn added, "Let's hear him out. Sir, you spoke of… unconventional explanations, but we have yet to actually hear yours. Can you spell it out for us? What do you think is happening?" Quinn knew from his years of courtroom experience that very often so-called experts could hang themselves, given enough rope. Yet there was nothing overtly sinister about the man in the turban, Tony Quinn had to admit to himself. Doctor Durga seemed sincere in his concern. *Nutty, but sincere.*

Durga seemed to notice Quinn for the first time. He spoke only to him, ignoring the others. "You… you are different than the others. You perceive more."

Quinn shrugged. "I'm open-minded. That's all."

"No, it's more than that," Durga said. "You somehow… you see more than a normally-sighted man would. Despite your handicap you are the least blind person in this room. How is that possible?"

That was way too close to home for Quinn. He coughed uncomfortably and shrugged again. He remembered another courtroom tactic: *when you're put on the defensive, turn the tables. Attack.* "I asked you a direct question, Doctor Durga. What is your explanation for these events? All I 'perceive' is a runaround. What do you want us to do?"

"To set right a grave injustice." Durga's voice was firm. "You are planning to bring a series of indictments against a man, Salvatore Costello. These charges are false. The injustice about to be committed is upsetting the natural balance. I know that the longer you pursue your vendetta against an innocent man, the more unnatural events will follow."

"And here we go again!" Warner had been holding back but his exclamation of contempt was almost inadvertent. "This man is clearly working for Costello. Somehow he… he…"

"Somehow I *what*, Commissioner?" Now it was Durga's voice that

"Shut up, swami!"

held contempt. "Called the lightning from the heavens? Summoned the beasts to do my bidding? What device or trickery could accomplish this? I certainly do not carry any such miraculous object. Have your men search me. Right here in this office."

"Do it, Commish." This was McGrath. "Have the swami stand for a frisk. He's bluffing, but I'm not. Hell, I'll do it myself." He stood up. "Arms out, Mandrake."

"No, don't." Tony Quinn had been watching Durga very closely from behind his dark glasses, all his enhanced senses focused on the turbaned man in white. Now he spoke up. "I agree with the Doctor. He's not responsible." He turned to face the self-proclaimed mystic, careful to keep his eye-line level while he turned, as a blind man would. "But I fail to see how the police and the district attorney could be wrong about Sal Costello. We have a witness."

"Produce him," Doctor Durga said. "He is lying. I will prove it."

"Of course," McGrath snorted, disgusted. "Produce him. That's just what Costello wants, after us playing cat-and-mouse for the last month trying to keep him safe in hiding."

The deputy mayor leaned forward. He addressed Warner directly. "Jerome… how sure are you of your witness? Is there a chance that the Doctor is right? Could we have made a terrible mistake?"

"I'm sure." Warner's voice was tight. "Monday morning an eyewitness will swear in open court that Salvatore Costello's guilty of murder, racketeering, extortion, and blackmail. Nature or the bogeyman or whatever will just have to get over it."

"There is no help for those who refuse to accept it," Doctor Durga said, his voice sorrowful and pitying. He rose to go and this time no one stopped him. The room fell silent for a moment.

Finally, Quinn cleared his throat. "Commissioner? Could I have one of your men take me to my car? This has all left me a bit fatigued."

And *Tony Quinn's done all he can,* he thought. *Now it's the Black Bat's turn.*

Silk Kirby had a gift for getting into places where the rules said he shouldn't be allowed to go. It was a knack he had used many times during his career as a confidence man, and it served him just as well in his current role as an aide to the Black Bat.

Right now he was putting it to use infiltrating Doctor Durga's luxury apartment building on Sutton Place. He'd already done some discreet surveillance of the entrance from across the street; Silk had circled the building and decided his best bet was the main entrance in front. There was a doorman, and it looked like he was screening visitors, but Silk had ways of getting around that. He riffled through the selection of business cards he carried in his wallet and chose one that read:

DOCTOR G. LUDWEG KIRBY, M.D., PH. D.
UNITED STATES PUBLIC HEALTH SERVICES
PRIMARY INVESTIGATOR

On each side of this impressive-looking title was emblazoned a white star in a blue circle. *Official* and *patriotic,* Silk thought. *That should do it.*

Then Silk took a deep breath, exhaled, and shifted his posture, straightening himself into an almost military bearing. Arranging his face into the expression of a man on Important Business, Not To Be Trifled With, he set off across the street towards the doorman.

The doorman looked up as he approached; opening his mouth to say something, but Silk cut him off. "Dr. Kirby," he said, handing the doorman the business card. "Here for the inspection." He glanced around. "What happened to the corpsmen?"

"Sir?" The doorman looked at the card, then up at Silk, nonplussed. "I'm afraid I don't…"

"Toxic mold," Silk said. "Building down the street has three cases in the hospital already. Federal law says we have to test every residential building on the block. Should be a couple of medical corpsmen helping out with the sampling, they were supposed to meet me here." He shrugged. "Probably traffic. Oh well, they'll be along. What's your name, young fellow?"

"Uh…Jerry. But you can't…I wasn't told of…"

"Of course not," snapped Silk. "We always do surprise inspections. Have to, by law. Can't have any attempts to fox the medical staff. You think your landlord wants to deal with a mold scare? If we find toxins on the property it could cost him thousands of dollars in safety upgrades. You know him better than I do, but I'll wager he hates to part with a dollar. When was the last time *you* had a raise?"

"Well, Buckner's an old skinflint, for sure," the doorman admitted. "But still…"

Silk waved him to silence. "Hold on, there," he said, and leaned forward. "Open a little wider. Hmmm. Funny color there on the roof of your mouth. Lean back a little there, young man." The doorman obediently leaned back, his mouth yawning wide. Silk made a show of inspecting the doorman's mouth. "Hmmp. Ah. Ah-hah. That's enough. Jerry, have you been feeling achy in your joints? Dry around the eyes? Coughing a little more than usual?"

"Er..." The doorman was looking a little frightened now. "What are you saying?"

"Not saying anything specific...*yet.*" Silk put a point on it, which made the doorman even more nervous. "Have you got a washroom here? I mean for yourself."

"Well, yes, there's a little one for the staff under the hall stairs. But..."

"Jerry, this is important." Silk tapped the doorman on the chest with a forefinger. "You need to go into that washroom and *scrub*. Face, hands... really, you should take your shirt off and scrub your entire upper body. If there's any cleaning solution, something with alcohol, it probably would help to rub that on your hands afterward."

"Oh my God. Are you saying..."

"I'm saying it's the easiest way to avoid a week of tests for mycotoxin poisoning. Step on it, now, Jerry. I can mind the door here for you while I wait for the rest of my team." Silk smiled. "You shouldn't be more than five or ten minutes. And for God's sake, when you get back out here, be careful who you shake hands with. A man in your profession ought to invest in a pair of gloves." Silk looked at his watch. "Quickly now, Jerry. If you're not scrubbed up by the time my colleagues get here they might overrule me and then it's the hospital for sure."

"Yes sir!" The doorman disappeared down the hall. Silk counted ten, then stepped into the building and, after a quick glance at the glass-fronted building directory, headed for the elevator, noting with pleasure that it was one of the new self-service models. He didn't think Dr. G. Ludweg Kirby could have persuaded both the doorman *and* an elevator operator to step away for an alcohol scrub at the same time, even for just five minutes.

Doctor Durga's suite was on the seventh floor, the top. A broad-shouldered man dressed in an ill-fitting business suit stood by the door. He looked up sharply as Silk exited the elevator. "No visitors without an appointment, bud."

"Unclench yourself, big fella," Silk said cheerfully. He was back to his own rakish self, G. Ludweg having served his purpose. "I'm not here for the swami. I have a date with the lady of the house."

The big man looked skeptical.

"G'wan," Silk said. "Tell her that Silk Kirby's out front. She'll see me." When the big man hesitated, Silk added, "Come on, what can it hurt to ask? Think of the fun you'll have kicking me down the stairs if I'm wrong. And don't you get bored just standing there? It's a chance to stretch your legs."

After a moment, the big man nodded. Silk suspected it had been the boredom argument that had swung it. *You don't have to be a fake swami to do a cold reading,* he thought, a trifle smugly.

A few seconds later, the big man was back. "C'mon in. She'll see you." His manner had marginally thawed, now that Silk had been approved.

Silk nodded and smiled, another old grifter's reflex; *cultivate allies, always be nice to the help,* and stepped into the foyer. It was expensively appointed, with several hanging Oriental tapestries draped over deep-brown mahogany paneling.

"Hello there, Norrie. I thought I must be dreaming." It was a stunningly beautiful olive-skinned woman dressed in a raw-silk kimono, a print with golden intertwining dragons against a scarlet background. He hair was jet-black, done up in a French twist. "I half-expected Idaho Bob to be with you."

"You know better than that, princess. He's still got at least three years on his sentence." Silk's voice hardened. "Where you put him. They'd have got me too if I hadn't run."

"Norrie, don't." The woman looked pained. "You know better than that. Bob would have killed both of us. He was crazy."

"He was." Silk sighed. "I wasn't sorry to see him go down for ten-to-fifteen, I admit it. But why didn't you wait for me? You *disappeared,* Vangie. Dropped off the face of the earth." He waved a hand at the Oriental tapestries. "And now this mysterious queen-of-the-orient crap. How'd you ever get hooked up with this Durga guy in the first place? 'Vandyha Naffir'? Seriously? Are you kidding me? You're from Teaneck for Christ's sake."

"It's not…" Vangie looked sad. "Don't be like that, Norrie." She came closer, and Silk allowed her to enfold him in her arms. She laid her head on his chest. Her hair smelled of violets. She shuddered with tension for a moment and then melted into Silk's arms.

The sense memory of it, of how it had once been between them, was overpowering. He wanted to kiss her hard. But he didn't. "What are you into, Vangie?" Silk asked softly. "What's Durga's game? What's the grift here?"

She just shook her head, still against his chest.

"I can help you, baby." Silk took her by the shoulders and looked searchingly into her eyes. "I have a friend who's taken down a lot bigger guys than your pal in the turban. But you gotta give me something. Did he burn those people yesterday? How is he doing it? Is it a weapon?"

Now it was Vangie's turn to pull back. "And what the hell do you care, Norrie? What's in it for you? I know the legendary Silk Kirby doesn't do anything that isn't profitable. You looking to cut yourself in? Is that it?" She shook her head and let out a small, choking sob. "I hate all you men. All you ever want is…"

"That's not fair, Vangie. I never gave you any cause for that kind of talk, and anyway, it's not like that any more." Silk heard the growing desperation in his voice and cursed himself for a weakling. *Damn the woman.* Two seconds with her in his arms and he was forgetting the whole point of getting up to the apartment in the first place. "I…it's complicated. I can't get into it all right now. I help people, that's all you need to know. I'm tryin' to help you. Really. You just have to trust me."

"I can't…" She looked up at him, her eyes bright with tears. "He's crazy, Norrie. Crazier than Bob. Crazier than anyone. This is… it's big, it's extortion and murder and I'm so scared. I don't know how to get out. I only know pieces of it. But I know he burned those people up yesterday. It's something to do with the mayor's office, and Sal Costello."

There was a noise from the door. Vangie stiffened, her eyes going wide. "Oh, God. He's here."

Silk turned to see Doctor Durga enter, flanked by the big guy from the hallway. "And who is this?" Durga's voice was deep, faintly tinged with suspicion. *He's got the voice for it,* anyway, Silk thought sourly. *That must knock 'em flat at the séances.*

"He is a news writer, for one of the Western papers," Vangie said. Silk had to suppress the urge to whistle appreciatively at the vocal change. Vangie's "Vandyha" voice was even more convincing than Durga's. No wonder the act had worked all over Manhattan high society. "He bluffed his way in. I was just telling him to leave."

Silk looked at Durga, then back to Vangie. Her eyes pleaded with him: *Don't blow this for me. Just go with it.* He nodded. "Heard about your press conference today," he said, breezily. "Thought I'd come see what was up. Get a jump on the other guys."

Doctor Durga nodded slowly. "No interviews," he said. "My art is a private thing. I will have another press conference tomorrow morning. That will be soon enough for you. Brick, escort the gentleman out."

The gorilla nodded and clamped a hand the size of a canned ham on Silk's shoulder. "Let's go."

Brick? That's his name? Really? Silk thought, but all he said was, "Hey, easy there, I'm going. I got a job to do too, you know, we're all friends here. Take it easy." Over his shoulder he added, hoping Vangie would get it, "I'll see you later, then. Like we talked about."

Doctor Durga just grunted, but Vangie gave him an imperceptible nod. That would have to do, Silk decided. He let himself be pushed out into the hall and across to the elevator. When the elevator door opened, Silk stepped in, and Brick nodded, satisfied. He stepped back and the cage doors slid closed, leaving Silk alone. *Now what?*

Silk knew he had to take it to Quinn. *I shouldn't have held out on him,* he reflected. *But I hate telling him about stuff like that, like what we were into back when we were running with Idaho Bob. I'm not that guy any more.*

His thoughts boiling, Silk stepped out onto the street, almost bumping into Jerry the doorman, whose face was pink and freshly scrubbed. "Hey, sorry about that, wrong address," Silk said brusquely. "My mistake. Turns out it's the next block. Good hygiene is never wrong, though," he added, and gave Jerry a clap on the shoulder. Then, before the beleaguered doorman could respond, Silk was walking briskly down the sidewalk. *Got to find a pay phone and call the boss. He should be back by now.*

"Kirby." A voice came from the alley. "Hold it."

Silk turned to see a man standing in the alley with a gun aimed casually at his midsection. "Hey there, Norrie," he said. "Sal Costello sends his regards. Back here nice and slow, now, and don't even think about yelling or running."

Professional, Silk realized. Knew better than to get close enough for Silk to make a grab for the gun, but still close enough that there was no way for Silk to run.

So, since he had no choice, Silk went. Nice and slow.

Night had fallen at last, and Tony Quinn was glad of it.

He was the Black Bat now. This was when he felt most fully himself; moving along the rooftops through darkness that was, for him, as clear as noonday. His clothing was matte black, as was the hood that masked his acid-scarred features. It covered his entire head, but for the eyes. Twin gunbelts crossed his chest, each securing a spring-loaded holster; on the right was a standard .45 automatic, and on the left was the Bat's grapnel gun. Around his shoulders was a black scalloped cloak that billowed out like bat's wings. Perched on the cornice of a brownstone apartment building, he was a black shadow against a black sky; from the street he was invisible.

Three stories below him, he watched Deputy Mayor Brewster standing near the building's front stoop. Occasionally Brewster would check his watch and the Bat had to suppress the urge to check his own. The Black Bat was playing a hunch, tailing Brewster; it was all he had left to try, since Carol's inquiries had proved fruitless and Silk had disappeared some hours ago. "Following a lead," he'd said, according to Carol and he had yet to call in.

That just left his hunch. "First principles," Quinn had said to Butch and Carol. The group had re-convened in Quinn's study, after Quinn and Butch had returned from the aborted press conference at City Hall. *"Cui bono?* Who benefits from the effort to create a supernatural scare?"

"Doctor Durga?" Carol suggested.

"That was my thought, too," Quinn admitted. "But after talking to him earlier today... now I'm not sure. The natural suspicion is that Durga's a charlatan trying to turn a profit somehow, but I honestly can't see how. Today Warner practically accused him to his face of faking the whole thing to put pressure on the D.A.'s office and Durga, he wasn't *angry*, he didn't huff and puff like one would expect. No show of outrage at all. Just... sorrowful. He didn't strike me as a man who is only looking out for himself. He's not a con man. He.... I don't know what he is. But he's not looking to turn these events to his advantage, at least not yet. So who does that leave?"

"Costello?" Butch hazarded.

Quinn nodded. "Has to be. This certainly isn't his style but it's to his benefit. And the greatest threat to Costello is the witness. That's what the whole charade is aimed at. Forcing the witness out of protective custody and into the open."

"But...." Carol looked doubtful. "Tony, I know you're sure it's him, but.... Have you thought about other explanations? Seven people are dead. Have you thought about any sort of other link between them? Some common factor the coroner missed?"

"You mean, some *specific* reason those people were targeted?" Quinn considered it. "We've been over all that. There's no link we could find. Two politicians, three waitresses serving drinks, a radio producer, and a stenographer from the D.A.'s office. No affiliations between any of them; the two councilmen weren't even in the same political party. And not one of them had any kind of tie to Costello. No, I think it was random. Showing off what could happen if the city doesn't play ball."

Carol still wasn't convinced. "If it is Costello, isn't this a little… I don't know, *baroque* for him? Lightning and swamis and wild dogs. Why not just the usual strong-arm tactics? Threaten someone. Break some legs. Why all the hocus-pocus?"

"That's the question, isn't it?" Quinn steepled his fingers. "I don't know. But the weak link here is Brewster. Costello showed up uninvited to the Deputy Mayor's party just before the chaos broke out, and it's the Deputy that Durga's putting pressure on, not the D.A. So I think its Brewster that is going to be getting the Black Bat's attention tonight."

To Quinn it had seemed obvious. But now, watching the figure standing on the sidewalk below him, the Black Bat was having doubts. What the hell was Brewster doing?

Then a small tan coupe pulled up to the sidewalk. The window rolled down and the Bat's trained hearing could pick up the raspy smoker's wheeze of Lieutenant McGrath. "Still on record that this is a bad idea, sir."

Brewster stepped forward and opened the car door. "I've taken every precaution. I haven't been followed. There's no one around."

Of course, Brewster hadn't accounted for someone on the roof, the Bat noted with a quiet smile. Then he saw the direction the car was taking, and swore. Damn it, he hadn't reckoned on Brewster getting into a car. By the time the Bat could reclaim his own vehicle two blocks down, a battered, nondescript sedan with a supercharged engine, he would have lost them. Gritting his teeth, he sprinted diagonally across the rooftop, reaching the opposite corner of the roof just as the coupe was rounding the block.

Tony Quinn had not been a natural athlete in his former life. He was fit enough for a young attorney; he had played a few rounds of golf now and then, and if he had to sprint for a taxicab it didn't leave him as winded as some of his colleagues would have been. But life as the Black Bat was proving far more strenuous. Since the operation that had restored his sight and granted him the other enhanced abilities that aided him in his nocturnal crusade, the Black Bat had trained himself relentlessly, exercises designed not just to build muscle but also to increase speed, agility, and gymnastic skill. After all these months, he was well into Olympic-class territory, but this was going to be tricky even for him. He was counting on not just his new-found physical prowess but also his other senses,

"What the hell was Brewster doing?"

the enhanced eyesight and also the highly developed 'proximity sense' he had carefully honed over the last year that let him read the almost imperceptible air currents around him as easily as a pearl diver senses waves in the ocean.

But all this was subconscious, a flicker of memory. Consciously, the Bat was watching the tan coupe disappear down the street and calculating angles as he ran for the building's edge. *Fire escape...lamppost...there. That was the one.*

Then he launched himself off the edge of the roof, three stories in the air.

It seemed suicidal. But the Bat had been training for exactly this. He spread his arms, his cape grasped in each hand. The ribbed cape billowed out behind him and with a sharp THRAP! the leathery fabric instantly filled like a sail. The fall turned into a diagonal glide. Just as he felt the briefest hesitation in the air currents beneath him, as the glide threatened to spill over into a fall, the Bat released the cape and thrust his hands forward. His gloved hands caught the horizontal bar of a street lamp and his body swept upward into an elliptical arc, his bootheels aiming for the sky. He let go of the lamppost at the highest point of the arc and his body shot upward, feet-first, cape trailing behind him. The Bat drew his knees up to his chin and then thrust his feet sharply out, hunching his shoulders forward, twisting in mid-air so that his hands were able to grasp the looming railing of a fire escape attached to the next building. He swung up on to the fire escape and took the iron steps to the roof, three at a time.

In this way, running along the roofs and leaping from building to building, more or less parallel to the route the car took, the Black Bat followed the coupe as it threaded its way down the darkened city streets.

The Bat had been practicing this method of rooftop gymnastic navigation for weeks and had discovered that he was able to match the speed of most cars in typical city traffic. Even at night when there were fewer vehicles on the road, he found that, as long as the buildings weren't too far apart and there were no parks or playgrounds along the route, just by leaping and swinging from building to building he had been able to keep ahead of Butch in a follow car even when Butch was going thirty miles an hour. The Bat could see the rooftops as clearly as a normal man would have in broad daylight, and his ability to 'read' air currents had gifted him with an unerring aim for whatever handhold he dived for.

This was the first time he'd tried to follow an actual suspect vehicle, though, as opposed to the training sessions with Butch. But it was working.

The Bat was able to keep pace with the coupe and was feeling only slightly winded. Beneath the cloth of the mask, the Black Bat's teeth bared in feral exultation. *This is what I was meant for,* he thought. *This. Not a courtroom. Maybe the acid was... Not a blessing, never that, but maybe...destiny?*

The train of thought was abandoned as the Bat saw the coupe slowing. They had arrived.

The feel of the neighborhood had changed. There were fewer lampposts, and no residential buildings. This was commercial, the warehouse district. Near the East River. Suddenly the Bat realized where they were. His jaw clenched in frustration. *The damned fools. This is the same safe house the office was using when I was a prosecutor. They're supposed to* rotate *them.*

He knew which building they were headed for now and swung up towards that rooftop without bothering to keep track of McGrath and Brewster in the coupe. A quick bounce off a decaying wooden windowsill and a mid-air somersault later, the Black Bat was hoisting himself over the corrugated iron surface of the warehouse roof edge. There was an open skylight about ten yards away, and the Bat could hear voices. Concentrating his enhanced hearing, and careful to make no noise himself, the Bat crept closer to the opening.

As he neared the skylight, the murmur of voices resolved into discernible words. "It's your deal."

A grunt. The riffle and slap of cards being shuffled.

Babysitting duty, the Bat realized. Two cops, playing cards.

He risked a peek over the edge of the skylight opening. Two bored men in shirtsleeves sat facing one another over a card table. Just to the left of the elbow of one of the men, a gun in a holster lay on the table. Another holstered gun dangled from a shoulder strap that had been carelessly hung on the back of the other man's chair.

There was a knock. Instantly both men reached for their pistols.

The knock came again, this time in an odd rhythm; one-two-three, one, one. A longer pause. Then, one, one-two-three.

Morse code; the letters *D-A*. Beneath the cloth of the mask, the Black Bat's mouth curled into a grimace torn between amusement and annoyance. *They haven't even changed the knock!* He made a mental note to find a way to bring up the need for security updates with Warner, if he could think of a good excuse for Tony Quinn to raise the subject.

The two men visibly relaxed. One let out a sigh and rose to answer the door, moving out of the Bat's field of view.

The hooded eavesdropper strained his ears and heard McGrath's familiar growl. "Hey, O'Hara. How's it goin?"

"Quiet. I think she's getting a little cabin fever, but you can't blame her for that."

She? So the witness was a woman. Interesting.

The Bat heard Brewster clear his throat. "So where's your witness?"

"I'll get her, sir," the man at the table volunteered. He stood up and moved out of view of the skylight as well. The sound of a knock and a door opening. Then he was back. Then the Bat saw a blonde woman in her forties step into view near the card table.

McGrath's voice. "Evening, ma'am. The Deputy Mayor wanted to stop by and offer his thanks for helping us out with your husband."

The Black Bat's eyes widened in shock. **Husband?** *Could it be?*

Then Brewster stepped into view and offered his hand to the woman. "Arnold Brewster, Mrs. Costello. I'm pleased to meet you. We appreciate everything you're doing for us."

"I'm not doing it for *you*," the blonde woman said. "This is self-preservation. And yes, payback." Her voice sharpened. "After I'd caught him with that foreign floozy…"

"Nevertheless," Brewster went on, "we're very grateful…"

The Bat heard McGrath grunt. "Sir, we really shouldn't spend too much time here."

Then the Bat's hypersensitive hearing picked up something else; not a sound so much as a thrumming vibration that was felt more than heard. Coming from above.

He looked up. Something, some kind of giant flying craft, was approaching. It was matte black against the night sky, and would have been invisible to anyone other than the Black Bat and his enhanced vision. The air appeared to ripple under it like a heat mirage as it passed, and masked vigilante swore softly under the mask. Somehow, Brewster had been followed, and now this thing, whatever it was, was coming to unleash the lightning.

The Black Bat's decision was instantaneous. He took a deep breath and dropped through the skylight opening.

McGrath and the other cops were taken completely by surprise. The Bat had his own gun out before any of the others could reach their pistols. "I'm not here to hurt you! But you have to listen to me." His voice was a harsh rasp, utterly unlike Tony Quinn's normal urbane tones. "Sal Costello's lightning machine is coming for your witness. We have to get all of you out of here…Now!"

McGrath was just opening his mouth to argue the point when there was a flash of light from above, and suddenly the walls exploded in flames.

Silk was taken back to Durga's building, but not to the penthouse this time. Instead, the man with the gun had marched him down the alley and past a row of stinking garbage cans to a door set into the rear wall of the building. There, the gunman had unlocked the door and shoved Silk down a short flight of concrete steps, to a dank little basement room with one naked light bulb hanging from the ceiling. There, two other gunmen were waiting. They quickly and efficiently lashed Silk to a wooden kitchen chair with a length of clothesline.

Silk shook his head ruefully. Couldn't fault them for their professionalism. The whole thing had taken less than five minutes, from the gunman first calling Silk by name to Silk being trussed up in the chair. He was placed with his back to the door to the alley, but he heard it creak open. Then a portly, florid-faced man in a pinstripe suit stepped around Silk and stood facing him, his eyes cold with appraisal.

Silk gave a brief nod. "Mr. Costello?"

"That's me." Costello pulled up another chair and sat, a gunman flanking him on either side as courtiers would a king. "The question is, who are *you?*"

Silk shrugged, or tried to, but his arms were so tightly bound it came off as more of a squirm. "Nobody special."

"You work for somebody. You're a player." Costello rubbed his jaw. "I don't know you, though, and I know everybody. That makes me nervous."

Silk tried another shrug. He was testing his bonds, as well, trying to make it look casual. They were unyielding. There was no way he was going to break loose without help.

Costello leaned forward and smacked Silk sharply across the jaw with his open palm. "Hey. I ask a question, I get an answer. Or you get pieces of you broke off." There was no anger in Costello's voice. Just annoyance.

Silk tasted blood at the corner of his mouth. *Son of a bitch can hit.* "Ask your partner who I am."

"You mean the swami?" Costello snorted. "He ain't around."

"Not Durga," Silk said, patiently. "Your *partner.*"

Costello raised an eyebrow, then looked up at something behind Silk.

Vangie stepped around and joined Costello. She slid in between

Costello and the gunman flanking him on the left and draped herself over Costello's shoulder. Then she smiled at Silk, a comfortable feline smile.

"You always were smart, Norrie," she said.

"Not as smart as you." Silk let his bitterness show. "I completely fell for the act. Scared little girl, trapped by the big bad magician. Durga doesn't know anything at all, does he? He's on the level. It's you pulling the strings. Like always, like you played Bob and me way back when. And I went for it again, sap that I am."

"Doctor Durga is a great man," Vangie said, putting mock sententiousness into it. "He helps people banish their negative energy, he frees them from evil. I am merely the channel through which his magic functions." Then her voice sharpened. "Of course it's me. That damn fool actually believes he has magic powers."

"Why wouldn't he?" Silk snorted. "You can make anyone believe anything. Well... any *man*. You did a cold reading on me so slick I didn't even catch you doing it. Told me everything you thought I wanted to hear, just like you would any mark at a séance. You only made one mistake; when you told your gorilla to come get me, he used my *real* name. Durga didn't know it. I told the guy in the hallway my name was Silk. Nobody but you ever called me Norrie. If not for that one little slip... I completely bought it. Hell, I was thinking you still loved me." He nodded at Costello. "But I guess you got a new fella."

"I do indeed." Vangie leaned down and whispered something in Costello's ear. He nodded and motioned to his men and they exited, leaving Vangie alone with Silk.

Silk said softly, "Why are you doing this, Vangie? Killing folks. Burning people. What's Costello got on you?"

She threw back her head and laughed. "Oh, my God. Men are so stupid. All of you." Then she leaned forward and faced Silk, her eyes flashing with anger. "That's why I'm doing this. Because I'm *smart*. Smarter than you. Than *all* of you. Do you know I have two doctorates? Physics and engineering. Yeah, that's right. Vangie from Teaneck is a *scientist*. I studied acoustics and photons and electricity and I figured out how to make them work together. My storm cannon can focus light so intensely that it can set the air itself burning. Did you know that if you put coherent light through the right lens, you can burn metal? I can do it. I can do it from a mile away. I should be working for the Army. But they just *laughed!*" Her voice was ramping up into a shriek. "I offered my work to the War Department and they *laughed* at me! Called me 'adorable' and 'spunky' and sent me packing. Because women aren't allowed to be smart! We're just supposed to be pretty and let the men do all the work!"

Silk stared. *Jesus Christ. She's as crazy as a basket of snakes. How did I never see this?*

Then Vangie seemed to gather herself. "Well, I can be pretty and let the men do all the work. Like you, and Bob, and Sal. Even that imbecile Durga. You do the work. I keep the money. And I *invest* the money." She shrugged. "My devices are expensive. The focusing lens in the storm cannon is made of diamond; it's the only material strong enough. Unfortunately, I couldn't afford a diamond the size of a dinner plate. It takes the kind of financing that only a nation can support. But the War Department laughed me out of the room when I tried to show them the plans. They wouldn't pay for one. That left crime." She spread her hands. "It took ten years to figure out how to build a compound lens from smaller diamonds, and get enough of them to create a prototype. What I skimmed from you and Bob was just the start."

Silk licked his lips. He tried one more time. "Vangie... I understand why you thought you was frozen out. I can even see why you sold out me and Bob. But... what happened at the party... those people burning like torches... none of *them* ever did anything to you. Seven people dead... why? Just to help your boyfriend beat a racketeering rap? Scare the mayor?"

"Oh, please." Vangie rolled her eyes. "It's simple. I was grifting with Durga. I used my optic and sonic devices to create illusions for him. That, along with me cold-reading his visitors and feeding him answers, that's how I worked it; without him even knowing it! We were building up a nice little nest egg, his rep was building. And he wasn't lying! That's what sells it. He *believes.* He's dumber than a box of hammers, Norrie, really. The poor dear became convinced he had supernatural ability. So pretty soon he's the toast of New York. The money was really starting to come in…. then we met Sal Costello." She paused. "And he had a *lot* of money. I decided that was faster. So I talked to Sal. You know how I can talk to a man, Norrie."

Silk winced at that. He knew, all right.

Vangie's smile was predatory. "So now Sal's with me, and I can afford to build my cannon *and* the launch platform. That was all I wanted, honestly. I needed to have a demonstration model if I was ever going to get anywhere with the research." She shrugged. "If that silly bitch he was married to had just taken her lumps, it wouldn't have been a problem. But no, she has to go squealing to the district attorney. Sal was at his wit's end; she'd been with him for sixteen years, she knew everything. Hell, she kept the books at the beginning." She looked smug. "Nothing makes you more attractive to a mark than being a rescuer, you know that, Norrie. I told him we could aim Durga at the Deputy Mayor and I'd field-test my storm cannon. Presto, the gods want Sal Costello free. Meanwhile, I let certain interested parties know about my weapon and told them to watch the papers for a demonstration."

Silk stared, frozen with horror. Just business. That's all it was to her.

Vangie was getting warmed up now, enjoying her story. She had been longing to boast to someone, Silk realized. "Brewster's a believer, you know. It was his wife that got Durga invited to all those toney Upper West Side parties. It's working, too," she added. "Sal got word that Brewster's asking to be taken to see his mystery witness. When he does, we'll be there." Vangie chuckled and then made a pistol gesture with her thumb and forefinger. "Bang comes the lightning."

Silk paled. She was going to do it again, unleash death from the sky, unless he could stop her. But how?

Vangie stepped out of view for a moment. When she returned, she was carrying an odd metal device under one arm; some sort of cross between a tuning fork and a tommy gun. She aimed it at Silk. "No lightning from this one," she said, "but it's just the test model. You know how some opera singers can break glass just with the power of their voices? I got to thinking about that, and I wondered what I could break if I built a gun that fired a beam of concentrated sound. Turns out there are all sorts of interesting effects. I can't really break anything with this, but I can cause terrible pain." She flicked a switch.

Agony exploded in Silk Kirby's skull, a thick red bolt of pain that entered through his ears and jaw and shot down his spinal column, then flared out through his shoulders and thighs. Silk screamed and his back arched in the chair, his entire body racked with uncontrollable spasms.

Vangie kept the sonic gun trained on him for a full thirty seconds before she shut it off. Silk slumped, and only the clothesline that bound him to the chair kept his body from sliding to the floor. He groaned. His ears felt like they were bleeding out.

"You see, now?" Vangie said. "I can't shatter glass with it, but I can do that. And it doesn't even make any noise! The range is out of human hearing. Dogs can hear it, we had some fun with them earlier, but humans can only feel the pain. Pity it doesn't have the range of the storm cannon. After about thirty feet, it's only good for scaring somebody's poodle. From a distance, it just makes people mildly uncomfortable, although the more sensitive ones can feel something of what I just gave you. But at close range... well, I don't know how long a person could last. I've never really tried it out at close range like this on someone. Never had a reason." She leaned forward. "But I have a reason *now*, Norrie. I want to know about your mysterious friend, the one you were going to enlist on my behalf. I want to know why you were nosing around. I want to know what your grift is." She flicked the switch again.

Silk spasmed again as the red wave of pain engulfed him like a flash flood. *So stupid...should have told the boss...going to die now because I was embarrassed to tell him about Vangie...stupid...stupid...*

Then everything went black.

The Black Bat whirled his cape around him in an effort to keep the heat and smoke at a distance. The entire building was burning. He saw Mrs. Costello on her knees a few feet away, coughing. The air above her shimmered and the Bat knew that the lightning weapon was about to strike again. He launched himself directly at her and the two of them crashed through the flaming wall into the hallway. Behind them came another thunderflash and the room they had just been in was gone, replaced by an orange-and-white inferno.

The Black Bat thought he heard McGrath shouting through the crackle of flames, but he was effectively blinded by the white fury of the flaming building around him. No way to see if any of the others had gotten out. The Black Bat closed his eyes and let his other senses guide him, feeling his way through the air currents. With one hand he pulled Mrs. Costello to her feet and enveloped her in his cloak, shielding her as best he could from the fire, and together they stumbled down the hallway. A few feet further down and the Bat was able to open his eyes. The wall at the far end of the hallway had collapsed and it was open to the sky. Then, in front of them, again he could see the telltale shimmer.

No choice, the Bat thought grimly. *I guess we'll see if all that training was good for something.* He fumbled out his grapnel gun with one hand and yanked Mrs. Costello to him with the other. Then the Bat took aim at the row of warehouses across the street and fired. The four-pronged harpoon shot up and out, trailing a length of thin nylon cord, embedding itself in the opposite warehouse's upper wall. He shouted, "Hang on!"

The mobster's wife barely had time to let out a small squall of protest before the Bat had triggered the grapnel's rewind mechanism and, just as the hallway exploded around them, they were airborne, flying across the darkened streets four stories below. She screamed and struggled but the Bat hardly noticed, he was so focused on calculating angles and hanging on to both her and the grapnel gun. The wall was coming up fast, too fast; they were going to smash against it like bugs on a windshield. The Black Bat swung his legs up and out, trying to twist and divert their momentum. The cord continued to rewind on to the reel, adding to their speed. The Bat clamped harder to Mrs. Costello with his left arm and thrust out his bootheels, kicking out against the side of the warehouse that suddenly loomed before them, and half-swung, half-wrenched the woman up and around, and in that same moment losing his grip on the grapnel gun. *No...!*

But that last kick had done it. In an ugly, tangled somersault the two of them swung in a sloppy arc back up and in, to land in an untidy heap on the warehouse roof. A second later, the grapnel gun landed next to them and with a hissing click the last of the cord rewound into the reel, the harpoon having snapped off. Across the street, the Bat could see the entire upper two floors of the former safe-house were a mass of flames. Down below, at street level, several policemen were milling around the front of the building, coughing. The Bat could see McGrath, and one other he recognized. So it looked like some, maybe even most, had gotten out. At least that much had gone right. He looked up.

The craft was circling, still seeking its prey. The Bat pulled Mrs. Costello back from the edge of the roof, deeper into the shadows. "Keep still," he told her. "You're the one it wants. Drawing attention to us will just get you killed."

The woman nodded, her face a pale soot-streaked mask of terror. The Bat looked up, getting his first clear view of the thing.

It hovered over the flaming building, questing this way and that, circling, barely forty yards or so over the warehouse roofs. It was some sort of dirigible. Small, barely two hundred feet long. It looked to be a rigid, zeppelin-style craft, but with modifications the Black Bat had never seen before; parts of it seemed more like an autogiro, but it was hard to be sure; even with his special vision, it was difficult to make it out against the smoke and the night sky. There were two giant canvas screens suspended from the center gondola, so that the whole craft had the appearance of floating just over a folded kite. *Camouflage,* the Bat realized. The screens were matte black, reflecting no light at all. It would be invisible in the night sky. *It's invisible right now,* the Bat realized. *Floating above like that, even in the light of the fire, no one can see it but me.*

"It was some sort of dirigible."

He had to get up there, while it was still hovering, confused, before it started firing its hellish lightning gun again. But how?

Behind him, he could hear Mrs. Costello's voice, small and terrified. "Who *are* you?"

First things first, the Bat realized. *Get the witness to safety.* "A friend," he said, still using the Bat's rasping tones. "Are you hurt? Can you walk?"

"I…yes. I'm all right. Thanks to you," she added. "You saved my life. That was… amazing."

"I wouldn't want to have to do it again." The Bat grimaced under the mask. He had to pursue the flying craft somehow, but he didn't dare just leave Mrs. Costello here on the roof. Nor could he trust her to the police below in the street. Sal Costello still had plenty of his regular goons looking for her, he was certain. And Costello had city government wired. Quinn was sure of Warner and reasonably sure of McGrath, but putting the woman back into police custody felt too risky.

Of course, the alternative he had in mind was risky too. But to the Black Bat's way of thinking, it was a risk worth taking. He fumbled a card out of his pocket. "Get down to the street. Find a phone and call this number. Someone will come for you."

Mrs. Costello stared at the card. "Anthony Quinn? The guy that used to be D.A.? I thought he was crippled after that courtroom bombing."

"Just blind," the Bat said. "But he still consults with the police once in a while. It's not important. The important thing is that he's the only one I can think of at the moment who could put you up in a safe place, because I'm sure your husband doesn't have *his* phone tapped. One of his household staff can pick you up. Quinn's helped me before." He could see her nod, buying it, but he tried not to think of what McGrath would make of it all if he found out. "And for God's sake stay in the shadows, away from everyone, even the police. I'm hoping there's a phone somewhere in this building and you can just wait here." He strode over to the roof access door and, blessedly, it was unlocked. He opened it and gestured her in.

"But… what about you?" She goggled at him. "Where are you going? Who *are* you?"

"Nobody special. Please hurry, Mrs. Costello," he added. "Right now there's a good chance they think you're dead. That's our only advantage. Leave the rest of it to me."

She stared at the caped figure for a long moment, then nodded and went into the building.

The Black Bat once again turned his attention skyward. The craft was still there. Somehow, its camouflage screens were hiding it from the police in the street, despite the light of the fire. The Bat squinted. Even with his special vision he was barely able to make it out. If it hadn't been hovering so low, he wouldn't have been able to see it at all. Whoever had designed those hanging screens had to be some kind of optics genius.

Okay, he mused. *You have to get up there. Never going to get another shot at it. Except it's across the street, three hundred feet up, and you broke the grapnel. You've got to figure it out in the next minute or two before the damn thing starts shooting again, or just sails away. What've you got? Is the grapnel gun a total loss?*

The Black Bat knelt and retrieved the gun from where it had fallen a few moments before. He turned it over in his hand. The cord was still good, and the reel mechanism. He unsnapped the reel from the gun and pulled out the broken stub at the end of the line where the grapnel had been. Hundred and fifty feet of line on the reel. Costello's flying death machine was half again that distance up from him at least. If he could find a way to launch himself *up;* shorten that distance somehow?

The Black Bat strode to the roof's edge and looked around, calculating speed, distance, air currents. He saw little to help him. It was the warehouse district; there were no projections on the buildings, no flagpoles or lampposts. Just flat wooden building fronts, slanting metal roofs... *power lines.* Suddenly galvanized, the crimefighter stripped off one of his gauntlets and held his bare hand out over the street, closing his eyes, concentrating every iota of his enhanced senses to try and read the air currents. With the heat of the fire?

Maybe. Maybe he could do it.

Or he'd end up a black-caped stain on the pavement below. No choice. No one else could do it; no one else had his training or his visual advantage. The police had no idea this craft was responsible for the fire. With a crowd of cops who could see nothing in the sky above them, once again it would be put down to freak lightning. And the Black Bat was on foot. Even traveling over the rooftops using his special skills, he knew that once the thing rose and sailed away there would be no following it. It had to be now.

Quickly, the Bat uncoiled a length of the extra-strength cord from the reel. He knew the auto-rewind was intact, and all he needed was a projectile, something that could serve as a bolo. He scanned the rooftop. There. A length of pipe coming up through the roof. A vent chimney. He wrenched it loose from its rusted mounting and it came loose at the joint. Now he had a length of pipe about a foot long. He hefted it. Was it heavy enough? Yes. He knotted the end of the cord around it, then swung it experimentally. His aim would have to be perfect. He had advantages a normal man did not, but even so…

It's crazy. Don't care. Can't be helped. He clenched his jaws, stepped back from the roof's edge a few yards, then ran towards it and leaped out over the street, once again with his black scalloped cape clenched in each hand to serve as a sort of glider for the few seconds he would need it. The length of pipe was also in his left hand, the reel gripped in his right, each wrapped with a fistful of cape. A few feet of nylon cord connected them.

Once again the cape billowed out and filled like a sail. The Bat arced out over the street in a steep glide. He swung his booted feet forward and just as the glide was about to collapse into a fall, he let go of his cape and dropped down, feet-first. His bootheels struck the power line that had been his objective and the line bowed down like a trampoline stretched between the two poles. Using the line as a springboard, combining the momentum of the leap with a thrust upward using every iota of energy he could summon from his leg muscles, he launched himself straight up towards the deadly airship floating above. Arms at his sides, now, he arrowed up towards the airship, in a high arc that carried him over the fire… and its updrafts, which, as the Bat had calculated, helped his upward momentum. At the height of his arc, at the precise moment before his momentum evaporated completely and he would fall downward again, he hurled the length of pipe at the airship, thumbing the release on the reel so the cord trailed freely behind.

The Black Bat was aiming at a very specific spot between the two hanging screens just under the airship; there was a gap of maybe two feet, and a strut just behind that gap. It would have taken spectacular, superhuman aim to throw something and hit a target that small, especially while hurtling through the air in freefall five stories above the street.

Fortunately, the Black Bat's extranormal abilities had gifted him with exactly that degree of superhuman aim.

The length of pipe flew true, shooting into the gap between the canvas projection screens. As the length of cord reached its end, the pipe snapped back, exactly as the Bat had hoped, and the improvised bola wound around the strut three times. The line snapped taut and the Bat gave a quick double yank on the reel, triggering the auto-rewind. Then he hung on with both hands for dear life as he swung crazily back and forth under the airship, the cord snaking into the reel, pulling him upward with remarkable speed.

Jesus it's coming in too fast…smash your hands on that strut and it's all over…only chance is dead-stick landing..come on, you trained for this…

He shot up through the gap. At the last possible moment, the Black Bat let go of the reel and grabbed the strut it was wrapping around. The reel bounced off the steel of the strut and smacked the Bat a painful blow to the wrist, then the last of the cord wound into the reel and it snapped against the strut and stuck. The length of pipe dangled from an inch or so of cord just to his left.

The Bat gripped the strut and hung for a moment, panting. Then he swung his legs up and over, and after a few seconds' scramble he was safely sitting on a larger crossbeam that was part of the web of metal struts that supported the hanging screens.

Looking down the length of the airship's belly, he could see why there was a gap. A few yards away, poking out of a square opening in the skin of the ship, there was what looked to be some sort of multiple-lens camera projector aimed straight down. The lightning gun. Had to be.

Careful not to lose his balance, the Black Bat tapped his armpit to make sure he hadn't lost his .45. He drew it out and, with the gun clenched in his right hand, began to crawl towards the opening where the lightning cannon was protruding. Time to finish this.

Silk Kirby awoke in darkness, with a pounding headache. He was in an awkward position, sitting on the floor with his knees just under his chin. He tried to straighten his legs and found he couldn't as his heels bumped into the far wall. He was not bound, for which he was grateful, but he realized why as he tried to move. Everything hurt. The last time he'd felt this bad, Silk reflected, was that time in Chicago when Idaho Bob had gotten them into that brawl at Orsini's and a couple of the Grandinetti boys had tuned up on them.

Well, Vangie tuned up on me for sure, he thought bitterly. *Her and her damn tuning fork whatsis.* Slowly, painfully, he slid up to his feet. He still hurt but at least there was room to stand, and it was a blessed relief to straighten his legs.

Silk began to assess his surroundings. He was in a small room, maybe five feet by five feet; a little too big for a closet, more like some kind of supply room. He could feel shelves at his back built into the upper wall. To his left there was a tiny crack of light under what Silk assumed to be a door. He reached out, feeling for the handle, found it, and tried the latch. Locked, of course. *Oh well.* He rattled the door again. *Door feels weird. Light. Wonder if I could pop it out.*

"There is no escape," A voice came from the darkness. Silk heard clothing rustle. "We are trapped."

Silk turned. In the dim light he could make out the vague shadows of high cheekbones and a goatee. There was a tiny red glint from the ruby at the front of the turban. "Well, hello, Doc," Silk said with a cheerfulness he did not feel. "Welcome to the party. She zap you too?"

"No. It was... my tea." Doctor Durga's voice was dull with disappointment and betrayal. "Vandhya prepares it before my afternoon meditation. It must have been drugged. I awakened here a short while ago. I think the floor has occasionally dipped, and I heard engines for a time. I think we are on an airship." He exhaled a heavy sigh of defeat. "I have tried my arts on the door but it will not open."

"Yeah? I got my arts too, and we could try those." Silk was kneeling now, examining the doorjamb and hinges, more by feel than sight in the dim light. No keyhole, but it wasn't a bolt. Of course, he didn't have his tools. The boss had them in his Bat outfit; Silk had been teaching him lockpicking for the last six weeks. *Never leaving the house without picks again,* he vowed. *Got to get another set.* "You got any metal on you? Something thin. Paper clip, anything. Hair clip'd be about perfect," he added. "You got any hair under that thing?"

"Thing?" Durga sounded confused. "Are you referring to my turban?"

"Yeah, the turban. What keeps it on? Clip? Hairpin?"

"Certainly not." Now the voice was offended. "Properly wrapping a *pagri* is a skill. Perhaps your American women require pins and clips, but..."

"Great. As a turban jockey you're a genius." Silk let some of his exasperation into his voice. Vangie had been right, the guy really was a stiff. "But I need something metal to pick this lock."

"Ah." Durga caught up. "I see." He paused a moment, then offered, "My jewel has a pin. And a hasp that could perhaps be flattened."

"Great! Let's have it." Silk waited while Durga fumbled with the ruby at the front of his turban and handed it over. He took the stickpin ruby setting and turned it over in his hands. The pin was too short to do much good, but the hasp was long enough that Silk thought he might be able to slip the tongue of the door lock. He knelt and set to work.

The opening around the gun assembly was too narrow to admit a body, but the Black Bat had found a crawlway hatch next to the mounted lens cannon, and it was the work of a few moments to slip the lock with the special tools Silk had given him. He opened it carefully and climbed aboard.

He emerged into a maintenance crawlspace of some kind running the length of the ship's belly. He could feel the throb of the craft's engines now, though the sound itself was muted. *The entire design is based on stealth,* the Bat realized. *Engines muted, projection screens hanging below to fool eyes on the ground. It's as close to invisible as humanly possible. No wonder the attacks were dismissed as lightning.* Despite the blackness he could see everything about him clearly; a catwalk stretched before him, and on either side, the lower part of the hydrogen ballonets that kept them afloat. The gun would be useless to him here; he dared not take the chance of setting off the gas. Holstering the .45, he gathered his cloak about him and crept forward.

At the end of the catwalk was a short ladderway leading to a trapdoor set into the ceiling. The Bat looked up, and, removing a gauntlet, pressed his bare hand against the trapdoor, trying to sense any human activity above him. All he felt was the faint thrumming of the ship itself. Well, he couldn't just sit there. Either there was a person above him or not. He slipped the gauntlet back on and shoved the door open.

He saw an empty room with wooden benches set into each side of the wall, and above those, portholes looking out into the night sky. The lights were on but very dim, though to the Black Bat it might as well have been high noon. He hoisted himself up and out and checked his equipment belt, inventorying possible weapons. The pistol was no good. That left him… three of the glass smoke capsules, which weren't much use as a weapon but they would cover any action he took. The lockpicks. A pocketknife with a three-inch blade, which wasn't really meant to be used as an offensive weapon. Ammo clips for the .45. Now he wished he'd thought it through more when he was filling the belt pouches. A lead sap or some brass knuckles would have been helpful. He shouldn't have assumed the gun would be sufficient.

"Hey, who the hell?" A large man appeared in the doorway to the saloon, glaring. "How the hell did you get on board?"

"Bats fly," Quinn said, in the Bat's rasp. "Make it easy on yourself. Give it up. Where's Costello?"

"Give up my ass," growled the hulking figure, and charged at the Black

Bat. The Bat shifted and launched himself into the air, whipping his cape around the hulking man's face in the same way a matador teases a bull. He pivoted in mid-air and thrust his bootheel forward, where it connected solidly and shoved the thug headfirst into the bulkhead at the rear of the saloon compartment. There was a solid thud and the big man sank to the floor.

The Bat smiled beneath his mask and turned forward.

"Hold on there, we ain't done, ya caped jackrabbit."

The Bat whirled to see the big man coming at him again. "Okay," he rasped. "Plenty more where that came from." He squared his shoulders and braced himself. "Come get some."

Silk and Doctor Durga emerged from the supply closet into a small corridor. "Control room," Silk whispered. "Navigation."

Durga nodded to where light spilled from a hatchway to their right.

Silk shrugged and inched forward. Now they heard voices.

"The whole top of the warehouse is *gone*," came Vangie's voice. It was nothing like the serene, spiritual tones she had used as 'Vandhya.' This was shrill and enraged and tinged with her Jersey origins. "They're dead, I'm telling you. The longer we hang around the more power we use, the more chance someone might see something they shouldn't. We don't dare take the chance of a screen failing." She softened her tone, putting seduction into it. "There's no way she got out, baby. Let's just go home."

"Cops got out." Costello's grunt was emotionless, unmoved. "We need one more shot. Down on the street. Take 'em out."

"The scope doesn't show anyone there but cops and firemen. The tracker you planted on Brewster went out with our first shot as he was talking to her for Chrissake!" Vangie was getting shrill again. "In the *same room!* They're both *dead!* Killing a bunch of firemen isn't…"

"*No!*" To Silk's complete horror, it was Doctor Durga. He shoved past Silk and strode into the control room. "No more killing, Vandhya! No more murders done in the name of the gods! This ends now!" He rose to his full height and pointed imperiously at where Vangie and Costello were standing in front of the ship's control panel. Behind them was a large glass viewport. Silk could see city lights and a river… not downtown. He recognized it after a second. They were over the warehouse district somewhere, looking out over the East River. "I command it!" Durga said, getting angrier. "By my arts I hold you where you stand!"

"Command *this*, Punjab," Costello sneered, and pulled a gun.

Silk didn't give himself time to think, but dived through the door at Costello, focused entirely on the mobster's gun hand. They struggled, and Silk realized sickly that the beefy ganglord's build was more muscle than fat. Nevertheless, Silk hung on with grim desperation, battering Costello's hand against the metal control panel, trying to make him drop the gun. Behind him, he could hear Vangie screaming something about *idiots* and *hydrogen,* while Durga continued to roar his angry ultimatums.

Costello's teeth were bared in a predatory grimace of triumph as he finally wrenched his arm away from Silk and knocked him to the floor. "Goodbye, punk," he spat, and pointed his pistol at Silk's face.

At that instant came three muffled explosions.

Suddenly the room was filled with smoke. A large body thudded to the floor close to where Silk lay, *Brick*, he realized, *from the apartment building,* and then Silk had a vague impression of a caped, hooded figure all in black whirling into the room, knocking Costello to one side.

From the floor, Silk grinned wide. "Meet the boss, Vangie," he croaked.

The black-clad figure pulled Silk to his feet. Through the roiling yellow smoke Silk could only see silhouettes; Costello struggling to his feet, Durga falling against a bulkhead, and Vangie reaching for some sort of gun, no, not a gun, a rifle, *the sonic weapon!*

"Boss!" Silk yelped. "We gotta go! *Now!*"

Then there was the high keening whine of the sonic rifle and red waves of pain shot through Silk's body. He thought he heard Durga scream. He saw the Black Bat flinch in controlled agony and pull a pistol, aim, not at Vangie but *out,* towards the front viewport. *No! No guns!* Silk tried to yell but he could hear nothing, just the rising whine of the sonics. The Bat grasped the heavy .45 by the barrel and hurled it with all his might at the glass viewport. The glass shattered. He hauled Silk after him and both of them half jumped, half-fell out the port, plummeting toward the East River. Behind them the sonics rose ever further into a nerve-scraping scream, and then there was a hiss of sparks and the entire airship exploded into a giant white-orange fireball.

In freefall, the Black Bat twisted and managed to get his legs below him, still grasping Silk by the shoulders. "Silk!" He shouted. "Point your toes! Otherwise from this height your ankles will shatter! Hit the water *straight!* Straight as you can!" Then he let go of Silk's shoulders and spun away, trying to straighten his body. Silk did the same, somewhat less gymnastically, and seconds later the two men plunged into the water. Flaming debris rained around them.

Somehow Silk found the strength to right himself and stroke for the surface. He saw the Bat, a few feet away, struggling. Tony Quinn peeled off the hood and cape and, freed of the extra weight, swam for the surface as well. The two men broke the water at almost the same time.

"Nice save, boss," Silk coughed.

"You too." Quinn grimaced. "Don't suppose you brought a car." He glanced over at the docks and the flaming warehouse beyond. "It'll be swarming with police over there. I suppose we could try for the other side of the river, but it'll be the hell of a swim. Are you…"

Suddenly Silk's face split in a wide, toothy grin. "Hey." He nodded toward the docks. "Cavalry."

Just a short distance south of the area where the warehouse was still blazing, Quinn saw Carol Baldwin standing on a dock, frantically gesturing at them. Quinn's convertible roadster was parked behind her.

"Can't believe I saw that before you did," Silk said, with a hoarse laugh.

They swam for it.

Quinn's mind was beginning to blur with exhaustion. With the threat gone, the last two days were catching up with him rapidly now. He hardly realized when they reached the dock, then Silk and Carol were pulling him up and he had a brief moment where he was in Carol's arms and to his delighted surprise, she was kissing him. He pulled away and saw Carol's eyes, bright and shining with promise.

"Don't *ever* scare me like that again," she said, in a voice somewhere between exasperation and delight. "When I saw the explosion over the river…"

"It was a near thing." For a moment he almost pulled her to him again, but now was not the time. "What about Mrs. Costello?"

"At the house. Butch has her. I came back down here as soon as I could. When we heard Mrs. Costello's story I knew you'd need help. A ride at least."

"That was smart." Quinn nodded. "You did very well. Costello's dead, but his organization is still there and she and the D.A.'s office can take it all down now, easily, while there's still a power vacuum. They'll be scrambling like rats and Warner and his men can scoop them all up."

"I'm just glad you both are all right. Speaking of… where'd you find *this* rogue?" She jabbed a finger at Silk, who flinched.

Silk spread his hands wide in mock martyrdom. "Hey, what'd *I* do? I was just tryin' to get a lead; looking up old friends." He thought of Vangie, and sobered. He finished weakly, "Never mind. Just…you should be nice to me, I had a rough day."

"Going off on your own." Carol glared at him, then back up at Quinn. "I'm so mad at both of you taking such stupid chances."

"I know. We're very bad boys and you are a wonderful girl." Quinn grinned, suddenly exultant at being alive, no, at *having* a life, having a purpose again, friends... and this woman in his arms. He heard more sirens. "Later for the post-mortems. Quick, get us home. Back way, the tunnel entrance. I need to change to respectable Tony Quinn before Mrs. Costello sees me in these wet clothes." His mouth twisted in a rueful grimace as he remembered something else. "And you'll need to help me with a story for McGrath about how the Black Bat had one of my cards."

They piled into the roadster and sped silently away, as the fires continued to burn.

The End

AFTERWORD

I was a pulp fan before I knew there were such things as pulp magazines.

Here's how I backed into being a pulp fan. I'd always loved books and comics and adventure, but pulps specifically weren't on my radar until the summer of 1975, when I was fourteen. That year, two things happened that literally changed my life.

The first thing was that my mother told me that if I wanted money, I better go earn some. So I started mowing lawns and discovered that the more work I did, the more books I could buy. Suddenly I had control over my income. I could build my own library.

The second thing was that our neighborhood grocery store changed magazine distributors. The new outfit carried much more lurid fare, and instead of *Better Homes and Gardens* and Taylor Caldwell novels, our local grocery was now stocking Marvel comics and the Bantam *Doc Savage* reprints and all sorts of sword-and-sorcery series paperbacks and …well, I could go on and on. If you're reading a book from Airship 27, I daresay you can recall a similar tipping point in your youth somewhere, that moment when you had the epiphany that *this* was the good stuff. I was hooked for life.

Because of this, I'm not really a purist about 'pulp fiction.' For those of us that came to it in the spinner-rack pulp revival days of the late sixties and early seventies, it all kind of swirls together—Doc Savage and Mack Bolan and the Shadow (with those brilliant Jim Steranko covers!) and TV tie-in books by Michael Jahn and George Alec Effinger… I never differentiated between them, and it wasn't until I was reading books like Peter Haining's *The Fantastic Pulps* and the *Weird Heroes* series from Byron Preiss that I finally started to grasp what pulp magazines once had been. To me, it was all one thing—the Steranko *Shadow* paperbacks, Ron Goulart's *Avenger* novels, Robert E. Howard and Ian Fleming and Edgar Rice Burroughs—they were just My Guys. There was a wonderful sort of scruffy, underground feeling about it all; those of us that loved this stuff endured a great deal of parental and academic disapproval, and it fostered a defiant punk-rock ownership attitude in response. And when it came to those delightfully trashy paperback books that I thought of as mine, even then, I always had a soft spot for the B-listers. My Robert E. Howard paperbacks were all plastered with *In the Tradition of Conan!* on the covers but the stories I liked best were his tales of the Puritan adventurer Solomon Kane, and Dark Agnes the Sword Woman. Every time I went to the store there were at least a dozen *Perry Rhodan* adventures on the rack but I preferred the more obscure *Cap Kennedy, Secret Agent of the Spaceways.* And so on. Probably part of it came from that defiant feeling, the enjoyment of going against the crowd; but most of it was just the joy of discovering something new that apparently no one else had found yet.

Today we are in the middle of a pulp renaissance. There are more pulp reprints and 'new pulp' revivals of old characters than ever, and e-book technology and the internet have made it economically feasible for all sorts of projects that probably would have been stillborn if they'd been attempted through the traditional publishing and distribution methods of my youth. Probably my favorite of the pulp reprint projects that have sprung up over the last decade or so is John Gunnison's *High Adventure,* a bi-monthly trade paperback series reprinting various lesser-known pulp hero stories starring folks like Ki-Gor the Jungle Lord, the Green Lama, the Phantom Detective… and the Black Bat.

There have been lots of paperback reprints of Doc Savage and the Shadow, and even a fair number of the Spider and the Avenger, but *High Adventure* was my first experience with these others. So much awesomeness that I never knew about! Honest to God, it felt like finding a whole extra room in your favorite bookstore. So when I saw Airship 27 ask for writers to submit *new* stories starring those characters, I was all over that. I sent in a sample piece and pitched a couple of plot ideas, Ron liked this one, and here we are.

I thought it would be a lark, something just for fun—and it has been *tremendous* fun—but it was no lark. I always tell my students in Young Authors that you need to make sure that your hero's challenge should come out of his character, there should be a reason your story is specifically about him. A story starring Doc Savage shouldn't work if you tried to put the Spider into the same plot, and vice versa. Heroes shouldn't be interchangeable.

Which is all well and good. But there were all sorts of gentleman adventurers with secret identities in the pulp era— from heavyweights like the Shadow and the Spider all the way to C-list oddballs like the Moon Man and the Patent-Leather Kid, and a great many of them commissioned by editors who wanted 'something to get the Shadow fans,' or something like that. The gimmicks changed but the basic idea of a costumed hero with a team of aides that included a wisecracking smart guy, a big strong guy, and a plucky girl was something that was done a *lot*. Additionally, there's also the overlap with comic books; the Bat dresses a lot like Batman and his abilities echo those of Daredevil and Doctor Mid-Nite. So the thing that ended up being the hard part was figuring out what makes a Black Bat story specifically a *Black Bat* story and not just a generic pulp adventure.

I asked myself what was special about Tony Quinn, what sets him apart from the others? Reading Black Bat reprints in *High Adventure,* I came up with these-- he's a former prosecutor, everyone thinks he's blind but he actually can see in the dark, and one of his aides is a reformed swindler. And also, I knew Airship 27 wanted something a bit more badass—the original Black Bat was a tamer version of the Spider, essentially, and when you want to do pulp adventure, 'tame' is definitely not on the menu. Especially, the Bat never really had a good solid supervillain in any of his sixty-some adventures.

Okay, so who's a good villain that plays into the Bat's unique qualities? I wanted something riffing on the idea of blindness, both actual and metaphorical, and different kinds of special sight. So it should be someone running a con, someone who operates in the dark. It's a short jump from 'swindler in the dark' to 'séance,' and that led me to the concept of Dr. Durga, a spiritualist scam artist who's playing for really high stakes and terrorizing all of Manhattan. And then I thought of the idea of Silk Kirby's grifter past catching up with him, and it all came together.

I ended up doing all kinds of research. I read about con men and spiritualist scams. I looked at hours of *parkour* and freerunning footage on the internet, trying to make sure the things I have the Bat doing are possible. Trying to figure out how Tony Quinn sees in the dark, I read up on night-vision goggles and how they work, and the properties of the infrared part of the spectrum. I looked at zeppelin blueprints and old

photographs of New York City and, especially, the history of laser technology (and was amazed to learn that lasers were first postulated by Albert Einstein in 1917, and that there were people trying to build them as early as the mid-1930s.) As wild as the action gets, everything in the story has some foundation in actual fact.

Most of all, though, I hoped to bring some of the visceral feeling of *my* pulp guys, the 1970s paperback crew, to a traditional 1930s pulp hero story. The story is set firmly in the thirties but I wanted to try to capture the hell-for-leather narrative drive that I remember so affectionately from the paperbacks of Don Pendleton and Ron Goulart and Donald Hamilton— that streamlined, stripped-down style that evolved when work-for-hire writers were getting paid based on how many books they cranked out rather than on how much wordage was in a story. That's what I was going for, anyway. I hope you enjoyed it.

I should thank some people. First of all, I appreciate Ron Fortier giving me a shot at all. Second, my beta readers Rin Adams, Sena Meilleur, Anne Hawley, and Tiffany Tomcal all offered helpful suggestions as I was working on the manuscript, as well as catching some embarrassing mistakes. Win Eckert and Adam Garcia both offered support and provided important information that led to me getting the gig in the first place.

And finally, my wife Julie, who married into all this fan craziness and not only listens to all my struggles with plot problems and character extrapolations, diatribes about pulp fiction and what it is and isn't, thoughts about the masked urban hero archetype and so on... but she claims to actually enjoy them. Fellas, trust me on this--when you find a girl that not only tolerates your weird fannish hobby but joyfully embraces it, you *marry* her.

GREG HATCHER - has been writing for one outlet or another for the last twenty-plus years, but this marks his first publication in an honest-to-God pulp anthology and he's still grinning about it. You can find his weekly column on the website ComicBookResources.com, as one of the regular rotating features on Comics Should Be Good. In addition to writing, he also teaches both the Cartooning and Young Authors classes for grades seven through twelve as part of an afterschool arts program in Seattle. He lives in Burien, Washington with his wife Julie, their cat Maggie, and ten thousand books and comics… including several 1970s adventure paperbacks by Norman A. Daniels, the guy that was the original Black Bat author under the pen name "G. Wayman Jones." Full circle.

DEATH ON THE RAILS

A Black Bat Adventure
by
Gene Moyers

The car shut down its headlights as it turned into the darkened side street. The only illumination came from two lonely streetlights. The others were dark, their glass shattered and neglected. Just as neglected as the large factory that loomed to the left. As the battered coupe slowly passed the darkened building it seemed to lean toward them, its air of abandonment obvious. The coupe eased to a stop near the rear of the building. As it idled there, nearly silent, the well muffled engine purring quietly, two men sat inside. The huge man behind the steering wheel whispered to his companion, "Are you sure about this, Boss? You're gonna need me in there." The well-built man next to him leaned closer. In the darkness of the car his face could not be seen beneath his wide brimmed hat. He replied, "Don't worry Butch; I'll be fine, besides I need you out here if things go wrong."

The big man clenched his fists on the steering wheel and nodded silently. His companion removed his hat and pulled a black silk mask over his face. As he did he continued, "Go to that filling station we passed a few blocks back. Call the police and give them the message we decided on. Then come back here and wait for me near this alley. Hopefully things will go quietly. I may be able to get him alone and take him without a shot."

Butch shook his head but said, "Whatever you say, Boss."

The other man got out of the coupe and removed his overcoat and tossed it back into the seat. He was tall and dressed head to toe in black. A gun rode in a holster at his waist. He closed the door quietly and nodded before fading into the shadows of the alley behind the silent factory. Butch put the coupe in gear and it purred quietly away. He drove quietly back to the main street and down two blocks to an all-night filling station where he parked behind it. He went inside to make a phone call. The man on duty jerked his finger at the telephone on the wall and went to use the restroom. Butch put in a nickel and asked for police headquarters. In moments he was connected and spoke urgently. "Listen! Dutch Marley and his new gang are in the closed appliance factory out on Carmody Road. They're planning a big job. If you get there in a hurry, you can get them all." When the voice on the other end asked his name, Butch hung up and headed back to the coupe.

The black clad figure glided down the alley. His uncanny eyesight made dodging glass on the ground from broken factory windows easy. When he reached a fire escape on the back wall he paused to listen. The only sounds came from a distant cricket chirping. Nodding, he jumped to the lowest rung of the ladder and climbed to a metal platform with a set of steep stairs leading up the back of the building. A minute's climbing bought him the factory's roof. Peering over the edge he looked for movement but the darkened roof was empty. He climbed over the roof ledge and ducked under the elevated water tank on the roof then paused to look carefully around before moving on.

The figure in black hugged the shadows as it moved across the rooftop. When it glided from under the raised water tank into the moonlight it was a flitting specter; when it was motionless it seemed to blend into the blackness. The figure knelt by a skylight and bent forward. Rubbing the accumulated dust away with a black gloved hand the figure bent over the glass and peered downward. A dim glow came from far below. The gloved hands moved to the catch and a moment later the skylight was slowly raised. Slowly a head leaned over the sill and stared through the beams and catwalks to the gathering below. The eyes peering down at the men far below could clearly see the men gather on the factory floor. If any of those men could have seen the hooded figure peering down at them they would have instantly recognized the Black Bat.

The Black Bat lifted the skylight higher and swung a leg over the sill. Silently lowering himself to a metal roof truss he balanced there a moment as he quietly closed the skylight behind him. Under the high factory roof it was very dark as he silently and sure footedly crossed to a catwalk. Once on the catwalk, he moved closer to the men below. When he was directly above them he stopped and took stock.

Although the scene was only dimly lighted by a lantern on a long table, the Black Bat's uncanny transplanted eyes gave him the ability to see clearly in darker places than this factory. There were six men gathered around the table. It had been cleared of the junk that cluttered the closed factory and several crates had been opened. The men were examining items taken from one of the crates. One of the men held up something in the light and laughed. The Black Bat could see it was a shotgun. Another man was opening another crate with a long screwdriver. From the crate he drew out another heavy looking weapon. He passed it to a heavy set man.

The Black Bat eyes gleamed in the dark as he recognized the man he had come for; Dutch Marley, former New York gang leader and wanted fugitive. Marley had cut a wide path through the New York underworld during prohibition and after its repeal. Eventually evidence had mounted against him and he had fled before being indicted. Word on the street was that he had gone west to Chicago. He had resumed his activities there until recently when he had finally been arrested for murder. Jumping bail, he had disappeared. Using his underworld contacts, one of the Black Bat's operatives had learned that Marley had returned to New York and was in the process of re-building his old gang. A week of tracking Marley had led the Black Bat here tonight. He intended to break up this little tea party and capture Marley.

As he watched, Marley held the weapon over his head and raised his voice above the whispers the men had been using, "Here it is boys. I told you this little job would be easy. With these choppers we'll make quick work of those guards." There were nods and whispers of agreement among his men. The Black Bat had seen enough. He glided across the cat walk to a ladder on the far wall. Silently he descended it and ducked behind a darkened piece of machinery. Making his way across the floor using cover of the darkened presses and lathes he was soon directly behind Marley.

Creeping closer he could see the men were wiping down their new weapons and pressing heavy .45 cartridges into magazines. Drawing one of his own .45 pistols from its holster the Black Bat stood up and took four quick steps forward. As the men looked up with startled faces, The Black Bat grabbed Marley from behind with his left arm while his right ground the pistol into Marley's back.

"Alright, everybody freeze!" he called out in a clear voice.

Everyone froze where they stood. Marley spat out, "What the . . ., who are you?"

One of the men whispered in awe, "The Black Bat!" There were intakes of breath and curses as the men tensed. Before any of they could go for their guns the Black Bat grated out, "Don't try anything or your Boss gets it. Everybody just take a few steps back and keep your hands where I can see them." There were grumbles as the five gunmen raised their hands and shuffled backwards. In turn the Black Bat shoved Marley up against the table. Keeping his pistol pressed against Marley's back he reached into the special belt her wore over his black clothing and tossed a pair of handcuffs on the table, "Put those on, Marley." Cursing, Marley complied while the Bat kept an eye on his men. They shuffled around, some looking scared while others were angry and defiant.

With Marley's hands cuffed in front of him, the Bat was reaching for the back of the fugitive's collar when he stopped short. There on the table in an open crate he could see metallic oval shaped objects that gleamed evilly in the light; grenades. He grabbed one and slipped it into his pocket followed quickly by another. Then grabbing Marley's collar he began backing away, "Alright, everybody stand just where you are until we're gone."

As the Bat and his captive stepped away toward the shadows the gunmen moved. The ones on the edges threw themselves left and right into the shadows. Simultaneously the remaining three went for their guns. The Bat, his gun still pointed at Marley had to snap off an un-aimed shot and missed. Meanwhile the three shooters had drawn guns and were firing wildly. The Bat jerked Marley off his feet and the two ended up behind the base of a dust covered lathe. Bullets ricocheted overhead and whined into the darkness. Black Bat holstered his pistol and crawled across the cluttered floor dragging a cursing, protesting Marley along with him.

Marley's gunmen had rushed back to the table as the Black Bat disappeared in the darkness. One grabbed a Tommy gun and slipped a magazine into it. Another picked up a shotgun and began thumbing shells into the gun. As they did a third man shouted, "Spread out!"

Knowing he had little time the Bat scuttled toward the back of the building dragging the unwilling gangster with him. As they crossed an aisle between rows of machines, fire stabbed out of the darkness followed closely by the boom of a shotgun. The Bat didn't bother returning fire; he just dove forward to the ground. As he dragged the cursing Marley farther away, more gunfire followed and then a crashing bang!

A bright flash lit up the factory, but instead of fading back to darkness the factory floor was now lit by a yellow glow and the Black Bat could hear the crackling of flames. One of the bullets flying around must have hit something flammable, perhaps a partially empty barrel of chemicals left behind. Whatever the reason, the factory was now on fire. Marley was screaming about getting out as the Black Bat jerked him to his feet. They ran to an open metal stairway and climbed. Above the factory floor the Bat could see the fire burning near the center of the floor. Fed by empty crates, accumulated trash and dirty machinery, it was growing even as he watched.

Butch waited a few minutes and then started up the battered coupe. As he turned onto the street going back toward the factory he heard an explosion and saw the factory's windows glow with light. He shook his head as he turned down a street to get around behind the factory; it looked like he should have called the fire department as well.

Ducking his head as a bullet ricocheted off a nearby metal brace, the Bat pulled Marley higher toward the roof. Moments later the Bat and his prisoner reached the top of the stairs and were confronted by a locked door. Smoke rising from the fire was trapped near the roof and Marley was coughing violently. His eyes watering from the smoke the Bat jerked a .45 from its holster and fired two quick shots into the door near the lock and kicked it open with his foot. Coughing, both of the men stumbled out onto the roof. The Bat had planned to go out the back of the factory into the alley but now he would be forced to use the rear fire escape. Pushing Marley ahead of him he headed for the curving top of a ladder he could see in the moonlight.

He reached the edge and peered over the side of the building. The ladder went down about eight feet and ended at a platform with steep metal stairs leading further down. He turned just as a shot flashed from the open door to the roof. He pulled Marley down to the roof and snapped off a quick shot at the doorway. At least one of Marley's men had followed them. Visibility was getting worse as there were now plumes of dark smoke rising through every vent, skylight and of course, the open doorway. The fire was growing. Black Bat was in a spot. He couldn't get Marley over the roof's edge without making them a target. He also couldn't leave Marley alone nor could he maneuver to get at the hidden gunman while dragging him along. Marley must have come to the same conclusion because he leered at the black clad form, "So, what are you gonna do now, tough guy?"

The Black Bat was silent for a moment before inspiration struck. As he reached into his pocket he calmly said, "You'd better get your head down." When Marley saw the grenade he blanched and buried his head in his hands on the dusty roof. Pulling the pin, The Bat lofted the grenade toward the center of the roof. It landed with a clatter and immediately exploded. The roof was lit for a brief second followed by the bang of the grenade going off near the base of one of the metal legs supporting the elevated water tank. As he had passed under it, the Black Bat remembered squishing through a wet spot from water that had puddled underneath it. As he pulled the pin on the second grenade he desperately hoped that it still contained enough water to do the job. The second grenade landed near where the first one had gone off and rolled up against the leg before it exploded. There was another flash and bang followed by a moment of silence and then a huge grinding screech as the water tank tipped to one side in slow motion and slammed to the roof with a huge crash.

Instantly a wave of water swept across the roof. It went everywhere including down the open stairway door. Black Bat jerked Marley to his feet and turned to the ladder. Behind them there was a creaking and tearing as the now empty water tank broke through the weakened roof. He looked back for a moment before pushing the cursing Marley up and over the ladder.

Lieutenant McGrath had just been leaving the station when the call came in. He should have been home, but his wife was out of town, so he had stayed late to catch up on paperwork. Hearing the name Dutch Marley had changed his mind. Marley had been a notorious gang leader in New York for years. The police had worked hard to get evidence against him to no avail. When they finally did get solid evidence and an indictment, he had unceremoniously skipped town. The word was that he was back but no one had definitely seen him recently. This new tip was almost too good to be true. He gathered up two car loads of officers and set off for the factory with sirens screaming.

With the sirens and lights clearing the way the police reached the factory in minutes. As they pulled up out front, McGrath could see the place was on fire. He shouted for the driver to call for the fire trucks as he drew his revolver and waved his men forward. Just as he reached the front door it banged open and a coughing, hacking man bent over at the waist came staggering out. McGrath grabbed him and shouted, "Where's Marley?" The man coughed and pointed behind him, "He was in there, *cough, cough,* with the Bat." Startled, McGrath shouted in surprise, "The Black Bat?" He shoved the gagging man at a uniformed officer and shouted, "Let's go." Dashing forward he ducked low as he entered the smoky warehouse.

As he crossed the darkened threshold, there was a distant explosion somewhere above. McGrath tried to look upwards but all he could see was smoke. He pulled his handkerchief from a pocket and held it over his nose. As he did, he gasped out to his men, "Spread out and look sharp." There was another explosion somewhere above. McGrath cursed under his breath as a deafening crash shook the entire building. In a flash, water poured down over everything and everyone. He was knocked to his knees as gallons of dirty water cascaded over him knocking his revolver out of his hand. He got to his feet spluttering and spitting. He was soaking wet and mad as a wet hen. He staggered back out the door cursing, "It's the Black Bat! He did this deliberately! I'll get him if it takes me the rest of my days!"

There was chaos for a few minutes. The cascading water hadn't totally put out the fire but it had slowed it enough that the fast arriving firemen had a head start on putting it out. Several other police officers had been caught in the deluge but were unhurt. The rest were rounding up the scorched and soggy gunmen that had escaped the building. In the end the police arrested four known criminals but McGrath was furious to see that neither Marley nor the Black Bat was among them. Once back at the station, booking the suspects and writing reports took quite a while. It was two hours later when McGrath finally made his weary way home. He changed and took a long shower before going to bed. His last thought as his eyes closed were that that Black menace had got the best of him again.

The doorbell rang. McGrath's eyes shot open. Who could that be? The doorbell rang again. He threw back the bed covers and sat up. At this time of night it must be something important; probably an emergency downtown. The doorbell continued to ring steadily. As he threw on his dressing gown over his pajamas he shouted, "I'm coming already, damn it!" Making for the stairs he flipped on lights as he went. The doorbell went silent. He reached the front door, unlocked it and jerked it open yelling, "All right, what's so dad blasted important?" Something heavy propped against the door fell inward and rolled against McGrath's feet. His mouth dropped open as he stared down into the dirty and angry face of former gang leader Dutch Marley. Marley was trussed up with ropes on his hands and feet and he was mouthing probably unrepeatable things through the gag in his mouth. This did not really register on Lieutenant McGrath, though. All he could see was the black bat symbol stamped on Marley's forehead.

"I'd really give a lot to see the look on Lieutenant McGrath's face right now," said the big man behind the wheel of the dark car as it slid quietly away from the curb. The tall figure next to him in the darkened car pulled a black hood off of his head and replaced it with a wide brimmed hat pulled low over his face, "Yes, I imagine he's plenty angry about now. But when he gets his wits back the first place he'll go is . . ."

"To Tony Quinn's place," finished his hulking companion.

"That's right so you'd better get us there first." The driver nodded and pressed the accelerator down. The car sped through the empty streets. Soon it was turning onto a quiet side street in an expensive residential section of the city. It slowed next to a gate in a high wall. The tall passenger got out but leaned back in to speak to the driver, "Thanks Butch. You did well tonight. McGrath would have had me if you hadn't been right there to pick us up." Butch O'Leary smiled back, "It wasn't much Boss. I wish you had let me go in with you though. There were a lot of those guys."

"It was important that the police be alerted, and fire department as it turned out. Now get going, I'll call you tomorrow." He closed the passenger door and watched the car purr away. He then turned and made his way through the gate into the rear garden of the estate. He entered the garden house at the rear of the property and closed the door behind him. He didn't need a light, his extraordinary vision let him find the iron ring and lift the concealed door in the floor of the garden house. He descended closing the door behind him and followed the darkened tunnel for many yards until he reached a ladder at its end. Climbing it, he exited through a concealed entrance into a brightly lit windowless room.

The room was outfitted as laboratory. It was filled with cabinets and equipment. There was a microscope, a small x-ray machine, cameras, cabinets filled with chemicals and shelves lined with books. It was the secret laboratory of the Black Bat. As he removed his black costume a concealed door in one wall opened and a slender, middle aged man with thinning gray hair entered. As he watched the tall man change clothing he spoke, "Did all go well, sir?"

The tall man straightened and brushed his hair back. As he did the scars around his cheeks and eyes became very apparent. Other than the scars, Anthony Quinn ex-district Attorney was quite handsome. He smiled and said, "Very well Silk. We bagged Marley and broke up his new gang. Several of them were probably picked up by the police. Butch picked me up as planned and we gift wrapped and delivered Marley to Lieutenant McGrath's house. In fact, I wouldn't be surprised if we don't have company soon."

Silk Kirby's eyes sparkled as the former confidence man and now valet to Tony Quinn asked, "Should I make some coffee for the Lieutenant?"

They exited the hidden room and entered a warm, well-furnished study. Quinn turned and closed the concealed door, "No Silk, I don't think that's appropriate for a pair of honest, early retiring citizens. In fact I think we'd better set the stage for our soon to be visitor." Quinn turned and hurried up the stairs. Silk went through the lower floor turning off lights and securing doors and windows. When he finished he went to his room and changed into pajamas and robe. He could hear the former DA in his room changing. He smiled and retired to his bed to wait.

Fifteen minutes later Quinn's sensitive ears heard a car pull up out front. He nodded. He closed his eyes and pretended to be asleep. Down

"Did all go well, sir?"

stairs an angry Lieutenant McGrath pushed through the gate and up the walk to the large Quinn house. Once at the door he pounded on it with his fist. A moment later he did so again. He raised his hand a third time when he heard a key turn in a lock. The door opened and the suspicious face of Silk Kirby looked out, "Who is it? And what do you want?"

McGrath grated out, "Open up Kirby. I want to talk to Quinn." Silk widened the door opening and peered out, "Lieutenant? Do you know what time it is?"

"Yeah, I can tell time. Now lemme in!"

Silk pulled the door open wide and McGrath brushed past him. "Okay, where is he?" He looked triumphantly at Silk. "He isn't here, is he?"

Silk looked surprised, "Of course Mr. Quinn is here. He's upstairs asleep."

McGraths' face fell and his jaw dropped. He squinted at Silk, "Oh yeah, let's go see." He then turned and stomped up the stairs with Silk just behind protesting loudly. Reaching the second floor he turned down the hall and walked directly into Quinn's room without a knock. As the door banged open Quinn turned over and looked in the direction of the open doorway, "Who is it? Silk, is that you?"

McGrath opened his mouth but no words came out. From behind him Silk spoke up, "No sir, it's Lieutenant McGrath. He insisted on coming in." Quinn looked confused, "Lieutenant? What time is it?"

McGrath finally found his voice and stammered, "Uh, it's late I know, but I thought you'd want to know that we finally caught up with Dutch Marley. We arrested him tonight"

Continuing to stare at the door Quinn questioned, "Dutch Marley? He's back in town? How did you catch him?"

"Uh, we got an anonymous tip. We caught him at a factory over on Carmody Road. It looks like he was up to his old tricks getting a new gang started."

Quinn smiled, "Well, that's good news. He's been wanted a long time. But couldn't this have waited until tomorrow, Lieutenant?"

McGrath looked uncomfortable, "Well uh, Since you did so much work on his case when you were DA I thought you'd like to know that we finally had him," he finished lamely.

Quinn nodded, "That's thoughtful of you but since I'm no longer D.A., I won't be prosecuting him, as much as I'd like to." He threw back his covers and groped around for his dressing gown. Silk stepped past McGrath and handed it to him. "Shall I have Silk make you some coffee?"

McGrath backed out into the hall, "Uh, no thank you. I have Marley down in the car and I have to get him to the station. Sorry to have bothered you." He turned and left quickly. Silk followed him down the stairs and closed the front door after him. He met Quinn coming down the stairs. Laughing he said, "He was muttering under his breath all the way out the door, sir. We really got him that time" They both laughed.

Three days later Silk ushered a tall, well dressed gentleman into Quinn's living room. "Commissioner Warner is here to see you sir."

Quinn stood up and held out his hand to empty air, "A pleasure Commissioner. What can I do for you?" Warner moved around and shook the hand, "Tony I've come about Dutch Marley. You've heard that we've arrested him?"

Quinn nodded, "Yes. Lieutenant McGrath was kind enough to make a special trip out here to let me know. It was very thoughtful of him." Silk made a valiant effort not to grin behind his hand as he scratched his face.

"Yes. Well, Marley's extradition hearing is tomorrow and I thought you'd like to attend."

Quinn's surprise was real this time, "Extradition? We have warrants on him here for racketeering and conspiracy. They're several years old but still valid. Who wants him extradited?"

Warner answered, "The state of Illinois. It seems that's where he's been hiding since he fled here. Recently though, he was arrested for murder. He broke out of custody before he could be brought to trial. Illinois wants him back in Chicago very badly. Judge Hoskins will hear the arguments tomorrow. Are you interested?"

"Absolutely! What time is the hearing?" Quinn asked grimly.

The next day at ten o'clock Quinn, holding Silk's arm, entered court room "B" in the municipal court building. It was crowded. As he took a seat in the rear of the visitor's section with his cane across his knees and Silk next to him, he could see many police officers, reporters and other interested spectators in the room. Quinn didn't look around but his eyes behind his dark glasses missed nothing. Marley sat at the defendant's table next to what must be his lawyer. The judge entered and the proceedings began.

Although it was interesting to hear from the Illinois prosecutor what Marley had been up to while on the lam, Quinn was interested in only whether he would be tried here in New York or in Chicago. Eventually the judge had heard representatives from all parties. He looked thoughtful as he scanned the court room. His eyes landing on Tony he spoke, "I see that Mr. Quinn is here today. Mr. Quinn, would you be so kind as to come forward and assist the court?" Surprised, Quinn stood up, "Of course your honor." He made his way forward, stumbling a little over other spectators shoes. A bailiff held open the little swinging gate separating the spectators from the bench and lawyer's tables for him. Once in front of the bench, the judge questioned, "Mr. Quinn, you were with the D.A.'s office during the Marley case. What do you think?"

Quinn spoke up, "Well your honor, we worked very hard on that one. Marley fled because we had a strong case. The evidence is still on file. I believe all the witnesses are still available. If tried here, I believe the D.A. can convict Marley on conspiracy, racketeering and extortion. It was, and still is a strong case."

The judge mulled this over, "These are strong charges, but you don't have a murder charge against Mr. Marley, do you?"

"No, your honor. We were never able to connect Marley directly to any murders although there were strong suspicions against some of his men."

The judge thought for a few moments and then spoke, "Although the charges by the state of New York pre-date those of the state of Illinois, the charge of murder is certainly more serious and should take precedence. I therefore rule in favor of the state of Illinois and direct that the prisoner be extradited to Illinois and handed over to the legal authorities there. Please see to that, Commissioner Warner." He stood up and banged his gavel down once,."This court is adjourned."

There was an immediate stir as everyone started talking at once. Marley was led away by a bailiff. Various lawyers were either arguing or shaking hands. As Quinn moved toward the rear of the court room, McGrath materialized by his side to open the swinging gate for him. As Quinn passed through it swinging his cane slightly back and forth McGrath let it go. Quinn saw it coming but didn't try to block it. The gate swung shut and hit Quinn in the legs. He only partially blocked it with his cane. As it struck he cried out, "Ouch!"

Watching carefully McGrath immediately apologized as he looked disappointed, "I'm sorry, Quinn. I slipped."

Smiling Quinn looked straight ahead as he replied, "That's all right Lieutenant. I'm getting used to it." Silk materialized at his elbow and helped lead him through the crowds as McGrath glowered at them.

In the car headed home silk inquired, "What do you think, sir?"

From the back Quinn replied, "Well, it's over one way or another. From what I understand they have a good case out in Chicago. Marley will be punished for his crimes. I'm not picky about who does it. On the way out I heard Commissioner Warner assigning McGrath to take Marley back to Chicago."

Silk laughed, "That will keep him out of our hair for a while." Quinn nodded.

Two nights later the Black Bat watched from a rooftop as Griff Halder walked cautiously down a darkened street. He paused at the mouth of an alley and looked furtively around before slipping into it. The Bat turned and glided noiselessly through the maze of clutter on the building roof. He reached the rear of the building and looked down. Although extremely dark the Bat could see the alley as clear as day. Halder emerged from the alley and looked around. Then pulling a cigarette lighter from his pocket he lit it and turned to the building on his right. Using the lighter's meager illumination he located a door at the rear of the building and knocked. There was pause and then the alley was flooded with light as the door opened. Halder entered and the door closed. The Bat's eyes narrowed. Years before Halder had been a trusted member of Dutch Marley's organization. Trying to track down the last remnants of Marley's gang had brought him here to this rooftop tonight.

The Black Bat considered the alley fire escape for a moment then turned and moved to the side of the building. The building across the alley was at the same level and about six feet away. The Bat stepped back about fifteen feet, took a deep breath and ran toward the edge. With a mighty leap he cleared the raised ledge and soared across the alley. He landed on one foot, tucked into a ball and turned his landing into a roll. Coming to one knee, he listened for several moments but heard nothing. Standing up, he made his way quickly to the small structure housing the stairway down into the building. It was locked but the Bat had the door open in a few moments. He entered the darkened stairway and started down.

As he reached the fourth floor, he drew one of his pistols and listened. He saw no lights and heard nothing. He repeated this action on the third floor with the same result and again on the second floor. When he reached the first floor, his attention was immediately drawn to a thin band of light coming from under a closed door near what looked like the back door to the building. Gliding noiselessly to it the Black Bat pressed his ear to the thin panel.

After being blinded by a gangster's acid and before the miraculous surgery that had given him new sight, The Black Bat had spent a year as a truly blind man. During this time he had developed to a high degree his senses of touch, smell and hearing as compensation for his sight. His sensitive hearing made it easy to make out the low voices on the other side of the door.

"I told you, the gas masks are no problem. And I can get you some tear gas grenades in a couple of days, but those others are going to be tough to get that quickly."

"Not good enough. I need everything in three days."

"And I told you I'll have to call my contact at Camp Reid to see if he can get them."

"All right, I'll pay you for the other stuff now. If you can't get those other grenades, we'll go without them."

"Fine, let's see the cash."

With suspicious eyes counting money on the other side of the door, the Black Bat judged the time was good for an entrance. He pulled out his other .45, reared back on one foot and slammed the other into the door just above the knob. The door flew open and slammed against the wall. Two men stood in the middle of the room. Griff, the larger man, was just handing a stack of cash to the shorter man in front of him. Both men had shocked looks on their faces. Before the Black Bat could say a word, Griff dropped the money and ducked behind the smaller man, reaching for a gun as he did. The other man threw up his hands and shrieked, "Don't shoot!"

The Bat couldn't get a clean shot at Griff; grimacing behind his mask he sidestepped and brought his pistols up. Behind the man, Griff had cleared leather with a revolver and was bringing it up. The vigilante yelled, "Don't do it!" Griff ignored the warning and squeezed his trigger. The Black Bat fired at the same time, their bullets crossing in flight. Griff's shot skimmed past the Bat's arm punching a hole through his short cape. The Bat's bullets found their mark in Griff's chest. His revolver clattered to the floor and he fell backwards. The Bat's guns twitched to the other now terrified man. He fell to his knees and pleaded, "Don't shoot Black Bat. I'm not with him."

The Bat advanced to Griff and bent down on one knee. The gunman's eyes were open and his breathing was fast and thready. When he saw the hooded face staring down at him he tried to smile, "Guess I wasn't fast enough, but we're . . ." his voice faded and his eyes closed. The Black Bat shook his head and stood up. He turned to the other man, took two steps and pointed one of his pistols between the man's eyes, "I just killed a man and I'm not too happy about that. Are you going to disappoint me too?"

The man turned pale, "Look Black Bat, I'm just a businessman. This guy came to me with an offer and . . ." The Bat cut him off, "Don't waste my time. You supply equipment to criminals. Griff here came to you trying to buy equipment. Just what was he going to do with gas masks and grenades?"

Licking his lips the man stuttered, "Uh, I'm not sure."

The gun was shoved forward until the warm muzzle pressed gently against the sweating man's forehead, "If that's all you know then you're of no use to me. Maybe I should just kill you now and be done with it."

"No! No! I know what they had planned."

"They? Who are they?"

"Halder! Halder said he and his friends needed special gear."

"How many gas masks did he want?"

"Five."

"What did he want them for?"

"When I asked what they were up to, he laughed and said, 'a jail break.'"

The Black Bat paused for a moment with his mind racing, "What else did he want?"

"Look I told him that those would have to come from an army post. That takes ti…"

"What was it?"

The man gulped, "He wanted army smoke grenades."

The Bat stood up and looked down at the man. He was tempted to tie him up and leave him for the police but decided it wouldn't do much good. He hadn't really committed any crime worth speaking of and he certainly wouldn't tell the police anything. He walked to the door and said over his shoulder. "I know who you are. Stay out of trouble. I'll be watching." He disappeared into the darkened hall leaving the shaking man staring at the body on the floor.

The next morning Quinn called Commissioner Warner's office and was quickly connected, "Tony, how are you and what can I do for you this morning?"

"Fine Commissioner, I'm just calling to see how Dutch Marley's extradition is going."

"Quite well. We'll be rid of that no good very soon."

"I'm glad. Do you mind telling me when it's happening?"

"Not at all, Lieutenant McGrath is taking him by train to Chicago on Monday."

"I hope security is good."

"Certainly, the Lieutenant is taking two of his best plain clothes men with him. Further, the convoy to the station will be heavily guarded and I've got three squads of men searching the train and passengers as they board for hidden weapons."

"Well, that is reassuring commissioner. I'll sleep better knowing that Marley is in good hands."

"Yes, I'm sure everything is going to be just fine."

"Yes, so am I."

Quinn hung up and was thoughtful for a moment. Warner had said Monday: three days from now, just when Halder had said he needed the gear. He looked up at Silk, "Get hold of Carol and Butch. We have plans to make."

Two hours later Carol, Silk and Butch were all assembled in Quinn's living room behind closed drapes. When she stepped into the room Quinn gazed affectionately at the petite blonde woman. Not only was she a competent aide in his fight against crime she was much more. It was she who had arranged for the miraculous operation that had restored his sight. In addition Quinn harbored strong personal feelings for her, feelings he couldn't express freely as long as he wore the black mask to combat crime. Carol in turn was very much in love with Tony. She was patient though; she knew that eventually their time would come.

Quinn quickly restated the happenings of the night before and his conversation with Warner that morning. Then he gave them his conclusions; "The police are sending Dutch Marley back to Chicago on Monday. Lieutenant McGrath is escorting him along with two other detectives. I believe that some of Marley's gang are going to attempt to break him out during the train trip. We need to stop them."

Carol asked quietly, "Why do you think Halder was planning a break out?"

Quinn replied, "Years ago he was Marely's right hand man. It's got be more than a coincidence that he's planning some kind of jailbreak just as his old boss is being extradited out of state."

Butch looked thoughtful, "Why do you think it'll be on the train?"

"Two reasons: the jail is too heavily guarded as will be the convoy to the

"We are going along to look after things."

station. Also the gunman wanted the gas masks and grenades within three days. That's just before the train leaves."

Carol inquired, "So what's the plan?"

"We are going along to look after things. Tony Quinn can't do it openly so I'll need you and Butch to go along as passengers. Carol, I want you to get a compartment on the train. Butch, you get a seat, a Pullman berth if you can. You two are going along. I can't be seen because McGrath will be immediately suspicious; however the Black Bat can certainly make an appearance." As he finished Quinn let a small smile cross his face.

Silk spoke up, "What about me, sir?"

"I'm afraid you have to stay behind, Silk." Before the smaller man could protest, Quinn held up a hand, "McGrath knows you too well, Silk. If you were aboard the train, he'd automatically assume I was nearby. He's already too suspicious of Tony Quinn for my taste. We can't give his suspicions any more fodder. He's never met Carol or Butch. They can ride the train unsuspected of being my eyes. Also, you have an important part to play right here."

Silk looked interested but suspicious. Quinn smiled and continued, "Carol, you and Butch go out and see to those tickets and pack your bags. Silk, you and I are going to put on a little drama. First though, you're going out to make some purchases." When he had elaborated what he had in mind to Silk, the ex-confidence man was smiling.

The lower concourse in Penn Station was chaotic at 4:30 p.m. Tony Quinn circulated through the crowd. He wore a long trench coat with the collar turned up, dark glasses and a scarf. The crowds of people brushed past him without a second look. He made his way to the track where the *Midwest Zephyr* was soon to depart. He found an out of the way pillar behind which he could observe the platform where boarding was in full swing. There was a heavy police presence. The police were taking threats seriously. Men were being searched while women had to hold their purses open for a cursory examination. Glancing to his left he could see the baggage car being loaded with crates and luggage. There, a policeman was keeping a close lookout to see that no unauthorized person stowed away.

While he watched, Quinn made out the large figure of Butch O'Leary being stopped and searched as he showed his ticket to the police. Quinn nodded. He didn't see Carol. She must have already boarded. Glancing at his watch Quinn was about to turn away when he spotted a familiar figure queuing up to board. It took him am moment of observing the thin, hard faced man before he recognized him as a known ex-con named Duran. Nodding, he pushed away from the pillar and merged with the crowd.

Aboard the train Carol was opening her purse and digging around inside when there was a knock at the door. She opened it and Butch slid inside. "Spot anything," she asked. Butch shook his head, "Not much. McGrath, Marley and two detectives are in a day car just ahead of the dining car. Marley is handcuffed to one detective; the other two are sitting just behind. I'm two cars back from you in a lower Pullman berth. When they make them up, I should be able to get out quietly if I have to."

Carol nodded as she held up a small automatic pistol she had pulled from the hidden compartment at the bottom of her purse. She reached back in and came up with a leather sap that she offered to butch. "It's a good thing they didn't heft the purse. It might have seemed a little heavy. Butch just smiled and banged his fists together, "No thanks. These'll do." Butch left to return to his seat.

At 5 o'clock exactly the train began to move. McGrath stood in the vestibule of the last car. The conductor walked alongside the slow moving train looking forward. As the train gathered speed he swung aboard and closed the door. He nodded to McGrath, "Well, we're off, Lieutenant. Everything went smoothly. No one's aboard who doesn't belong." McGrath nodded and returned to his seat. As the train pulled by a powerful electric engine entered the tunnel leading out from under Penn station, it was observed closely by the black clad figure clinging to the tunnel roof.

Quinn had waited for the right moment and slipped inside a few minutes before. Removing a black cloth bag from a pocket of his trench coat he quickly removed his hat and coat and stuffed them into the bag. He attached the bag to his waist. Under the trench coat he was dressed in black pants, matching long sleeve shirt and black rubber soled shoes. Finally he pulled a black silk mask from his pants pocket and slipped it over his head. Tony Quinn had vanished, replaced by the ominous figure of the Black Bat.

From his belt the Bat pulled out a light weight cord, weighted on one end. Whirling it around, he looped it over a light fixture high up the side of the tunnel. Using this he climbed up the wall to the light. A quick blow with his pistol butt shattered the light and left the Bat clinging to it in darkness. Grasping an overhead conduit containing power lines the Bat boosted himself up until his feet could get a grip on the light fixture. He clung there waiting patiently. He didn't have long to wait; less than two minutes later the Zephyr entered the tunnel. It was still traveling slowly as the black clad figure dropped to the roof of a passing passenger car. He landed with a thump.

Atop the car the Black Bat lay flat for a moment listening for any cries or other signs of alarm. Satisfied that he was undetected, he looked forward and back to judge his position then began crawling forward. The darkness of the tunnel was no impediment, his vision made it easy to move from car to car. When he judged he had reached the correct car, he worked his way over to the edge and looked down the side of the car. It was well illuminated by light streaming from the passenger windows. It took but a moment for the Bat to see a cloth fluttering from one illuminated window. He continued until he was directly above that cloth marker. Unwinding another thin but strong cord rope from around his waist he attached it to a metal hook he drew from his belt. He planted the hook on a lip at the edge of the roof and pressed it until the tip of the hook was lodged firmly in the soft metal. Dropping a length of rope over the side the Black Bat carefully lowered himself over the edge of the moving railway car.

Carol was patiently watching the window. She had hung the arm of one her sweaters out the window and pressed the sash down on it as instructed. When she saw the rope snake past the window she hastened to lift the sash fully and pulled her sweater clear. Moments later a black clad figure lowered itself into view. The bat's feet found the window sill and a few seconds later he was safely in the compartment and closing the window.

Turning, the Bat saw the look on her face and smiled casually at her, "See, a piece of cake." Carol just shook her head and mumbled something about "crazy stunts." Quickly she brought the Bat up to date on what she and Butch had seen. He nodded, "It's kind of early yet. We aren't due into Chicago until nearly noon. If they make a move, it will be late tonight." He rubbed his chin thoughtfully, "Probably somewhere after Pittsburgh, but before dawn. I guess we'll just have to wait and see." He paced across the small room. "It bothers me to have you and Butch do all the scouting ..."

"But you have to stay out of sight," Carol finished for him. The Bat nodded and sat down. Carol smiled as she opened the door to leave, "I'll bring Butch back."

Butch and Carol were soon back and the trio firmed up their plans as time passed quickly. Butch was briefed and turned down the offer of the third .45 that the Bat had brought aboard. Carol and Butch had arranged to be in different dinner seatings so they could get a look at more people. Then Butch and Carol left to mix with the passengers. There was much coming and going as the passengers settled in for their journey. Butch spent some time in the lounge car sipping coffee and sizing up his fellow passengers. Carol moved from car to car looking casual, smiling at people and saying "hello." The Bat tried to wait patiently wishing he could get out and look for familiar faces. He had carefully described the ex-con Duran to Carol and Butch but wished he were able to keep an eye on him directly.

Fleetingly, he wondered how Silk was getting on. They had worked hard on their preparations but the combination of questions and answers was endless. They couldn't cover every eventuality. In the end it would all depend on Silk's quick mind and his ability to ad lib. Fortunately the ex-confidence man was smooth and glib tongued.

By seven o'clock the train was pulling into Trenton for a brief stop. McGrath was off the train early. He greeted the Trenton detective who was heading up the squad of police there. Commissioner Warner had used his influence with every major police force along the route to put a presence in at the stations and check out suspicious characters attempting to board the train. After a brief word with him McGrath made for a telephone booth in the waiting room. He put in his money and was connected to the long distance operator.

The phone rang and Silk answered, "Mr. Quinn's residence."

Just what he'd expected thought McGrath; a stall, "Kirby, is that you? This is Lieutenant McGrath. Let me talk to Quinn, it's important."

"Oh, uh Mr. Quinn is in the shower sir. I can tell him you called though. I'm sure he'll return your call as soon as he's able."

McGrath nearly chortled with laughter. To himself he said, "I knew it. He's not there. I've got him now." Aloud he said, "I need to talk to him. Get him out of the shower if you have to."

On the other end of the line Silk was ready. He stood in front of a long table that had been placed in front of the telephone. On the table, were no less than four record players. All were turning and had records on the spinning tables. More records sat on a table nearby next to a recording unit. All records had handwritten labels attached to their centers. Silk smiled as he dropped the needle on one spinning record. He spoke into the phone, "Well, I'm afraid that's not possib . . ." From the speaker there came a distant crash and an irritated voice yelling out, "Damn! Silk where's my robe? I thought you laid it out . . . and who moved this chair?"

Silk yelled out loudly to the empty room, "Just a moment sir. I'll be right there." Then he spoke into the receiver again, "I'm sorry Lieutenant. We have a minor emergency here. If you can hold the line for a few minutes I can get Mr. Quinn for you." The speaker yelled out "Silk!" again.

In Trenton, McGrath who had heard everything fumed, "No I can't hold. This is long distance. Tell Quinn I'll try again later." He then hung up annoyed. He had been sure that Quinn would be out. The Bat was around here somewhere he could feel it; and if the Bat was here Quinn was here. Grumbling he glanced at his watch and hurried back to the train. The conductor was calling out, "All Aboooaaard!"

Back in Quinn's house Silk was chuckling as he stopped one of the record players and lifted off the vinyl disc. He set it aside and looked with pride at the set up. He and Quinn had spent most of yesterday afternoon recording bits and pieces of conversations on the discs. With preparation and some quick reactions Silk was prepared to keep McGrath's suspicions at bay all night if necessary. He rubbed his hands together and laughed aloud, "So much for Act I. We'll have to see if McGrath needs Act II as well."

Once past Trenton, Carol ate dinner during the first seating. She noticed that McGrath ate alone. At Philadelphia a lot of people got on and some off while the electric engine was exchanged for a powerful steam locomotive. McGrath again was quickly off the train consulting with watchful local police on the platform. When travel resumed, Butch ate dinner in the dining car. The two remaining detectives along with Marley ate dinner. Butch took note of a watchful McGrath hovering nearby. After dinner Butch adjourned to the lounge car where he caught sight of a man strongly fitting the description of Duran that Quinn had given him. He watched him and eventually followed him back to his seat noting its location for future reference.

Eventually he made his way to Carol's compartment. He knocked and was admitted. After giving his report to the Bat he asked, "We've only spotted one guy. What happens if we can't spot any more of them?"

The Bat replied soberly, "We'll just have to stay as close to Marley as we can and wait for them to make their move."

Butch wasn't too happy with this, "And what if they managed to get gas and smoke grenades?"

"I don't think they did. We broke up their contact on that one. They didn't have much time to set up another buy. If they did get some gas we'll just have to cope. You brought that large handkerchief didn't you?" Butch nodded his assent. "If they use gas use that handkerchief to cover your face. It might be a good idea to use it anyway if trouble starts. There are a lot of witnesses about and we need to protect yours and Carol's identities."

Butch nodded and stood up, "I'll go and see what Carol's up to." He slipped out the door into the corridor. He headed toward the rear but couldn't find her in any of the second class cars or the lounge. He frowned and headed forward. As he did he got some suspicious looks from one of the detectives and interestingly a dark haired, fairly well dressed man was eyeing him over his newspaper. As Butch hurried forward he felt a little guilty. Perhaps he had been too obvious in his comings and goings. Darn it! It was hard to be inconspicuous when you were his size. As he passed through the Pullman cars he had to work his way through uniformed porters who were making up the sleeping berths. Once clear of that congestion he moved forward into a car of first class compartments and was about to knock at Carol's door when he spied her blonde head at the end of the corridor gesturing to him. When he reached her she whispered, "There's something fishy going on."

Butch whispered back, "What?"

Just then they both heard a door open and the loud clacking of the wheels on the tracks and the roar of wind was loud in their ears. Carol's eyes opened wide and she reached behind Butch to twist a door knob then she pushed him backwards. Butch was too large to push easily but he sensed that Carol was scared and he threw himself backwards. Carol tumbled after him and they both ended up jammed in the tiny restroom. A moment passed and finally Butch whispered, "What was that about?'

She whispered back, "I saw the conductor heading toward the baggage car. I followed him on a lark and saw him meet someone in the vestibule of the baggage car. I could only see them through two sets of glass and couldn't hear what they said but I saw a man pass the conductor money and he passed something small and metallic back. I think it was a key?" There was a fast thinking silence as they both thought about what that meant. Finally Butch whispered, "What did this guy look like?"

Carol answered, "I couldn't get a good look at him but he was definitely blonde haired and was wearing a light colored suit."

"What do you think the key was for?"

"I'm guessing it was for the baggage car."

"Right, we'd better go tell 'you know who' about this."

Carol nodded and opened the door to peer into the corridor. She nodded and was gone. Butch waited a full minute and left casually. Minutes later they were all back in Carol's compartment. When he had listened to their story the Bat spoke, "Blonde man, gray suit. Okay that might be another one of them. I think I should take a look at the baggage car just in case."

Carol frowned, "But how are you going to get back there. Do you want us to create a diversion?" The Bat smiled and simply pointed at the ceiling with one hand. Butch accepted this easily but pointed out that they would be pulling into Harrisburg any minute. The Bat nodded, "We have to wait, but they can't do anything either. When we pull out of the station I'll go over the roof. Carol, circulate around and look for anyone suspicious and watch out for this blonde man. Butch, you go back and keep an eye on Duran." The two nodded as they all heard the whistle blow and felt the train start to slow.

It was after nine o'clock as they pulled into Harrisburg. Pullman berths had been set up and the train was starting to settle down. As he made for the station platform, McGrath could see many of the second class passengers were starting to doze in their seats. Once on the platform he made for the waiting room. There he went straight for the phone.

Silk was sipping coffee while sitting in a straight back chair near the phone when it rang. He immediately turned on all the record players and answered the phone, "Mr. Quinn's residence."

"It's McGrath again. Is Quinn there?" He had heard Quinn's voice but he just couldn't believe that he really was still in New York. He had to know for sure.

Silk responded quickly enough, "Yes, he's here. If you'll hold the line I'll bring him to the phone." McGrath looked disgustingly at the receiver; could he be wrong?

Silk waited nearly a minute took a deep breath and dropped the needle on the third spinning record while he held the telephone receiver near the speaker, "Hello lieutenant, nice of you to call." He quickly lifted the needle.

"Trying to find something to say McGrath responded, "Hello Quinn just thought I'd call you with an update."

Silk dropped the needle onto the far left player, "That's very nice. How are you?" He winced, that was just a little bit stilted.

McGrath seemed not to notice, "We're in Harrisburg. No sign of any trouble. Everyone's settling in for the night." While McGrath was speaking Silk was frantically shutting off one recorder and substituting one of the spare phonograph records sitting on the table for one he quickly pulled off the record player.

"Well, thanks for calling, Lieutenant. It's been nice talking to you."

McGrath looked disgustedly at the receiver in his hand, "Well I thought you'd like to know how things were going, Quinn. Sorry if I bothered you."

Silk dropped the needle on the far right hand player, "Goodnight Lieutenant, thanks for calling."

McGrath slammed down the receiver on its hook, "Rich dilettante! You'd think I was disturbing him from something important. What's a blind man got to do this time of night, anyway?" He grumbled all the way back to the train.

In New York Silk sat down heavily. He wiped some perspiration from his receding hairline and whispered, "Well, Act II was a little shaky but the audience bought it . . . I hope."

As the train pulled away for the station and gained speed, the Bat pushed the window sash up and grabbed the rope hanging from the roof of the car. Within seconds he had clambered to the roof and was moving forward along the top of the train. He could tell when he had reached the baggage car because there was no light from windows reflecting off the rapidly moving ground alongside the rails. Leaning over the side he found a set of steel rungs set into the side of the baggage car. Using the rungs, he carefully lowered himself until he could reach the door to the vestibule. He opened it, swung in and closed it behind him. He could see through the glass in the end door that the next car's vestibule was empty. Turning, he put his ear to the baggage car door and listened. His keen hearing clearly heard the sounds of movement followed by thumps, and then a high pitched screech.

The Black Bat cautiously opened the door and looked in. Halfway down the car a blonde man in a light grey suit was peering into a just opened crate. He had a crowbar in his hand. The Bat entered, closing the door softly behind him. Drawing his .45s he took several steps down the car and commanded, "Drop the crowbar and put up your hands!" Startled, the man jumped backwards. He raised the crowbar and then saw the Black Bat and his pistols. He hesitated a moment and then the crowbar clattered to the floor of the car. The Bat advanced on him. When close he could see the man was of middle age with hard eyes and a weak chin. The Bat motioned him back with his guns and stepped up to the open crate, "So what do we have here that's so important?" He risked a quick glance into the crate. Lying on blankets he could see the metallic forms of long guns. He flicked his glance quickly back to his captive before he could move, "Ahhh, that's how you got your guns past the frisks. Clever; nobody was searching shipped crates. All it took was a bribe to the conductor and there you go." The man pressed his lips together and said nothing.

The Black Bat's mind raced. If this man was opening the crate, his pals would be along shortly. He might be able to hold them up, but without support from Butch or Carol he could not get word to McGrath. Seeing the side loading door behind the crook he got a quick inspiration. He gestured with his guns, "Turn around and get that door open."

The man's mouth fell open in surprise, "What?"

"You heard me, get that door open!"

"Look, you can't make me jump. The fall will kill me!"

The Black Bat smiled, "I wasn't thinking of that but, it is a good idea if you don't do just what I tell you. Now get that door open!" The man turned and began fumbling with the large door latch. When he finally got it open, he looked back at his captor. The Black Bat holstered the gun in his left hand while indicating with the other what he wanted done. The man swore and grabbed hold of the door handle. It took some work but finally with a huge heave the door slid open a foot; immediately cold air and the roar of the rain filled the car. The man continued to jerk the door back until the door was open nearly four feet. The blonde gunman stepped back from the door and looked scared. The Bat also stepped back from the crate and gestured at it with his pistol, "Okay. I want you to start throwing those guns out the door."

Several expressions flitted across the crook's face; surprise, disbelief and anger in that order. He stepped to the crate and tried to protest, "Look, this isn't . . ." The Bat cut him off by raising his pistol and thumbing the hammer to full cock. The blonde man paled and quickly reached into the crate. He came up with a Tommy gun clutched in his hands. The Black Bat spoke loudly, "Out the door!" Cursing the blonde man turned and threw the gun out the door. He then returned to the crate under the Bat's watchful eye and plucked out another Tommy gun. The Bat gestured and the second gun followed the first. The third time he came out with a sawed off shotgun. The Bat shook his head as this too was thrown through the open door into the night.

His next trip into the crate brought out a rubber gas mask and a soup can sized cylindrical object. The Bat kept his face neutral. It looked like the gang had gotten their special gear after all. A gesture, and the man tossed them through the open door. Three more masks came next. As the man was pulling a pistol from the crate, the Bat's uncanny hearing detected a slight noise behind him. Before he could turn, something hard and moving fast struck him in the shoulder. He grunted and staggered forward. His arm partially numb, he barely kept hold of his gun. The blonde man dropped the empty pistol and tear gas grenade he was holding and lunged at the Bat. One hand went for the Bat's gun hand the other for his throat. His momentum threw the two of them across the car and against the wall.

The Bat got his free hand on the hand at his throat and pried it loose. As he did this, he saw two men rushing down the swaying car toward them. The roar of the train through the door had covered the noise of their opening the far door. He shifted his weight as the first man rushed him and lifted his foot into the man's mid-section. The Bat couldn't hear the woof of air leaving his lungs but he saw him double over and stagger to one side. The blonde man used this opportunity to hammer the Bat's still partially numbed arm against the wall of the car. His pistol was knocked from his grip and went skittering across the floor. The Bat then lifted his knee into the blonde man's groin. He too doubled over.

The Bat turned and met the last man with a left to the jaw and a weak right. The last man was Duran. He staggered and then waded back in arms swinging. The Bat ducked one blow and took another to side of the head. He fought back with two quick jabs and left hook. Duran was caught with the hook and took two steps back in pain. This happened just as the now recovered blonde man launched himself at the Bat. As the Bat was rammed back by the force of the blonde man's charge he saw Duran scrabbling for the Bat's dropped pistol as the second man, now recovered, lunged forward.

His options few, without time to draw his second automatic, the Bat let himself be shoved backwards. As he reached the open door he pushed himself to one side. Grasping the door latch he let himself be carried through the door by his attacker's momentum and he swung to one side of the door. Unfortunately the blonde man's momentum carried him straight through. His yell was barely heard as he disappeared into the darkness. Hanging onto the latch with both hands the Bat did not move. In a moment a head and arm protruded through the door. The hand held his recovered .45. The Bat was ready and with an accurate boot kicked the gun out and into darkness as well. Having bought a minute the Bat swung

"...the blonde man ...threw the gun out the door."

his feet sideways scrabbling with them to find a purchase along the bottom edge of the car. His toe caught and he pushed himself upwards a foot or two. As he did, he felt the door sliding closed. He hung onto the outside latch with both hands as the door slammed shut.

The closing of the door actually benefitted the Bat. There was a two inch sill directly under the doorway. He got his feet onto this and rested for moment taking the strain off his arms. When he was ready, he took a deep breath, let go of the latch and lunged upwards. He had only one chance but his strong, black gloved fingers successfully grasped the upper edge of the baggage car. It was the work of a few moments to pull himself up and sprawl safely on top of the car.

There was no time to regain his breath. The Bat ran down the top of the train. When he came to a gap between cars, he leaped. In less than a minute he had reached the rope over Carol's compartment. Seconds later he was inside the car. Once there he brought her up to date and sent her out to alert Butch. She found him walking forward from the lounge car. He was frowning. He had seen no sign of Duran and was getting concerned. They passed through the Pullman cars whispering to each other. Most berths were occupied as it was now well after ten o'clock. She briefed him then moved back to check on the police and their charge.

Butch moved to the forward end of the car as if to use the washroom. He chanced a look into the next car and saw two men in suits moving slowly along. One of them was Duran. As he watched one of them opened a washroom door. The other moved slowly along listening at each compartment door. Grimacing, he was tempted to charge in and sort them out with his bare hands. Wisely he realized they might be carrying guns and he retreated ahead of them. Taking cover in his berth, he stuck his head into the aisle and watched for them to enter his car. When they did, he jerked his head quickly back and flipped the curtain closed. As he lay there silently, he could hear the two moving slowly down the aisle. They moved quietly but paused to listen periodically. The footsteps paused just outside of his berth for several moments then moved on.

Butch waited for a few minutes then slipped out of the berth and headed forward to let the Bat know where they were. He did not notice one of the men lean back into the aisle and see him slip quietly away. He grabbed his partner's arm and the two men reversed their course and followed Butch forward. He reached Carol's compartment and was just raising his hand to knock as the two gunmen came into sight. They saw each other simultaneously. Duran called out in a friendly voice, "excuse me but could you help me?" The friendly tone did not fool Butch, his eyes were fixed on the hands both men had in their coat pockets.

Butch wasn't always quick witted but he had quick reactions. He immediately turned and ran forward. Both men drew pistols and ran after him. As he ran the big man desperately looked for a place where he could wait and ambush the two men, counting on his strength to over-power them in the narrow aisles of the train car. He found nothing and continued.

Black Bat was waiting alertly for word from his friends. He clearly heard Duran call to Butch. He did not recognize Duran's voice but he was suspicious when the two men thundered past the compartment door. Jerking the door open he recognized Duran as he disappeared around a corner. The Black Bat drew his remaining pistol and ran in pursuit.

Remembering the Bat's story, Butch continued on toward the baggage car. He reached it with the two men not far behind. Thankfully the door was still unlocked. Butch threw himself through the door and slammed it shut. He did not lock it but instead took cover behind it in the corner of the car. Duran and his partner slammed through one vestibule and across the coupling to the baggage car vestibule. Duran put out a hand to stop his pal from opening the door. Before he could say anything though, he caught a glimpse of a black clad figure behind them. Turning, he raised his gun and fired through the glass windows of the doors. The Black Bat fired almost simultaneously.

Glass in the upper halves of both doors shattered. The Black Bat ducked as did his opponents. They continued to exchange shots, each of them jumping up to let off a snap shot before ducking down again. Of course the roar of gunfire rang the length of the first class compartments. Panicked people ran out into the long corridor screaming for help. Within a minute the entire train was in an uproar. Pajama clad people spilled out of Pullman berths and second class passengers asleep in their seats were jerked awake by the commotion. This included McGrath and the officers guarding Marley. They jumped to their feet and drew their revolvers. McGrath was torn. Instinct told him to run toward the trouble. Training told him to remain with his prisoner. This kind of commotion was just the sort of diversion that a gang might try. Gritting his teeth he ordered his men to hold their places.

With bullets skimming just above his head Duran's companion decided to retreat into the dubious safety of the baggage car. He opened the door and ran crouched through it. Duran was right behind him.

When the gunman appeared, the waiting Butch grabbed him up in both mighty hands. He then slammed the gunman against the half open door slamming it shut in Duran's face.

The Bat saw the baggage door open and then slam shut. He jerked his head back as Duran flung another shot at him. When he looked again Duran was gone. He took a chance and charged through the door of his car. He could clearly see into the vestibule of the luggage car. It was empty. But the external door was swinging open. He ran to it and looked up. A figure was just disappearing atop the car. Ignoring the crashing sounds coming from the baggage car, he holstered his gun and swung out onto the rungs that ran up the side of the car.

Inside the baggage car Butch ignored the punches being thrown at him and picked up the disarmed gunman. Lifting him completely off the ground he tossed him forward into a pile of luggage. Bags flew in every direction. By the time the man picked himself off the ground Butch was there. He dodged a kick and again grabbed the man, spun and threw him into a wall. This time he could barely get to his knees. Butch finished him off with a straight punch to the jaw that left the man unconscious before he crashed into another pile of crates and slid to the floor.

The Bat lifted his head above the edge of the car. Duran had run back to the next car. He turned and fired when he saw the shadowy head rise over the edge of the car but it was dark and the swaying of the car made him miss. He missed again as the Bat threw himself over the edge onto the roof. The Bat drew his pistol and snapped off a shot from the prone position but Duran was running down the length of the train and he missed. He got up and ran in pursuit. Duran leapt across the gap between two cars and threw a snap shot behind him. The Bat sprinted to catch up and leapt the same gap. As he landed, he crouched down, aimed low and fired. Duran jerked and stumbled grabbing his leg as he fell. The Bat's last shot had clipped him in the leg. The Bat holstered his now empty pistol and advanced down the swaying train.

Duran, lying near the edge of the roof, got to his knees and fired his last shot. The Bat ducked under his shot. Duran pushed himself to his feet as the Bat advanced on him. He threw the now empty pistol at the Bat who barely ducked under it. Favoring his leg Duran leaned in and threw a punch. The Bat blocked it and returned a jab with his other hand. The two then stood toe to toe atop the swaying train, the wind tearing at them, and traded punches. Hampered by his wounded leg Duran could not put his full weight into his punches. He quickly realized this and changed tactics.

He threw himself forward attempting to knock the Bat off his feet. This should not have worked as the Bat was braced and ready; unfortunately the train swayed into a turn at exactly that moment.

Both men tumbled to the top of the car and rolled toward the edge. They ended up with their feet dangling at the edge of the roof. Duran was on top, his hands gripped around the Bat's throat. The Bat gripped Duran's hands in his fists and finding purchase with his feet, he heaved Duran up and over his head. Duran flipped over and landed hard on his back, with a thump that forced his breath from his lungs. He rolled over gasping for breath and attempted to get to his feet. Still gasping to get his breath back he lost his balance and slipped toward the side of the car. The Bat flung himself forward. As Duran fell outwards he caught the edge of the car with one hand. The Bat slid forward toward him on his stomach his arms outstretched yelling, "Take my hand!" Duran reached for him with his free hand, but his other hand, wet with blood from his leg slipped off the roof's edge and he disappeared into the darkness below.

The gunfire had caused an uproar aboard the train. McGrath and his men tried to calm the crowd while keeping a close watch on Marley. With frightened people crowding the aisles, none of the detectives noticed a dark haired, well dressed man slipping an automatic out of his pocket. He kept it low as he worked himself behind the police lieutenant, noticed by no one but Carol. She drew her pistol but kept it concealed next to her body. She hesitated to start a gunfight in the crowded car. There was too great a chance of an innocent person being hit. Debating her options she jerked her head up at a woman's scream. On the other side of the car outside the windows a man's legs were scrabbling against the window. Everyone turned to look just as the man plummeted past the window. This distraction was enough. The well-dressed man stepped forward raising his pistol. With no clear shot Carol improvised. She ducked and screamed at the top of her lungs, "He's got a gun!" Instantly there was panic. Some people ducked, several women screamed. McGrath spun around and clubbed the rising gun out of the man's hand with his own revolver and then landed a powerful left cross to the his chin. In an instant McGrath and another detective wrestled the cursing man to the floor of the car and handcuffed him. Carol saw none of this. She had slipped her gun back into her handbag and was pushing forward through the crowd.

Carol made it back to her compartment just as the Bat lowered himself down to her window. She opened it and helped him inside. "What happened?" she asked.

The Bat sat down wearily, "I shot it out with Duran. He was wounded. I tried to grab him but he fell off the roof of the car."

Carol said grimly, "I know. We all saw it happen right in front of McGrath. There was another man also. I warned McGrath and he got him."

The Bat said worriedly, "McGrath saw you?"

She shook her head, "No. I got away clean, but where's Butch?"

"The last I heard he was bouncing the last gunman around the baggage car." At these words there was a knock on the compartment door and Carol quickly admitted Butch. The large man had a pleased look on his face. The Bat inquired mildly, "Everything go okay?"

Butch smiled, "Yep. I've got that wise guy hogtied back in the baggage car. What did I miss?"

Not much. I think that just about wraps things up. Now all we have to worry about is making a quiet exit." Carol stood up and went to the door, "I'll go see what's happening." While she was gone, Butch and the Bat compared notes.

Carol was back in minutes with news, "McGrath has ordered the train stopped at the next possible town. We'll be there in minutes." Butch nodded his head and slipped out the door to reach his berth. The Bat stood up, "You and Butch should be all right. Just look confused. The next big stop is Pittsburgh. Get off there and rent a car. I'll see you at home." Carol nodded.

Minutes later the train began to slow. As it did the Bat raised the window and slipped over the edge. He lowered himself to arm's length and as the train slowed into the small station he dropped away. Fortunately he was on the opposite side from the flood lit station. Rolling down the grade he stood up and disappeared into the shadows.

With the train stopped, people flooded off to the platform. The few police detectives could not stop them although McGrath grew red in the face yelling at people to stay on the train. He had to break into the small closed station to summon police from the nearby town. They eventually arrived and a full search of the train was done. They found the tied up man in the baggage car. Both prisoners were turned over to state police that also soon showed up. Carol and Butch were both questioned as were all the other passengers, but no one paid them any special attention.

When he got time, the suspicious McGrath made another call. One of the prisoners had claimed to be attacked by the Black Bat and McGrath was furious that he had been so close to the masked man once again and hadn't even caught a glimpse of him. The sleepy long distance operator finally connected him to the New York number he asked for.

Silk sat dozing by the table full of equipment. He jerked awake at the first ring of the phone. He quickly checked his carefully placed recordings and started all the record players. He wasn't in any hurry to answer the phone. After all, any honest person would be sound asleep at one o'clock in the morning. Finally, he picked up the receiver and said sleepily, "Quinn residence."

Barely able to restrain himself McGrath spoke sharply, "Let me speak to Quinn, and he better by God be there!"

Silk summoned up a frosty voice and replied, "Mr. Quinn is asleep lieutenant. Do you have any idea how late it is?"

"I know how late it is. If I'm awake, everyone else needs to be awake too. Now wake him up."

"Fine. Hold the line please."

Silk smiled as he set down the receiver. He then wandered off into the kitchen. He poured himself a glass of water and took his time drinking it. Finally when he judged enough time had passed he returned to the phone. Speaking loudly he said, "Here is the phone Mr. Quinn." He then lowered a needle onto a spinning record. Quinn's sleepy voice came out of the speaker, "Hello. McGrath do you know what time it is? What's going on?"

McGrath gritted his teeth. He had been so sure Quinn wouldn't be at home. He had been certain that even now Quinn was lurking around nearby in the shadows, "Quinn. I'm halfway surprised to find you at home."

Not sure if he had a response to this at his fingertips, Silk grabbed frantically at his records. He flipped a record onto the floor and frantically replaced it with another. McGrath spoke louder, "Quinn are you there?"

Silk lowered a needle and the recorded voice said, "What can I do for you Lieutenant?"

Sarcastically McGrath replied, "Well, I thought you might be interested to know that Marley's men made their move. We've got what's left of his men in custody. The rest we're not sure about. Although one of them claims the Bat was here tonight. What do you think of that, Quinn? Oh, I forget, you don't know anything about the Bat, do you?"

Quickly Silk lifted one needle and dropped another one. Quinn's voice came through clearly to McGrath, "It's late Lieutenant and I'm very tired. Can we speak again tomorrow?"

McGrath looked at the receiver in disgust, "Fine, Quinn you get your beauty rest!" He slammed own the receiver and left the phone booth to return to the train. As he stalked past impatient passengers, he could be heard muttering, "I don't know how he did it, but Quinn's involved somehow; I'm sure of it."

Silk sat back in his chair. Slowly he reached forward and turned the record players off. He wiped his forehead and muttered, "That concludes Act III and tonight's performance." Then he smiled.

Two days later Tony Quinn sat sipping coffee in his living room as the doorbell rang. He didn't turn his head. He knew who it must be. Silk answered the door, "Good afternoon Lieutenant. Can I . . ." McGrath pushed past him into the living room. He glared down at Quinn, "Well I'd tell you what happened but I'm sure you know every detail already." Quinn turned his blank eyes in the general direction of McGrath, "Yes, Lieutenant. I spoke with Commissioner Warner yesterday. I understand congratulations are in order. Marley is successfully in Chicago police custody and you captured two of his would be saviors. You have my compliments."

McGrath simmered, "We actually captured three of them. We found another down the track a ways with a broken leg. He claims the Black Bat threw him off the train. But you wouldn't know anything about that would you Quinn?"

"How could I lieutenant? I was here in New York the whole time. You and I spoke, remember?"

McGrath stuck out his jaw, "Yeah, we did. Maybe you're the Bat, Quinn, and maybe you're not. One of these days I'm going to find out the truth." With that he clapped his hat on his head and strode to the front door. Silk opened it politely for him. He closed the door and walked back to Quinn. He was trying not to smile but could not hold it in. Quinn too started smiling. Soon both were laughing out loud.

The End

TICKETS PLEASE,

I guess it's not surprising for someone who loves the old pulps to be a history nut and nostalgia fan as well. And so I am. One of my historic loves is railroads. I love trains. They're interesting, romantic and a big part of our American history. Think of all wonderful stories and movies out there that center around a journey by train. As a boy I can remember watching lots of old movies with train robberies, battles and gun fights atop train cars and aboard burning baggage cars. Trains are definitely fun, so the idea of adding an exciting train trip to a pulp adventure was certainly a no brainer. I just don't know why I didn't think of it earlier.

Anyway, few months ago I was watching a movie based on a novel, by one of my favorite authors of the 1970s Alistair MacLean, called *Break Heart Pass*. Although it is technically a western, it is basically a mystery set on a train trip through the mountains. It has sabotage, mysterious deaths and a "what's it all about" plot. Not to mention lots of action in, through and on top of the moving train. When I finished watching it, I knew I had to write a pulp story set on a train. The only problems were which hero to write about and coming up with a plausible storyline.

I considered a train robbery (always a crowd pleaser), a hero protecting someone from an assassination plot and even having an innocent vacation trip interrupted by a sudden murder. The trouble was they all seemed forced. I had to figure a legitimate reason why a hero would be on the dangerous train trip. Finally I decided on a jail break. If the hero had captured a crook and turned him over to the police who were extraditing him to another state; now we have a reason for the trip. Then if the hero got word of a jail break on the train: Voila! We have a story.

Once I had a basic plot, the only decision was which hero would be best for the story. I considered several of my favorite characters; Purple Scar, Moon Man even The Green Ghost but I finally settled on The Black Bat. He was perfect for this story. He prefers to capture the bad guys if he can. He also has a relationship with the police and a unique relationship with a special police officer: Lieutenant McGrath. This also gave me the added storyline of McGrath constantly trying to prove Tony Quinn is secretly the Bat. It also gave important parts for Black Bat's assistants to play.

With the hero picked and a good plot the story practically wrote itself. I chose an early version of the Black Bat's adventures as a model. Before

WWII the Black Bat often fought criminal masterminds and gangsters; later on it was the Nazi menace and eventually ordinary criminals in conventional mysteries. The pre-war stories had a good 30s flavor and that's what I wanted. The story wrote smoothly and although I didn't break any personal records for writing a pulp short story, I came close. While there isn't a ton of mystery in this story, I believe what it lacks in mystery it more than makes up for in action. Interestingly, the part I had the most fun writing was the little scam set up for Lieutenant McGrath while on the train.

An additional benefit of writing about a new hero I've never written about is that I get to read up on him to get the flavor of his adventures. I had never read a Black Bat story until recently. I found them fun and easy to read. After seventy or eighty years some pulps read better than others. Most Black Bat stories were written by Norman Daniels, one of the better pulp writers, and his work stands up well after all this time.

So, another classic pulp hero to mark off my writing list; and a good one at that. I had fun with the Black Bat and got to write an adventure on a train as well. What more can a writer ask for. I'm also pleased to add my name to the list of Airship 27 authors who have written about his exploits. I hope you enjoy reading *Death on the Rails*. See you next time.

GENE MOYERS - studied European and Medieval history at the University of Oregon. He is a former U.S. Army armor crewman. He worked in the High Tech industry for some time and ran a store front and internet hobby shop for several years.

An avid military gamer and role player, his favorite game was *Daredevils* set in the 1930s. His love affair with the 1930s and pulps in particular stem from his first time reading a *Shadow* novel as a boy. Although interested in writing since a teen, he did not turn to serious writing until 2000. He is the co-author of *GURPS Crusades* published by Steve Jackson Games. He has written a story published in *Ravenwood volume II* by Airship 27. He has also written stories that will appear in the future volumes of *Moon Man*, *The Purple Scar*, *Domino Lady* and *The Phantom Detective* all for Airship 27.

When not working on Airship 27 projects he is busy writing horror adventures for his swashbuckling character set in Colonial America. Gene currently lives in Beaverton, Oregon with his wife and three lazy dogs.

THE MAGNIFICENT ANDERSON

A Black Bat Adventure

by
Gordon Dymowski

Sunlight streamed through the windows of Tony Quinn's mansion as a well-dressed dark-haired man strode up and down the room. Sipping his morning coffee, Quinn looked well-pressed in a sharp suit and well-combed dark, wavy hair. Only the dark-lensed glasses that Tony Quinn wore seemed out-of-place. Only a cigar-shaped man in a rumpled suit observing from a corner seemed out of place.

"And as I was saying, Mr. Quinn," the dark-haired man gestured in a dramatic fashion. "My efforts to investigate this Black Bat for my film have met with several attempts on my life. A near-miss by an unmarked car, a stray gunshot, and several mishaps at the theater have me perturbed."

"The great Randolph Anderson, bad boy of Broadway, perturbed?" McGrath, the cigar-shaped man, snarled. "Tell Quinn exactly *why* you're doing a film on the Black Bat."

Almost on cue, Anderson turned to Quinn and his manservant (in reality, his trusted aide Silk Kirby) and described with great enthusiasm, "The Black Bat is an interesting subject; a dark avenger taking justice into his own hands. I am rather interested in profiling such a figure from a variety of perspectives...."

"It helps that you are the lead on *Tales of the Dark Cloak*," Handing his cup to Silk, Quinn grinned. "I'm a big fan of your work."

"Thank you," Anderson shrugged. "But it's one of a variety of radio roles which I perform. In fact, I feel a certain....affinity with the Black Bat."

"Of course, you're talking to the right guy," McGrath suspected that Quinn was secretly the Black Bat, but could never prove it. "Of course, why Commissioner Warner had me babysit this pompous jerk..."

"Belay yourself, sir!" Turning on his feet, Anderson scolded him. "Mr. Quinn would be another, equally dramatic subject: a young, crusading district attorney fighting a vicious crime lord. Blinded by acid, he rebuilds his life and rededicates himself to serving as a beacon of justice!"

Flashing a silent smile, Quinn realized it *was* an accurate description of his life. Thankfully, Anderson did not know how Quinn's sight was restored by the surgical implantation and manipulation of another man's eyes. Thanks to that operation, Quinn could see things in the dark as clearly as daytime. Now, with the aid of a former con artist, a fallen prizefighter, and the eye donor's daughter, Tony Quinn delivered masked justice as the Black Bat.

In a voice tinged with sarcasm, Silk asked, "But how would you portray the Black Bat? Nobody's really *seen* him, have they?"

Puffing his chest, Anderson grew more confident, "I see the film combining the lighting of our production of *The Revengers' Tale* and the perspective from our Hermes' productions. Have any of you caught our work on *Othello* with the Harlem Shakespeare Collective?"

Behind his dark glasses, only the fringes of tiger-striped scarring around Tony Quinn's eyes peered from the frames. Holding Quinn within his line of sight, McGrath observed carefully for opportunity that Quinn would betray himself.

"Gentlemen," Quinn waved his hand. "I still do not know why I am being involved. Even as an attorney, I do not think I can advise on this matter."

"Simple," McGrath stood in Quinn's eye line with little result. "Someone's trying to murder Anderson."

"Do not be so melodramatic, Lieutenant." Straightening himself, Anderson struck a pose tailor-made for a soliloquy. "My investigations into the Bat would make me a slightly obvious target. Of course, a sandbag did nearly fall on me at the theater, but there is a simple explanation: restoration work on the Oberon Theater."

"What about the threats by that Purity League? The near accident in Times Square?" McGrath asked, glancing at Silk. Shrugging, he turned and glared at Anderson.

Anderson flashed an arrogant grin. "The Purity League is merely nothing more than a group of fools. As far as Times Square…my ambulance was due for service. It was through sheer luck that the brakes took."

"Ambulance?" Quinn asked as Silk poured another cup of coffee.

"Simple really: my radio work finances my theatrical productions," Anderson explained. "To get from one station to another, well….I recently learned that there is no law that mandates that a person has to be sick to ride in an ambulance. It is cheaper and quicker than taking a taxi."

With a heavy sigh, McGrath buried his face into the palm of his hand.

Straightening himself, Anderson paused a moment, "This would be my first Hollywood film, and I am eager to focus on a notable individual. The Black Bat combines a healthy thirst for justice with a magician's talent for misdirection. Much like the Dark Cloak, the Bat dispenses the kind of two-gun justice not seen since the days of Prohibition. My alternative still remains to write a story, a fictional take, mind you, about a popular American, regardless of his origins. You remain my second choice, Mr. Quinn, and I hope you consider allowing me to profile you…."

Quinn laughed as he waved his hand. "Thank you, Mr. Anderson, but my life is not that interesting."

Muttering to himself, McGrath wondered what was worse: dealing with Anderson on a daily basis, or hearing the Black Bat compared to a piece of lurid radio drama. Either way, McGrath concluded he was dealing with hacks.

"Of course it is, Quinn," McGrath's voice came out in a sarcastic slur. "After all, Anderson's film will be about you in any case."

"Really?" Anderson's cherubic face broke into a smile. "Are you suggesting that Quinn and the Black Bat are…"

"One and the same." Pointing an accusing finger, McGrath grew more confident. "This guy really ain't blind…he's play acting. Even his errand boy here is in on it!"

In a moment of inspiration, Silk poured a bit of hot coffee onto Quinn's lap. Feeling the heat of the coffee on his leg, Quinn straightened himself, his voice grimacing in pain.

"I'm *so* sorry, sir," Silk reached for a nearby napkin. "Let me wipe that up…."

"No bother," Quinn waved his hand. "This suit needed cleaning anyway…"

"Well, I believe we had better leave," Anderson announced. "But allow me to invite you and your staff to lunch. I will be dining with my paramour, Ms. Vera LaMarche, as well as my producing partner, Mitchell Brushman."

"May I bring my bodyguard as well?" Quinn asked innocently. "Perhaps he might be useful if you're threatened."

"Of course," Anderson stated. "We will dine at the Sapphire Gypsy at approximately twelve o'clock. Your valet can come as well, although I doubt we will need his…services."

With that, Anderson strode out of the room. With an exhausted and exaggerated sigh, Lt. McGrath followed him. Silk watched through the window as both men entered a single car and drove off.

"Sorry about that, Tony." Grabbing a nearby napkin, Silk began wiping Quinn's leg. "I had to think of *something*…"

Smiling, Quinn turned and faced Silk. "It's actually rather relieving. McGrath won't let go of his need to prove I'm the Black Bat. I like how McGrath keeps me on my toes, and it's great that you can roll with the punches."

"Speaking of punches," Silk aimed a thumb toward the rear of the house. "I think Butch and Carol should be ready for us."

Heading the rear of the house, Quinn and Silk opened a secret door leading into a hidden laboratory. Inside, a tall blonde woman whose feminine curves belied her starched blouse and long skirt leaned against a bench cleaning the spectacles hanging from her neck by a chain. On the opposite end a large, muscular gentleman sat cracking his knuckles as if preparing for a fight. Dressed in his well-tailored suit, he had all of the trappings of a prizefighter.

"Good morning, Carol," Quinn greeted, and then turned to the large gentleman. "Have any news, champ?"

Butch O'Leary felt a particular sting of pride. After refusing to throw a fight, he was now Quinn's ally in fighting corruption. If helping Quinn in his crusade for justice meant making dents in the fight racket, Butch was glad to help. Although Butch had once believed that Quinn's accident would make him reluctant to fight crime, it had the opposite result: Quinn was now a nocturnal crusader hiding behind a dark persona fighting criminals and delivering justice by any means necessary.

Carol Baldwin, the shapely blonde now chatting casually with Silk, was the one aide who Tony Quinn felt *extremely* grateful to have in his crusade. If it were not for her, Tony Quinn would have lived in seclusion and inactivity as a result of his blindness. But it was her father's generosity in donating his eyes, and her gift of radical surgery which transplanted them to Quinn, that granted him the unique ability to see in the dark. But it was for more...personal reasons that Tony Quinn held Carol in such high regard, but as long as the Black Bat actively crusaded for justice, there would be no room for any measure of domestic bliss between the pair.

"Glad you filled us in Warner's visit yesterday," Butch stated as everyone sat down at the bench. "Gave us time do some digging."

"After all," Carol smiled warmly at Tony. "It's not every day a girl gets hired by a famous actress as a personal assistant."

"Count yourself lucky," Silk pointed a thumb at Butch. "After meeting Anderson, I wouldn't mind getting some boxing lessons from Butch."

Chuckling, Quinn's voice took on a firm, gentle tone. "At my request, Butch and Carol investigated separately to get a bead on what's happening while Silk stayed to maintain my cover. What have you learned?"

"Well, Brushman, Anderson's producing partner, is a nervous Nelly," Butch began. "I talked to some of my construction pals working the theater. He's Anderson's lackey; Anderson has the credit, Brushman does the work. Unfortunately, Brushman's been busy trying to get additional funding to maintain the theater where Anderson's putting on his play..."

"Maintain?" Silk asked. "Something Anderson forgot to share with us?"

"Yeah. Some local yahoos calling themselves the New York Purity

Brigade have been scrawling nasty messages on the theater's walls. Plus, it's delayed work on the Oberon for *months*. Plus, there are rumblings among the stagehands and hired help, and it's nothing I can pin down….."

"Nearly had an unfortunate incident," Carol chimed. "Thankfully, I managed to make my way into the entourage of Vera LaMarche, the infamous 'Buxom Bolivian' who is Anderson's current flame….and cause for divorce. It wasn't easy…"

"Speaking of which," Butch continued. "Rumor has it one of the play's investors is Jimmy 'Two Fry' Malvotti."

"Wait a minute," Silk's voice took on a confused tone. "Two-Fry Malvotti…the crime lord?"

As Quinn nodded, Butch scratched his head in confusion, "Why do they call him 'Two Fry'?"

"Remember the Ventura Diner shooting?" Silk loosened his tie. "Malvotti approached Ralph Sandoval, head of the East Side syndicate, and put a gun to his head. Sandoval's goons had been poisoned by the grill cook planted by Malvotti. Sandoval begged for his life, asking only if he could finish his burger and fries. Malvotti allowed him to eat everything except for two French fries before shooting him in cold blood."

"Malvotti's rap sheet's impressive: extortion, theft, larceny," Quinn explained. "Investing in the theater gives him some public credibility."

"He can also launder his ill-gotten gains," Silk continued. "It's no surprise that he's a rotten egg, but he wants to hide behind a curtain of respectability."

"I also had some….heated conversations," Butch clenched his fists, and everyone knew what he meant. "Had to get a little ugly, but word on the street is Malvotti doesn't quite need public attention right now."

"You know…" Carol's voice trailed off, and a hint of recognition gleamed in her eyes. "When interviewing for the position, by the way, I begin at lunch time, LaMarche received a call from someone named Jimmy. She pleaded with him to leave her alone, that it was over, but there was a hint of familiarity in her voice."

Stroking his chin in thought, Tony Quinn furrowed his brow, revealing more of the tiger-striped scars beneath the lenses of his dark spectacles.

Unclenching his fist, Butch continued, "Thing is my contacts tell me Malvotti's not too happy with Anderson poking around and asking questions. My contacts tell me Anderson's doing a lot of damage, putting a target on his own head."

"No wonder," Silk warbled. "Based on this morning's meeting,

Anderson is kind of a pompous jerk. I think he might have swallowed a dictionary when he was a kid."

"Not too far from the truth," Quinn explained. "Commissioner Warren gave me the details yesterday: Anderson grew up a child prodigy in Ohio. His past is wrapped in rumor and innuendo – read all of Shakespeare by age six, directed Ibsen plays at age ten. He came out of nowhere a few years ago, directing some challenging plays on Broadway, and received attention for a very controversial radio production of *The Island of Dr. Moreau*...as well as the voice of the Dark Cloak."

"Think he takes his role too seriously?" Butch asked. "Thinks himself the junior version of the Black Bat?"

Chuckling to himself, Quinn rubbed his neck. "I seriously doubt it. Anderson seems more bluster than boldness. But he is a problem, and thankfully, he'll keep McGrath busy."

"We also might want to keep an eye on Brushman," Carol shifted in her seat. "He came by for a brief moment yesterday during my 'interview.' He was brief, curt, and reluctant to deal with LaMarche. He kept pushing her to consider a role in Anderson's film, and she wanted nothing to do with it. Her exact words were 'I have better things to do with my time'."

"And *Othello's* not an option; production ends tomorrow night," Quinn's face reflected his deep concentration. "Besides, according to Warren, Brushman's been begging various people to invest in Anderson's movie, meaning that either the studio is reluctant to back his feature..."

Silk looked up, snapping his fingers. "Or there's an ulterior motive."

"Sounds like we need to get the skinny on what's happening," Butch offered.

"So Butch and I will head to the Sapphire Gypsy," Quinn's voice purred with confidence as he planned out their campaign. "Silk will watch outside. Carol..."

Rising from her seat, Carol turned to leave the room. "I need to get to work anyway. I'll be sure the 'buxom Bolivian Bombshell' makes it without the gossip columnists knowing."

As Carol left the room, Tony Quinn's eyes seemed to have a glint of enthusiasm despite being hidden by large, dark lenses. His lips curled into a small, yet satisfied, grin.

"So that's the plan; today, we meet the players and find out who's looking to murder Randolph Anderson..."

"And cure him of his fixation with the Black Bat?" Butch asked. "Seems like a mighty tall order."

"If it comes to that," Quinn stood up. "Given Anderson's reputation as a self-obsessed genius, he will find something else to occupy his time when this is over. Right now, he is in someone's crosshairs, and it's our job to make sure he's safe."

Emerging from the secret laboratory in Quinn's mansion, the three men heard the faint sound of Carol's car driving off. After shadow boxing, Butch went to help Silk prepare the car for their outing, and Quinn went to his room to get dressed.

After selecting and putting on an appropriate shirt and suit, Tony Quinn tied a necktie without using a mirror. A grin spread across his face, as he knew that at some point, the Black Bat would have to appear to dispense justice.

He had a team. He had a plan. He had a mission.

And that was all he needed.

As Butch gently guided Quinn into the Sapphire Gypsy, both heard a dry, dusty accented voice declare, "Well if Hitler missed the bus, it was only because that fool Chamberlain was driving it!"

With a soft whistle, Butch took in the opulence that was the Sapphire Gypsy Supper Club, a former speakeasy turned reputable social outlet. Deep in the well-to-do section of New York, the Sapphire Gypsy's white-and-gold marble walls betrayed its owner's wealth. As the midday sun burst through an elaborate skylight, the room glowed with an almost supernatural power. At one far end of the great hall was a well-stocked bar reflecting the venue's bootlegging past. At the other end was a large stage and dance floor, complete with new electronic equipment. A variety of round tables surrounded by chairs in preparation for the evening's busy activities stood between the bar and the dance floor. Most evenings, the place was packed with people eager to escape the current spirit of impending war; this afternoon, it was quiet, open for a select few of New York's wealthier residents.

From a table in the far corner, a striking raven-haired beauty stood up, her caramel-colored skin clashing with her low-cut ivory-white dress. Regarding both men with almond eyes, the woman waved enthusiastically and spoke with a soft accent.

"Mr. Quinn!" She yelped. "Please, come over. Randy's been telling me so much about you."

Guided by Butch toward the table, Quinn took a quick mental inventory. Although posing as a blind man, Quinn learned how to make a razor-sharp observation of his surroundings while maintaining a façade of sightlessness. Approaching the table, he saw Carol acting nonchalantly while Randolph Anderson bickered with a balding, pinched-faced man. Beside them sat a bored McGrath, cradling his head in his hands.

As Quinn and Butch approached, the woman reached out and took Quinn's hand into her own, shaking it. "My name is Vera LaMarche. Won't you and your bodyguard have a seat?"

"Why, thank you," Quinn reached for a chair and began seating himself. As Butch took a seat next to him, the pinched-faced man waved over a waiter.

"Please have the chef prepare his finest rib eye steak for Mr. Quinn," the pinched-faced man ordered. "Also, please bring his associate a grilled cheese sandwich."

"Actually," Quinn stated. "I'm quite in the mood for a grilled cheese sandwich myself."

Visibly disturbed, the pinched-faced man sat in silence. Butch shot the man a satisfied grin.

"You'll have to excuse old Brushy," Anderson announced. "Despite his rather sour demeanor, he is quite the charmer, and a great creative partner to work with."

"Randolph," Brushman countered. "You *do* know that I prefer *not* to be called Brushy."

"No problem," Quinn stated. "Mr. Brushman reminds me of an old law professor. Real pain-in-the-neck type."

Sensing the tension between the men, Vera LaMarche interjected, "So, Mr. Quinn, have you...I'm sorry, I was about to ask if you had seen my movies. How stupid of me."

With a gracious tone in his voice, Quinn responded. "I was fortunate enough to enjoy your films before my accident, Miss LaMarche. I loved *Hacienda Honey* and *Tropicana Sunrise*."

Vera gave a light sigh, "Thanks. Unfortunately, that contract with RKO was all-too short....I had more fun understudying in *Animal Crackers* on Broadway than in Hollywood."

"You worked with the Marx Brothers?" Butch beamed.

"Well....I understudied one of the minor roles. I had spent most of my time playing solitaire and turning down advances from two of the brothers."

Soon a waiter with a large tray approached the table, and placed a variety of dishes on the table: two large steaks, baked potatoes, and pineapples for Anderson, a bowl of consommé for Brushman, a bowl of chili for McGrath, and one Cobb salad each for Carol and Vera.

Cutting and shoveling a piece of steak into his mouth, Anderson mumbled, "Why don't you tell Mr. Quinn what brought you here, Vera?"

After chewing and swallowing a forkful of salad, Vera straightened herself. "Unlike what you may read, I actually *was* born in Bolivia. Left when I was seventeen."

"So I take it the title 'Bolivian Bombshell' has a basis in fact?" Quinn innocently asked, noticing both McGrath and Butch becoming increasingly fascinated with the actress. Brushman rolled his eyes skyward in disbelief.

Undaunted by his dark glasses, Vera attempted to make eye contact with Quinn. "I'm from a very small, very poor village. You have to understand, Bolivia isn't really a country; more like a loose collection of smaller states. We've had much political unrest; in fact I left to build a better life *and* to support my family."

"I remember reading somewhere…." Quinn began.

"Yes, we lost some land to Paraguay," Frustration was very audible in Vera's voice. "It was *not* a good experience, and I wish I had been there."

"What Bolivia needs is a chap like Churchill," Brushman bellowed. "Now *there* is a man who will unite a country!"

Ignoring Brushman, Quinn comforted Vera. "It's understandable…"

"No, it isn't, Mr. Quinn," Vera leaned forward. "My career was not just about fame and money, but supporting my family, my village. For all my life, I wanted to escape but now I feel obligated to give back. You don't understand….the papers are all focused on a menace across the ocean, but you're oblivious to your neighbors in the south struggling to survive."

An awkward silence passed amongst everyone at the table. As the waiter returned with two grilled cheese sandwiches, McGrath's eyes darted in search of a clock. Sitting back in her chair, Carol thought she saw a glimpse of sadness in Vera's eyes, but chose not to acknowledge it.

"I'm….sorry," Quinn offered. "I did not mean to…"

"You didn't."

Reaching out, Anderson took Vera's hand in his, a loving look in his eyes. "Vera, you know that I have supported you. In fact, let me direct you in *Taming of the Shrew…*"

Pulling her hand away from Anderson, she stated, "Randy, I'm sorry, but….I need…it's so soon after my husband's death…"

"Caught in the crossfire of a gangland shooting," Carol offered as if on cue.

Although poised to correct Carol, Vera thought better of that act. "When my husband died...Randy was a breath of fresh air. His own marriage was disintegrating with his heavy workload and with my own efforts to establish myself on Broadway."

"You were both the natural target of gossip rags," McGrath's voice slurred in boredom.

"Yes, vultures like Winchell, Parsons, and Hopper," Vera snorted. "When Randolph directed *Julius Caesar*, complete with brown shirted thugs, they ran him into the ground. He was gallivanting around in ambulances taking on radio work for money. When he chose to produce *Othello* in Harlem, I began feeling increasingly left out..."

"Makes sense," His lips curling into a soft smile, Quinn's voice grew warmer. "After all, if Anderson's obsessed with making a film about the Black Bat..."

"I do not like your tone, sir," Anderson's baritone voice echoed throughout the room. "I am not obsessed with the Bat. I am fascinated with him!"

"That's *another* thing," Vera turned toward Anderson. "You are much too focused on that...that...*vigilante*. With so much *evil* and *injustice* happening in the world, why focus on some stranger who takes the law into his own hands?"

Ignoring Anderson and LaMarche, McGrath leaned toward Quinn's ear and whispered, "Listen, while the egghead's grilling the dreamboat, I have a favor to ask..."

"I'm listening," Quinn leaned toward McGrath, his voice softened.

"Gonna send one of my boys with some legal papers; stuff Brushman and Anderson wouldn't let me see."

"How did you get them if they were reluctant to ..."

"Police privilege," Waving the fingers of his right hand in the ear, McGrath noticed Brushman attempting to moderate the other discussion. "Some kinda insurance scam, perhaps you could read them....or more accurately, have your bodyguard read it to you?"

"Of course," Quinn stated.

"And by the way, if your 'pal,' the Black Bat, emerged from the shadows," McGrath tapped his index finger on the table. "For one night, at least, capturing him would be above my pay grade."

As Quinn nodded, Butch gently prodded him in the shoulder. As both men turned, Butch muttered, "Don't look now...guess who showed up?"

"Vera! Baby-doll!" A voice yelled from the entrance. "Can *anyone* join this party?"

Everyone turned to see a burly, olive-skinned man in a sharp, pinstripe suit flanked by two plainer-looking gunsels. As the three men strolled toward the table, Anderson buried his face into his palm, and Carol wrapped a comforting arm around Vera.

Standing up and pointing an accusing finger, Brushman lectured. "Mr. Malvotti, you are *not* welcome in this establishment."

Visibly embarrassed, Vera rose and stood close behind Brushman. "Please, Jimmy, don't make a spectacle of yourself!"

Both of Malvotti's associates reached underneath their lapels, ready to pull pistols from holsters. Waving them back, the well-dressed gangster approached Brushman. "Come on, Brushy, I am only revisiting one of the haunts of my youth. I remember when this place was a speakeasy. Now, I'm only here to check on my investment."

"*Othello* is proceeding as usual," Brushman shrugged. "You will get your rewards tomorrow night, after the play closes. You know that."

Carol and Butch both looked at Quinn for some kind of signal. Both noticed his casual tapping of his index finger on the table. Both realized Quinn was tapping out commands in Morse code, signaling them on how to proceed.

Rising from his chair, Anderson bellowed. "I just simply cannot *believe* this! With everything that I have to do, research for my movie, a production about to end, and this miscreant decides to intrude on our..."

"Listen, bunky," Malvotti poked a finger into Anderson's lapel, his two escorts standing guard.

"That's *Mister* Anderson to you," Butch countered, with Brushman nodding in assent.

Inserting herself between the two men, Vera turned toward Malvotti and pointed a finger in his face. "Listen, Jimmy, and listen well, we are *over*. You were fun. I have a career..."

"You traded up, didn't you?" Malvotti snapped. "Maybe you can make up for it by giving me your secretary..."

Catching Carol's look of discomfort, Butch clenched his fist, ready to defend her honor. Quinn waved him back for the moment.

Striding toward Malvotti, Anderson's voice took on a low, harsh tone. "Listen to me, you thug. I am tired of being pushed around by my business associates and low-life thugs like you. Not even the Borgias, with all their corruption, could generate the amount of sheer contempt I have for a ruffian like you."

"I simply cannot believe this!"

Rising from his chair, McGrath approached Malvotti, "Say what you need to say and get out of here."

Straightening himself, Malvotti addressed the people at the table, "Look, all I am here to do is make sure that I get return on my investment. Brushy here came to me, wanted me to get in cahoots with this Shakespeare thing, told me it was easy money. I had a lot of cash from my legitimate business efforts."

"And some not-so-legitimate ones," Quinn corrected.

Surprised, Malvotti regarded Quinn for a moment, "So now, I'm ok with investing in a play, but Brushman's trying to get me to invest in Anderson's movie. I ain't a bank on legs, and I'm no sucker. So I thought I would get the drop on Brushy...as well as see my old girlfriend."

"Well, you've seen me," Vera's eyes burned with anger. "Now get out! I have moved on from our momentary...fling. I suggest that you do the same."

"Yeah," Malvotti's voice dripped with sarcasm. "I can see that; both you and your new chippie."

As one of the men reached for his gun, McGrath and Butch rose from their chairs. As McGrath reached for his pistol, Malvotti took a step back as the other gunsel approached Vera. With almost lightning speed, Butch rose and threw a right hook which caught the man square in the jaw. As he collapsed, Carol rose and punched the other man in the gut. With a sudden *whoomp*, the man collapsed and Carol reached into his holster and withdrew his gun. As McGrath drew his pistol on Malvotti, Quinn sat and turned toward the noise. Knowing how Malvotti would react, he tapped out to Carol and Butch to stand ready.

As Carol took aim at Malvotti, the sharp-dressed gangster turned to run out of the Sapphire Gypsy. However, as he took a single stride forward, a man in a valet's uniform entered, gun drawn square on Malvotti's chest.

Turning back toward the group, Malvotti sneered, "Wow, McGrath, smart move having your boy serve as a valet."

"Actually," Quinn rose, interrupting Malvotti's tirade. "That would be *my* valet, Mr. Malvotti, and unlike you, he is no boy."

As everyone rose around the table, Vera leaned into Carol's ear and whispered, "Are you *sure* you know what you're doing?"

"Definitely," Carol kept aim on Malvotti. "Girl's got to protect herself, you know."

Raising his hands, Malvotti backed away at a cautious pace. "Sorry...I only wanted to discuss Mr. Bushman's satisfaction with the vendors I recommended."

Everyone turned toward Brushman, whose face was scrunched into a painful grimace. Looking uncomfortable at recent events, Brushman's voice reeked of weariness and frustration.

"We are....very satisfied, Mr. Malvotti," Brushman's words burst in a heavy whine. "Be assured that not only are they keeping us happy, they will be earning a *very* healthy bonus with tomorrow night's closing."

An audible *click* broke the tension, as everyone turned toward McGrath aiming his police revolver at Malvotti.

"Move along, Two-Fry," McGrath snarled. "This is a private party."

Putting his hands down, Malvotti shot McGrath a nasty glare.

"Listen, copper," A sense of regret permeated Malvotti's words. "You can't stop me from keeping an eye on my well-invested dough, and quite simply, stopping me is way above *your* pay grade..."

Stepping forward, Malvotti emphasized his words by poking Tony Quinn's lapel, "And *you* listen, shyster; if you're such a high-and-mighty crusader, ask Brushman to show you his contracts and papers. Everything's on the up and up. Hell, have the cop read 'em to you. He probably needs a change from *See Spot Run...*"

Turning on the balls of his feet, Malvotti and his two gunsels strode out of the restaurant. A tense silence filled the room as everyone but Carol and McGrath returned to their seats. After handing McGrath the gun, Carol then made her way to her seat next to Vera LaMarche.

"Probably need to leave *anyway,* Anderson," McGrath waved to the dark-haired man. "I'll drop you off at the theater."

Eager to create a distraction, Anderson beamed, "Why don't you join us for today's rehearsal, Mr. Quinn?"

Feigning fatigue, Quinn sighed, "Perhaps tomorrow afternoon? But to be honest....Malvotti's invitation has me intrigued."

As his eyebrows arched, Bushman dismissed with heavy sarcasm, "There's nothing to that thug's accusations. Everything is in order."

"Then why not allow Mr. Quinn to review them, Marshall?" Vera LaMarche asked. "Are you so afraid of what he might learn?"

"Listen, just because my partner has taken on a peasant girl as a concubine...."

Rising to her feet, Vera took two long strides and slapped Brushman across the face.

"*I'll* handle it," McGrath yelled as he dragged Anderson out of the restaurant. Brushman raced quickly behind both men.

Slumping in her chair, Vera hung her head as a weary voice said, "I can't take any of this anymore: the manic lifestyle, the long nights…I can't stand Randolph anymore."

Comforting Vera, Carol wrapped her arm around her and said, "Don't worry, I know you have a lot of pending business this afternoon. Maybe we can focus on getting it done?"

Lifting her head, Vera flashed a fragile-looking smile.

As Butch helped him rise, Quinn apologized, "I am really sorry for what happened. You deserve to be treated with more respect."

"Thank you," Vera's voice took on a sunnier tone. "I really appreciate you coming."

With that, Vera LaMarche got up, strode toward Tony Quinn and Butch O'Leary, and kissed each man on the cheek. Within moments, both Vera and Carol left to take care of other business.

Turning, both men noticed Vera kissing Silk on the cheek as she left.

Taking a few steps toward Quinn, Silk asked, "What's next, boss?"

Even behind dark lenses, Quinn's eyes grew more intense.

"I'll call McGrath this afternoon to arrange for delivery of those papers," Quinn decided, then glanced at Silk. "Can you prepare my…. *outfit* for some extra curricula activity?"

Silk smiled knowingly and nodded.

Within moments, everyone left the restaurant – Vera and Carol left together, McGrath dragged Anderson toward the theater, and Silk drove Quinn and Butch home.

"Can you get me some coffee, Butch?" Carol asked.

As Butch went to the kitchen, Carol sat beside Tony Quinn in a secret laboratory hidden in the rear of his mansion. A clock on the wall declared the time to be 6:30 p.m. After a relatively quiet dinner, the two of them and Silk had retired to the rear. Both Silk and Quinn had split the copious pile that McGrath's colleague had brought them, and spent the past half hour reviewing overcomplicated contracts. Lifting his head from a pile of papers on the table, Quinn turned to Carol and flashed a smile. Although there was a strong affection between Carol and Tony, romance would have to wait until there was no more need for the Black Bat.

As Butch returned with a tray containing four cups of coffee, Quinn announced in a grim tone, "These insurance papers for Anderson's play are out of order."

"How so?" Butch McGrath asked. "Keep it simple…some of us ain't exactly glitterati, you know."

"If I read the papers correctly," Silk regarded his companions with great concern. "The production pays out high dividends on closing night, and higher ones if there's foul play. Right, Tony?"

Looking at his three comrades, Quinn reviewed a clause with one of the pages. "Right, most policies pay out after completion of production to cover costs. But some of these clauses don't make any sense. Some abstract quotes about 'creative works', a full payout plus percentages should there be any disruption in production….this reads more like a potential bill of sale than a contract."

All three looked up to see Butch, clutching a few typewritten sheets and looking frustrated. "These *are* confusing; the last time I heard *party of the first part* used this much was in that Marx Brothers opera picture."

Placing one set of sheets on the table; Quinn took the papers from Butch's hand and reviewed them.

"This is *Malvotti's* contract for the play!"

"Of course," Silk said. "Malvotti wants to be sure that he's not buying a pig in a poke. Trust me, I've been on the other side so long I know when I'm being played for a rube."

Placing the contracts down, Quinn thought aloud, "Malvotti's contract is interesting: no share of the profits, just direct return on investment. Standard clauses about disruption of production…but one clause stands out. It gives Malvotti 'proprietary control' over various vendors: food, transportation, construction…"

"So he's making money on the back end?" Carol asked. "He's avoiding profits from production but making it on other services?"

"That's just it," Quinn responded. "It's not much but I wonder if the effort is toward keeping a legitimate front. After all…"

"If Malvotti has control over activities around Anderson's play," Silk concluded. "It gives him a *lot* more room to cover his tracks. It's a great con: present yourself as a patron of the arts…"

"And you avoid charges of patronage," Quinn quickly sipped his cooling coffee. "So despite being a really good suspect, Malvotti has nothing to worry about."

"What about Brushman?" Silk countered. "He seems a bit…stuffy."

"He and Anderson have a love/hate relationship," Butch took several gulps of coffee. "Anderson loves Brushman, and Brushman hates Anderson. Seems tailor-made for homicide."

"But Anderson needs Brushman," Carol pushed her coffee aside. "Anderson's a bit…flighty. The kind of guy who acts first and asks questions later. Look at his behavior: leaving his wife for Vera, using ambulances to get around town…"

"But Brushman gains nothing if Anderson dies," Butch countered. "He's left holding the bag on paying off production costs, and *maybe* gets some pocket change."

"But he *does* acquire well-needed recognition," Quinn stroked his chin in contemplation. "Without Anderson, Brushman emerges from the shadows as a potential producer…can strike his mark upon the stage."

"All this is full of sound and fury," Silk rubbed his neck. "But it means we're back where we started…"

"Perhaps tomorrow's closing performance will provide some insight," Carol beamed. "On the surface, Vera has little motive, but I haven't learned anything working with her. She doesn't seem to reveal much to anyone, including Anderson."

"Even still…." Quinn regarded Silk. "Busy tonight, Silk?"

Silk grinned like a kid on Christmas, "We making a visit to Mr. Malvotti?"

Moving toward a locker, Quinn swung the door open, revealing a black costume. Hanging on a hook was a cape that was scalloped like bat wings, and a hood that covered his face. Removing a pair of crepe soled shoes from the base: Quinn removed the suit and various other accessories, including specially-gripped gloves and a belt with various compartments.

"Yes, we are," Quinn grinned at Silk as Butch and Carol left the lab. "I think it's time that Mr. Malvotti receives some special attention….from the *Black Bat!*"

"What are you trying to do, give me food poisoning?"

Jimmy "Two Fry" Malvotti shot up from the diner booth and pointed an accusing finger at the waiter.

"But sir," the thin, shabbily dressed man pleaded. "You *ordered* this. It's chicken fried steak!"

Forcing the waiter backwards, Malvotti paced toward the front window. Potential customers outside could see the words VENTURA DINER in large, black-and-gold letters, with a smaller sign announcing UNDER NEW MANAGEMENT taped beneath it. However, the scene inside had scared them away. Now that the diner was Malvotti's turf, it served as both his headquarters *and* a reminder to those who get in his way.

Pinning the waiter against the front door, Malvotti snarled, "Then make up your mind: serve me chicken or serve me steak! Not that breaded piece of gristle covered with glue!"

As the waiter turned and burst out of the door, two large men wearing suits grabbed him by the arms and dragged him into a nearby alley. Returning to the booth, Malvotti saw the chef behind the open counter, placing a nicely formed hamburger patty on the grill. As the patty sizzled, the chef turned and bent his head in apology.

Sitting back down, Malvotti pushed the plate away, looking up at two gunsels replacing those who escorted the waiter outside.

"So what happened at lunch?" croaked a large, bald-headed man who was accompanied by a lighter-haired accomplice.

Reaching into a lapel pocket, Malvotti's right hand whipped out into a wide arc, brandishing a switchblade. Bringing the knife's edge close to the bald man's throat, he threatened, "I don't pay you to be nosey; I pay you to follow orders."

As a variety of sulphur-coated adjectives and invectives emerged from Malvotti's mouth, one of the pair who nabbed the waiter burst into the diner. "Boss! The Black Bat! He ambushed us!"

"It's bad enough the guys I hired for Anderson are shirking their jobs," Malvotti rose from the booth and slammed the switchblade on the counter next to his plate. "Some jerk's paying them under the table to goof off… but now the Black Bat's on my case?"

Shifting on his feet, the lighter-haired man pleaded. "We gotta take care of this *and* Anderson! After all…"

Lurching forward, Malvotti grabbed the man's lapels and slammed him on the counter. An old, haggard-looking gentleman sitting at the counter continued to sip his coffee and read his newspaper, oblivious to what was happening.

"Listen and listen *once*," Malvotti's voice was a harsh whisper. "I put the cash from my business doings into this play to clean it up. They got that greasebag Capone on taxes, but I am going to be smarter. If Anderson dies, all I get is what I put in. No one, not even that Black Bat or that fuddy-duddy Brushman, is gonna stop me. Understand?"

The thug nodded his head, and Malvotti released his lapel. As Malvotti stepped back, the thug got back onto his feet, regaining his composure as his bald companion stood watch over the proceedings.

"Sorry, boss…." The light-haired thug shrugged like a chastised schoolboy.

"What about the Bat?" the bald thug asked as Malvotti removed a black paper seal that fell to the ground.

Opening it, Malvotti realized it was the shape of a bat!

"He's a dead man," A cold snarl spread on Malvotti's face. "I'll take *personal* pride in executing him myself."

"*Well here's your chance, Malvotti!*" A firm, confident voice filled the room.

Turning toward the rear of the diner, Malvotti and his crew saw a man dressed entirely in black, a scalloped cape billowing behind him. Covering his face was a hood that reminded Malvotti of an executioner. Strapped around the man's waist was a belt and around his chest was a leather holster rig with automatic pistols under both arms. As the brown-haired man got up slowly and ran out of the front door, he caught a glimpse of suction grips on the man's gloves.

"So you're the Black Bat…." As a snide smile spread on his lips, Malvotti pointed at the Bat.

"Get him, boys!"

All three thugs leapt at the Black Bat, who threw a swift right hook at the bald man's jaw. As the bald thug crumpled to the ground, his light-haired colleague withdrew a switchblade from his pocket. As he flicked the blade open, the Black Bat ducked and delivered a punch straight into the man's midsection. Dropping the blade, the man fell to the ground, and the Black Bat turned to see Malvotti attempt to sneak out of the diner.

With great speed, the Black Bat drew one of the automatic pistols from its holster and fired off a shot. Crumpling to the ground, Malvotti grasped his shoulder as he fell to the floor. As he looked up, he saw a perfectly round bullet hole in the glass of the diner door.

Standing over Malvotti, the Black Bat helped the gangster to his feet, only to grasp and shove him into a booth.

"You….you touched me!" Malvotti's eyes reflected great fear. "You *shot* me!"

Keeping steady aim at Malvotti, the Black Bat stood guard. "I deliberately aimed to crease your shoulder. Now, tell me about your beef with Anderson."

Out of the corner of his eye, the Black Bat saw the remaining thug reach into his lapel and pull a knife. Thinking fast, the Bat turned and fired a shot, catching his opponent in the chest. As he fell, the Bat saw the bald and light-haired thug escape out the back of the diner.

Turning back toward Malvotti, the Black Bat warned, "This gun has five shots left, and my other one's fully loaded. Tell me about Anderson… *now!*"

Moving himself into a sitting position, Malvotti kept a cautious eye on the Black Bat. Unnerved by the Bat's executioner-style hood and those blazing, intense eyes, Malvotti put on a brave face.

"His lackey, Brushman, wanted help: catering, stagehands, transport, etcetera." Malvotti's words were full of counterfeit bravado. "So he hired my boys at a price. A much cheaper price…"

"….and you become a major investor."

"That's right, I came into some cash, and wasn't sure how legal it was. So I decided to use the play as a way of….well, giving myself a little bit more respectability."

"And remove the taint of corruption from your ill-gotten gains," the Black Bat snarled, keeping the barrel of his gun trained on Malvotti.

"This afternoon, I wanted to see my old girlfriend, Vera. She took up with me after her old man died; really fun honey. However, she decided she needed a new sugar daddy…"

"And went with Anderson?"

"Yeah. She claimed it was to send money back to the people of her village, but she ain't exactly wearing cut-rate clothing, is she?"

"And the accidents?"

"Nothing doing. It would be a real knuckle-headed thing to do. Anderson's my meal ticket. Killin' him means I get zip. Nada. See the papers for yourself…."

Keeping quiet, the Black Bat holstered his gun, turned and headed for the back of the diner. Rising from his booth, Malvotti saw this as an opportunity and decided to ambush the Bat from behind.

After taking a few cautious steps, Malvotti was about to strike when the Bat turned and punched Malvotti, forcing him to the ground.

Opening a compartment on his belt, the Bat unfolded a black paper bat and placed it on Malvotti's forehead.

He then left the diner, deciding that the this affair, like Anderson's play, would end tomorrow night!

"Watch yourself, Mr. Quinn," Mitchell Brushman whispered as he and Butch gently guided Quinn through the front door of the Oberon Theater.

Outside, Silk stood guard with the car; after all, he *was* "on the job" as Tony Quinn's valet. Leaning against the automobile's hood, Silk observed

"Malvotti kept a cautious eye on the Black Bat."

workers replacing a wood panel with a pane of glass. On the opposite side, workers hastily painted over scribbled phrases like KEEP NEW YORK PURE and PURIFY HARLEM. Whistling softly, Silk took in the pleasant experience of springtime in New York: the hustle and bustle of city life, the gentle flow of cars moving through the streets...and if trouble arose, the newly reloaded pistol remained ready for action in a secret holster.

As Butch and Brushman guided him toward the main stage, Tony Quinn struggled to hide his reaction to the theater's interior. Butch whistled softly as they made their way through an ornate lobby which seemed carved from a single block of black-and-gold marble. In one corner, a lone worker scrubbed down a tall column, removing a thick coat of dust to reveal a lovely, ornate design. A group of men carried old, broken wooden chairs out of the main stage, replaced by new, cushioned seats filling the hall. Approaching the stage, Butch took in his surroundings noticing actors, directors, stagehands, and workers rushing through the burgundy-walled interior..

"If I ever get my mitts on this Purity League," Butch grumbled.

"It does seem a shame," Quinn whispered in response. "With all the troubles in Europe...."

As the three men approached the front row, Brushman broke off and went onstage, approaching Anderson. The dark-haired, cherubic-faced director was talking to two men holding mimeographed sheets. Both were impeccably dressed: button-down shirts with open collars, starched pants, and freshly polished shoes. The taller member of pair had dark brown skin, no hair but a neatly trimmed goatee. The other had a lighter complexion, and his face was long and gaunt. After Brushman spoke with Anderson privately, the director turned toward the two impeccably-dressed men, whispered guidance, and then invited Quinn and Butch to sit in the front row.

"And now, gentleman, I give you....Mr. Antony Quinn, attorney at law who is on special attachment to the New York police," Anderson introduced in a very robust tone, and then turned back to his actors. "You have the scene, my actors, please demonstrate the talent that has driven this remarkable production."

Making his way from the stage, Anderson sat on Quinn's left, with Butch hanging on Quinn's right. Soon, McGrath arrived from the rear of the stage, seating himself behind Anderson.

With that, the two men onstage dropped their scripts and turned toward each other.

Approaching the lighter skinned man, the bald actor asked in a smooth, baritone voice, "How shall I murder him, Iago?"

"Did you perceive how he laughed at his vice?" The tall, gaunt actor responded in an accident that Quinn couldn't quite place.

"O Iago!"

"And did you see the handkerchief?"

"Was that mine?"

"Yours, by this hand: and to see how he prizes the foolish woman your wife! She gave it him, and he hath given it his whore."

"I would have him nine years a-killing. A fine woman! A fair woman! A sweet woman!"

Sitting on the front row, Quinn maintained his façade of blindness, focusing on the rhythm and pacing of Shakespeare's words. Both actors managed to convey a myriad of emotions through their voices, their tones, their very being. To everyone's dismay, McGrath stifled a rather loud yawn. Turning back toward the cop, Anderson shot him a nasty glance, then turned toward the stage and waved his actors on in encouragement.

Straightening himself, the tall, gaunt man onstage asserted, "Nay, you must forget that."

"Ay, let her rot," the bald man's baritone voice took on an audible sneer. "And perish, and be damned tonight; for she shall not live: no, my heart is turned to stone; I strike it, and it hurts my hand. O, the world hath not a sweeter creature: she might lie by an emperor's side, and command him tasks."

"Nay, that's not your way."

"Hang her! I do but say what she is: so delicate with her needle! An admirable musician! O, she will sing the savageness out of a bear! Of so high and plenteous wit and invention!"

"She's the worse for all this."

"O, a thousand, a thousand times…and then, of so gentle a condition!"

"Ay, too gentle."

"Nay, that's certain…but yet the pity of it, Iago! O Iago, the pity of it, Iago!"

Rising from his seat, Anderson clapped for a few moments, and then waved the men off the stage.

"That is quite commendable, lads," Anderson lectured. "You have both captured the essence of the scene, with Iago's hidden agenda bearing bitter fruit as he lures his friend into emotional darkness over a perceived incident of infidelity…"

"Oh, Randolph," Brushman sighed. "Must you persist in elongating your pretentiousness?"

"Brushy, must you always be such a sour puss?" Anderson grinned at some perceived victory.

"Although I admire your direction," Brushman folded his arms and looked down his nose. "I sometimes believe that your expanded ego is the natural driver of these repeated attempts at homicide, one of which may lead to your imminent demise."

"Did both these guys both swallow a dictionary?" Butch mumbled to Quinn.

"Brushy," Anderson waved his arms as he spoke. "Perhaps it is wise for us to delay the inevitable creative disagreement as I think Mr. Quinn and his assistant would like to meet our players…"

As the two actors descended from the stage, Butch helped Quinn rise and guided him toward the two men. Looking back toward McGrath, Butch caught a glimpse of the cop looking for a potential misstep. Looking past toward one of the doors into the lobby, Butch thought he caught a glimpse of Carol but thought better of it.

Approaching the two actors, Quinn extended his hand as Butch led him forward.

Taking his hand, the tall bald man introduced, "I'm Benjamin Avery; I am very glad to meet you, Mr. Quinn."

As the two men shook hands, there was a slight discomfort on both Brushman and McGrath's faces. Neither man seemed comfortable with the two actors. Neither Quinn nor Butch made any remark.

"I am glad to meet you as well, and I must say," Quinn's handshake was firm and enthusiastic. "Both you and your colleague have done wonders with Shakespeare's words."

"Thank you," the tall, gaunt man approached and shook Quinn's hand. "My name is Andrew Royal."

"Interesting accent," Quinn remarked. "I can't quite place it…"

"My family's originally from New Orleans," Royal emphasized the *Nawlins* pronunciation. "We then moved and spent some time in Baltimore."

"That explains it," Quinn released the actor's hand. "Since my accident, I have gained a greater appreciation of the human voice. I do not think I have enjoyed theater or opera as much as I currently do."

"Thank you," Benjamin's voice radiated warm and acceptance. "I graciously speak on this production's behalf when I say that we truly appreciate any accolades for our work. In fact, I am proud to say that thanks to Mr. Anderson's efforts, I will be starting classes at Rutgers within the next year."

"Aren't you worried about…?"

"Adjusting?" Benjamin's voice grew in confidence. "Times are difficult, but the fight and struggle will be worth it."

Quinn understood exactly what Avery Benjamin meant. "Sometimes we fight the harder battles to win the sweetest victories."

Benjamin smiled back, and Andrew asserted, "You know, you're not like others, who find us a bit….strange or unusual."

"Is there any reason why I should?" Quinn asked.

Despite his dark glasses, Avery Benjamin and Andrew Royal noticed a kind of acceptance in Tony Quinn. This blind man didn't see the color of their skin, but could appreciate the fruits of their artistic efforts. Had they known of Quinn's activities as the Black Bat, they might have truly appreciated the irony.

As the two actors said their goodbyes, Quinn and Butch approached Anderson and Brushman, already knee-deep into an argument. "I must insist, Randolph, that you consider taking on additional protection before tonight's performance."

"I have, Brushy. In fact, I canceled my cameo on the *Hermes Theater Radio Playhouse*."

Brushman's eyebrows shot skyward. "Are you not afraid of the League?"

"The fact that a group of misguided cretins head into an already segregated area to foster race hatred….why, that's just as futile as Miss Parson's comments about my personal life."

On cue, Vera LaMarche's voice yelled, "Hello, darling!"

All of the men but Quinn turned toward Vera LaMarche as she made a grand entrance. She was wearing a low-cut black dress that emphasized the string of pearls against her caramel skin. As several stagehands turned, their hearts melted and broke with every step the striking Bolivian actress took. Behind her was Carol, dressed rather conservatively and adjusting her ill-fitting spectacles while clutching a notebook under her arm. Quinn signaled Carol by scratching his temple. Carol nodded and appeared to trip; the countersignal which meant that she had touched base with Silk outside of the theater, and trouble was brewing.

Surprised, Anderson responded in an almost absent-minded manner, "Vera! Darling! I…wasn't expecting you."

Wading through the row of seats, Anderson walked up the aisle toward

Vera and gave her an embrace. Both Quinn and Butch noticed that it seemed as if both actors were acting on cue.

"Of course, Randolph," Vera's soft, subtle accent seemed more pronounced "This is your closing night. I simply *had* to be here."

"But aren't you in rehearsals for..."

"Petruchio and Katharine can wait, darling..."

As the couple greeted each other, Carol noted the counterfeit affection between Anderson and Vera. Turning toward Butch and Quinn, the large boxer nodded, with Quinn remaining still. All three agreed something was amiss, but kept guard.

"Hey! What's the holdup?"

As everyone turned, a large, barrel-chested man entered the room accompanied by two thuggish-looking men. His gray suit looked rather gaudy against his tan, forged from many summers at Coney Island. A fetching black fedora hid a gradually receding line of black hair.

Brushman flinched as the gray-suited gentleman approached him, extending a hand. "Tonight is payday!"

As the two thugs watched, Brushman shook the gentleman's hand, and Anderson rushed toward them.

"Mr. Malvotti!" Anderson roared, pointing his finger in an accusing manner. "How *dare* you intrude on this production?"

Turning toward Quinn, Malvotti extended his hand, "I forgot to mention, I am really sorry to hear what Snape did to you, Quinn. He always *was* a bit of a..."

Inserting himself between the two men, McGrath removed his badge from a lapel pocket and showed it to Malvotti. "I would *reconsider* your tone, pal."

Malvotti shrugged, "Now Lieutenant, all *I'm* doing is keeping an eye on my investment....and speakin' of Shakespeare, who's the hack who's gonna rewrite this play into plain English?"

"Now see here, you miscreant," Brushman sneered.

"So it ain't you," Malvotti pointed his thumb at Anderson. "But what's the guy behind the Dark Cloak himself gonna do about this play?"

"Nothing," Anderson countered. "You know tonight's closing night, and I'm heading for Hollywood in the morning..."

"Black Bat's on your case about sticking your nose into places it don't belong. He gave me a bit of a visit, but I'm not afraid him. Still, you might want to reconsider your subject matter. Understand?"

"Now *you* listen, Two Fry," Curling his hands into fists, Anderson took a wide step toward Malvotti. "I do not take kindly to bullies or thugs. Rest assured that if you continue to harass me, Miss LaMarche, Mr. Brushman, or any of my entourage…we *will* take appropriate action…"

"You actually believe you *are* the Dark Cloak, doncha?" Malvotti snorted. "You actually believe all that 'web of crime ensnares the guilty' garbage…"

"Perhaps you should step off, pal," Butch growled, stepping toward Anderson, fists clenched.

Turning, Malvotti approached Butch and asked, "O'Leary, right? I saw you fight a couple of times. I can't believe you're still standing."

Catching a glimpse of Carol shaking her head, Butch stepped back unclenching his fists.

From the lobby, the group could hear a large commotion as men yelled "Let's take the theater!" and "Purify New York!" Within moments, a large group of white hoods and business suits entered the theater. Various actors and stagehands rushed out of the room, hoping to avoid any potential bloodshed. Pushing their way past the bodyguards, one of them held a gun at Randolph Anderson's head!

"You're coming with us!" The gunmen yelled. "You've sullied this town, and we're here to purify it!"

As McGrath strode, pistol clutched in hand, one of the hooded men approached and swung a wild punch. Feeling the full brunt of the fist on his jaw, McGrath stumbled and fell backwards, releasing the gun from his grasp.

Soon, a group of hooded men approached Anderson. Stepping backwards, Butch placed his hand on Quinn's shoulder. As the two men stepped away, Carol did the same with Vera, leaving Brushman confused as to what was happening.

"Do not touch me, you ruffians," Anderson yelled, cautiously regarding the pistol at his head. "I will go with you quietly."

"You better," the hooded gunman snarled.

Within moments, gunshots were heard outside of the theater. As the throng of hooded men escorted Anderson out of the room, both Butch and Quinn strode toward the exit. Noticing that Carol and Vera had already left, both men rushed outside where Silk was waving them toward the car. All of them caught a glimpse of Anderson being rushed into the rear of an ambulance.

After guiding Quinn into the back seat, Butch tumbled into the front seat as Silk started the engine. As the car rushed forward, Quinn touched a small button, opening a hatch on the seat beside him.

Keeping a watchful eye on his driving, Silk stated, "Caught those hooded crumb bums leaving an ambulance, of all things, so I took the liberty of firing a few shots at their window."

From a distance, the three men trailed an ambulance with three bullet holes, forming a triangle, in a rear window. Passers-by looked on as both vehicles raced through the city streets.

"They're heading toward Lunar Park!" Butch remarked.

"Sounds like it's show time, boss!" Silk yelled.

Removing several packages from the hidden compartment in the seat beside him, Quinn looked up as Silk pulled into a side road hidden by bushes. From a distance, the three men could see the hooded villains pulling Anderson out of the ambulance. Dressing quickly, Quinn switched from his conservative suit to a nearly black shirt and pants. After that, he changed into crepe-soled shoes, and special gloves with tips which helped him grip special surfaces. Removing his dark glasses, Quinn glared at events through scarred eyes, protected by a pane of Argus glass activated by Silk. Quickly, he placed a dark cowl over his head, revealing only his intense, piercing eyes. A pair of fully-loaded automatic pistols found their way into holsters beneath each of Quinn's shoulders. After wrapping a belt with several compartments around his waist, Quinn finished the outfit with a black cloak. In the mid-afternoon light, there was something dark, shadowy, and mysterious about the figure. As Butch and Silk emerged from the automobile, both men felt a sense of urgency, knowing that Tony Quinn had transformed himself into the Black Bat!

Pointing toward a smaller road, the Black Bat barked, "Butch, follow this small trail. Silk, stay here and keep watch. I'll follow them and see where they end up!"

As Butch went along the smaller trail, the Black Bat sped through a series of bushes and trees, finding himself alongside the ambulance. Waving an all-clear signal to Silk, the Black Bat ran toward a small clearing encircled by several trees. He watched as one of the hooded men threw a rope, its end knotted into a noose, over an overhanging branch of the largest tree.

Crouching behind some bushes, the Black Bat was surprised to find the throng of hooded men waiting for something to happen. Anderson was pushed forward, and a large hooded man pointed a finger in accusation.

"You have been found guilty of the crime of impurity," The man's voice yelled from within the crowd. "The verdict is that you, Randolph Anderson, shall be hung until you are dead!"

Springing from the bushes, the Black Bat rushed toward Anderson. Brandishing both pistols, the Black Bat turned to see a hooded man rushing toward him with a baseball bat. The Black Bat fired two shots, both knocking the bat right out of the hand. Pointing the other gun at the man's head, the Black Bat took a defensive posture.

"One at a time or all together, it does not matter to me!" A savage growl emerged from beneath the Bat's mask. "Stop this now, or I will make sure none of you survive this day!"

Although several of the hooded men ran away, the small crowd that gathered around Anderson continued to cheer as the leader placed the noose around Anderson's neck. Out of the corner of his eye, the Bat noticed a slight hesitancy on the hooded man's part, with Anderson giving him an almost subtle nod.

"String him up!" the hooded leader yelled, and several others pulled on the rope.

Anderson's body jerked upward as the men lifted him up, and the Black Bat aimed both pistols at the rope. Three shots from his guns frayed, and then split, the rope, causing Anderson to fall to the ground.

"How *dare* you defy justice like this?" Striding toward the hooded men, the Black Bat noticed them cowering with fear.

Aiming both pistols toward the men front of him, the Bat was surprised when Anderson yelled, "Mr. Bat…please don't!"

Turning toward Anderson, the Bat noticed Anderson taking a pleading posture. As the crowd began dispersing, the Black Bat returned one of his guns to a holster, keeping the other one aimed at Anderson.

Words rushed out of Anderson's mouth like he was a chastened schoolboy. "I hate to impose, but I would like to know how you *do* that with your voice? I mean, we do something similar on *The Dark Cloak* radio show, but that involves a coffee can and a bit of reverb…."

"What is the meaning of this?"

Standing in a nearly-empty park, Anderson felt a sense of dread at the intensity of the Bat's eyes. Only the gunsels who had a shootout in a hall of mirrors at Coney Island had a similar glare: a sense that nothing or no one would stand in their way.

Anderson's voice grew in confidence. "After all this time, I wanted to find a good way to meet you. I've been planning a film about you and yes, you are a public figure, so I am legally able to do so. So I took advantage of some of this so-called Purity League's controversy, hired some local actors…"

"So this has all been for your play?" the Black Bat aimed his pistol at Anderson's forehead.

Failing to appear calm, Anderson gulped, "Sadly, yes, the accidents and mishaps were real. The Purity League mostly exists as a way for narrow-minded men to relive their Victorian childhoods."

"And you took advantage of your colleagues by playing into their worst fears? You disgust me, Anderson: by treating these people as pawns."

"But that's not..." Shifting on his feet, Anderson sputtered. "That wasn't what I...."

"What did you think having men in hoods would actually *do* for the morale of your cast?"

Finding sudden courage, Anderson stood up to the hooded figure. "For the past few weeks, I have had several attempts on my life, for no other reason than I am running a play which is controversial."

Stepping forward, Anderson pointed an accusing finger in the hooded avenger's face. "Is there *no* depth to your ignorance? Do you *really* think that I would exploit my own cast? I only did what I did to gain insight into my attackers and their motivations. So please shoot me if you must, but understand that I am an artist, and I intend to see this project through."

After stepping away, Anderson shouted, "Oh, and another thing, I *will* make that film about you, but not about you as a legend, but as a model of corruption, about how one person's search for value, justice, or compassion, or even love, corrupts them. Good day, sir!"

As Anderson strode away from the area, a large man in a hood approached him. Quickening his pace, Anderson walked straight into a powerhouse right hook, catching him square in the chin.

Holstering his pistol, the Black Bat walked toward the hooded man as Anderson lay on the ground. As the suited man removed his hood, the Bat holstered his pistol.

"Thanks, Butch, we'll need to get him back to the theater."

"No problem," Butch responded. "Been wanting to do that for awhile now."

As Butch slung Anderson's body over his shoulder like a sack of flour, the Black Bat removed a small, black piece of paper from a compartment on his belt. Opening it, the Black Bat pinned the paper on Anderson's shirt. The paper had been cut to resemble a black bat, wings spread out, showing that Anderson had an encounter with the Black Bat!

Entering the secret laboratory in the rear of his mansion, Tony Quinn removed his mask and headed for the phone on a nearby table. Reaching for a pile of papers, he dialed the theater and asked for Brushman.

"...Anderson walked...into a powerhouse right hook..."

"Mr. Brushman, it's Tony Quinn. Bad news, my driver found Anderson stranded in Lunar Park."

"Oh?" Brushman's voice was tinged with slight disappointment. "It's three hours to show time, and Randolph *would* decide to take a sojourn in the park."

"He and my bodyguard will be escorting Anderson back to the theater," Quinn continued. "But unfortunately, I am a bit under the weather, so I will forgo the invitation. However, I would like for my valet and bodyguard to enjoy the show. I will have my attending nurse come in tonight."

A necessary bluff, to be sure, but Quinn had bigger plans. He had suspicions about who was attempting to sabotage Anderson's efforts, and wanted to bide for time.

In a sour-toned voice, Brushman condescended, "I *suppose* we can give them your seats, after all, we had made them available for you and a guest."

"I appreciate it," Quinn delivered an overdramatic sigh, hoping that Brushman was fooled.

"You are most welcome," Brushman countered, and hung up.

Placing the phone on its cradle, Quinn sat and reviewed the carbon-smudged copies of contracts for a few moments. Within moments, the phone rang again.

"It's Carol, Tony," a bright, female voice announced.

As a smile creased his lips, Tony's voice grew warmer in tone as he updated her on recent events.

"It's just as well," Carol countered. "Vera LaMarche just signed a contract with a major Broadway producer; she's moving ahead with *Taming of the Shrew.*"

"Which means that she and Anderson..."

"Are no longer a working concern," Carol countered. "In fact, she was planning on telling him tonight after *Othello.*"

"But you'll be there?"

"Yes and Ms. LaMarche has informed me that tonight will be my last night of employment."

"Disappointed?"

"Not really."

For a moment, Quinn thought he heard Carol smiling. He smiled back. One day, they would be together.

But the Black Bat's quest for justice came first as always.

Returning the phone to its cradle, Quinn resumed his review of various legal papers. It was a very intricate web of motives: Anderson wanting to protect his work, Malvotti seeking to launder money and protect his reputation….but LaMarche was no longer a suspect.

One down, two to go.

Malvotti was the most obvious suspect; after all, he had the most to lose. Even with such a minimal contract, he was engaging in a very precarious financial shell game. With his own dubious reputation, Malvotti seemed a likely candidate….especially since he and the Bat had encountered each other in the past.

And both men were eager for a rematch.

Placing the papers on the desk, Quinn began considering Brushman and Anderson.

"Brushman and Anderson have a love/hate relationship," Quinn thought aloud."Anderson loves Brushman, and Brushman hates Anderson. Almost seems tailor-made…"

"For a decent motive?" Silk's voice emerged from the laboratory entrance. "I left Butch at the theater to cover Anderson and keep an eye on things."

"Good," Quinn turned as Silk pulled up a chair next to him. "By the way, LaMarche is no longer a concern; she's just signed a contract and fired Carol."

A broad smile spread on Silk's lips.

"But Anderson needs Brushman," Silk explained. "Anderson's a bit… flighty. The kind of guy who acts first and asks questions later. Look at his behavior, setting up a fake attack by the Purity League, using ambulances to get around town…and Brushman doesn't gain anything if Anderson dies. He's left holding the bag on paying off from the production…"

"But he *does* acquire well-needed recognition," Quinn rubbed his chin, contemplating his thought. "Without Anderson, Brushman emerges from the shadows as a potential producer; can strike his mark upon the stage."

"All this is full of sound and fury," Silk announced. "But it means we're back where we started…"

"Not necessarily," Quinn rose, pulling the mask of the Black Bat over his face. "I'll work backstage. Ready to brush up your Shakespeare?"

Most men who faced the Black Bat did so with fear. Silk Kirby faced the Black Bat with a broad smile, knowing that this affair would be ending tonight!

Backstage at the Oberon, the typical rush of frantic activity was more fraught than usual because of closing night. Actors and actresses rehearsed their lines, carefully meeting the tricky rhythms of iambic pentameter. Stagehands of all types, from costumers to prop handlers, hustled to make sure that everything were in working order. Workers touched up the paint on stage scenery, hoping to suggest grand elegance on a shoestring budget.

Standing offside observing the activity, Randolph Anderson smiled, was grateful that Quinn and his staff found him in the park and helped him. Anderson was even more grateful that his wallet was intact. Every show he directed was a trick of some kind, focusing on unique lighting, or sound or even the play produced, but with *Othello* he had managed to pull off one of the greatest tricks in theater history. For a director to assemble two radically different audiences together under the rubric of Shakespeare was quite an impressive feat. Soon, he would be on a train to Hollywood, ready to sign a contract and bring the same genius to the movies. Given his intent to make a movie about an individual who faces corruption and injustice on a regular basis, Anderson felt himself swelling with pride. He would bring his own troupe over, make sure that they had a script, and make sure he had total control....just like he did over *Othello*.

Feeling a tapping on his shoulder, he turned to see Brushman, shifting on his feet and looking rather perturbed. "Randolph, Mr. Malvotti wishes to have a meeting with us."

"Now?"

"At some point before the play begins. I told him that we would meet in the back office. Is that all right?"

"Sure," Anderson turned, running his hand through his dark hair.

Opening night always brought a sense of excitement, and closing night brought a sense of danger – danger that a production might fall apart through sheer exhaustion.

Hoping to avoid that, Anderson made his way toward a pair of actors seeking help with their lines.

After picking the lock of the theater's back door, the Black Bat crept through the dark, making his way toward the back office. His dark outfit and cloak allowed him to blend into the shadows, concealing him from passersby. By now, Silk would have made his way around to the front, joined with Butch, and offered Quinn's apologies to the appropriate people. With Carol accompanying Vera LaMarche, the Bat was confident this affair would meet a sudden end.

Making his way toward an open door, he witnessed two well-dressed men entering the office. Standing still in the shadows, the Bat overheard their conversation.

"Now you know the drill," one voice said. "We wait for Anderson to show up, the boss give us the word, and …"

"Yeah…one question," another voice emerged, this one with the rasp of a heavy smoker. "Do we use guns or keep it silent?"

"Guns, we wanna be sure the Bat gets blamed, after all, *he's* the most likely guy..."

Slipping behind the two men, the Bat hid in a convenient dark corner by a file cabinet. With perfect clarity, the Bat's vision caught the general layout of the room; lights were on overhead but one of the men turned on a solitary desk lamp for illumination. Both men were dressed in suits reserved for those recently released from prison. One man was balding, and the yellowish stains on his fingers revealed that he was the smoker. The other, the leader, had dark, slicked back hair.

"What was that?" the balding smoker flinched, looking at the door.

Hearing the commotion outside, the dark-haired leader ignored it. "Settle down. You know the drill: we wait."

"What if Anderson doesn't…"

"Oh, *he'll* show up, the boss made special arrangements. He also made it clear that if anyone else was clipped, he wouldn't be *too* disappointed."

"Yeah, but what if the Bat shows up?"

"Not our concern. The plan is that we hide in that closet," the leader pointed toward a door in a corner of the room. "We wait for the signal, and then ambush Anderson. After that, it's a nice, hefty payday."

"Is it that simple?"

"Yeah, Joey, it's *that* simple. Now, let's get ready to…"

Both men heard the soft *click* of a gun safety being turned off. As the man named Joey took a step back, the leader felt something cold and metallic press against his back. Turning his head, he noticed the figure of the Black Bat outlined in the dim light.

"Thanks for the heads-up," the Bat growled. "Now, tell me, who hired you?"

Pivoting on his feet, the leader threw a wild punch at the Bat. Acting on instinct, the Bat ducked and missed the blow. Thinking fast, the Bat hurled a sharp, sudden left into the leader's gut. With an audible *whoof*, the leader exhaled and collapsed on the ground.

Quickly holstering his gun, the Bat grabbed Joey and pinned him to the wall. Squeezing Joey's throat with one hand, the Black Bat glared at Joey.

"Your eyes! There's something about your eyes...."

"I don't have time for this," the Bat's grip on Joey's throat got tighter. "*Tell me who hired you!*"

"I don't know!" Joey's breath reeked of cheap tobacco. "Jake...the guy you just knocked out... was my contact! I swear...he came to *me!*"

"To kill Randolph Anderson?"

"Yeah...we kill Anderson, leave no witnesses, and get paid twenty large apiece."

Knowing that he wouldn't get any further information, the Bat squeezed two pressure points on Joey's neck. After feeling a bit woozy, Joey found himself losing consciousness. Watching Joey's physical response, the Bat released him, and Joey fell to the floor.

Unsure of any further details, the Black Bat knew he had to act fast. Anderson would be led to an ambush, and the Bat removed a cord from his belt.

The Black Bat then realized who was coordinating matters....and resolved that this affair would end tonight!

Standing amongst the backstage hustle, Brushman waved toward Malvotti as Anderson stood impatiently.

"A business meeting. now?" Anderson's voice betrayed a deep outrage.

His face showing an impassive calm, Brushman demurred, "I didn't call this meeting. It must be important, Randolph....and have I ever steered you in the wrong direction?"

"Does '*Have you ever considered directing ballet, Randolph?*' ring a bell?"

Waving off his two armed escorts, Malvotti approached the pair of men, oblivious to the backstage activity. "We need to talk, Brushman."

"Agreed," The response came in Brushman's clipped, dry British accent. "We also need to talk alone, the three of us. Why don't we head toward the rear; there is an office that will provide ample privacy."

"Lead on," Malvotti growled. "But avoid any funny stuff."

Leading the way, Brushman led both men through a seeming maze of people, heading toward the rear of the theater. Seeing Brushman reach into the side of his jacket made Malvotti flinch, but Brushman shrugged as if he had forgotten something unimportant.

As they approached the door to the rear office, Anderson noticed the rear door cracked open.

Opening the door, Anderson examined it. "Some thief picked this lock."

"A deduction worthy of the Dark Cloak himself," Brushman sneered.

"Listen, you jokers," Malvotti said. "Never mind the gobbledygook. Let's get this meeting over and done with…."

Closing the door, Anderson sauntered behind his colleagues as they entered the rear office, a solitary desk lamp providing light.

"I think you gentlemen appreciate that, since this is closing night, we need to make appropriate….business arrangements," Holding a stiff posture, Brushman's voice betrayed no emotion.

"Can we please turn on some light?" Malvotti growled.

"In due time," Brushman stepped back. "But I must make something clear to both of you; neither of you will leave this room alive."

"Excuse me?" Anderson asked. Tensing slightly, Malvotti reached for a side holster.

Pulling his hand out of his jacket, Brushman drew a large, lethal revolver from a hidden holster. "I think you will find, Mr. Malvotti, that this piece of fine British craftsmanship can do incredible damage before you can reach for that cheap firearm you and your ilk prefer,"

"Listen, chrome dome," Malvotti pointed an accusing finger, and Brushman responded by thumbing back the hammer.

"Brushman….Marshall….why?" Slumping slightly, Anderson seemed chastened. "We were partners….in fact, we were going to do a movie together….everything was 50/50…"

"Really?" Brushman's scowling face took on a satanic glow in the desk light. Backing toward the closet door, he lectured, "It's always been about *you*, Anderson. Your cheap theatrics and self-aggrandizement have only been a detriment. I have had to clean up after you: the bankrupting performances, the Bolivian hussy who shattered your marriage. I had to keep up the pretense of begging for investors for your film while you were engaged in your usual juvenile antics. It's always been about the 'Magnificent Anderson', *not* the man with the experience who put you there…"

"But you *got* that experience through me," Anderson's voice grew more outraged in tone. "You had some experience, granted, but I helped establish your professional credentials. I earned the money while you got the reputation. You *do* realize how you got your professional reputation, don't you?"

Tightening his finger on the trigger, Brushman's lips curled into an angry sneer. "I got it the old fashioned way, I *earned* it!"

"What about me?" Malvotti snarled, his foot bumping into…something. "What was my role?"

"A wallet with legs, to use your cheap pulp-novel terminology," Brushman sneered. "But you were also a patsy. I arranged so many accidents while enforcing our contract that it made sense to frame you. Simply put, a gangster going after an actor/director interested in a vigilante makes all the sense in the world…"

"But what about Vera?"

"She is no longer your concern," Brushman said. "She has signed a new contract, hired a new agent, and intends to dump you like yesterday's refuse."

Anderson seemed dejected, and Brushman saw an opportunity. Reaching for the light switch, Brushman kept both men covered as he declared, "But my associates will insure that neither one of you will live to tell the tale."

As a bright overhead light turned on, both Malvotti and Anderson squinted and noticed two men, tied with a strong cord, unconscious on the floor. On both men's foreheads was a paper seal, the seal of the Black Bat!

Lifting one of the seals, Malvotti concluded, "Wait a minute…the Black Bat was here? Brushman, you're in deep. You need to get out. *Now.*"

"He is nothing more than a charlatan, a man who has listened to too many episodes of the Dark Cloak."

"Brushman, be reasonable," Malvotti countered, with Anderson looking on in confusion. "Shoot us if you have to, but if the Black Bat's here, you're in serious trouble. Even the boys in blue look away when the Bat's involved."

"Nothing more than smoke, shadows, and cheap theatricality," Straightening himself, Brushman grew more confident. "In fact, thanks to his gracious donation of two souvenirs, I can frame him for your deaths."

"*Cheap theatricality, Mr. Brushman?*" The Black Bat's voiced bellowed from a dark corner. "*Coming from a man who set up an ambush with two hired thugs, I consider that a compliment!*"

Startled, Brushman turned his head toward the source of the voice. Stepping toward the voice, Malvotti threw a wild punch in the air, and felt a sudden *thud* in his midsection. Crumpling onto the floor, Malvotti moaned as the shape of the Black Bat stepped into the light!

"So you're more than just Randolph's adolescent fascination," Brushman's voice took on a sing-song quality. "You really *do* exist."

From behind the impassive hood which covered his face, the Black Bat declared, "I'm not surprised that you're behind all these accidents. Once Anderson's gone, you get the glory…."

"…and enough money for me to return to England."

"Brushy? Seriously?" Anderson pleaded.

Swinging his gun hand wildly, Brushman smacked Anderson in the face. As both men tussled, the Bat withdrew twin automatic pistols from shoulder holsters, taking careful aim and firing at the wall just past Anderson and Brushman.

Both men stopped and turned, shocked that the Black Bat would open fire upon them. Malvotti merely crouched alongside the two unconscious thugs, unwilling to get involved.

"Both of you are criminal in your own way," the Bat's pistols were now aimed squarely at Brushman and Anderson. "Brushman decided to not only gain from your death, Anderson, but also took money from a known gangster to frame *him* for the crime."

"You're *defending* that filth?" The outrage in Brushman's voice was palpable. "I would have easily gotten away with it. It wasn't even illegal. All I wanted was to remove Anderson and his ego."

"And *you*, Anderson," the Bat snarled. "*You* acted recklessly, leaving a wake of bitterness and resentment!"

"Why, I don't think so, I…" Anderson paused for a moment. "All I wanted was to establish my reputation as a director, to make an impact on the theater before working on film. A film about a character that has made a direct impact on our culture…"

Holstering his guns, the Bat watched as Brushman turned the barrel of his revolver toward Anderson. Swinging his arm, the Black Bat grasped Brushman's gun arm while delivering a devastating punch straight into Brushman's mid-section. Dropping his pistol, Brushman clutched his stomach and leaned against the wall.

"But….you don't understand…" Brushman gasped. "Anderson was…. holding me back. With Anderson gone and the insurance money, I would have put that into another production….something other than that talentless hussy's desire for Shakespeare. I wanted to do something more ambitious, more reputable…."

"And so what are you planning to do now, Mr. Bat?" Anderson's voice took on a slight whine. "Malvotti's injured, Brushman's confessed, and I must admit that I am at a loss for what I am supposed to do next."

As the Black Bat's arm blurred, Anderson felt something hard smack against his face. Falling back toward the wall, he had realized that the Bat had pistol-whipped him like something out of a Cagney film. Anderson never noticed how swiftly the Black Bat had drawn his pistol.

Taking aim at Anderson, the Bat snarled, "You will leave town. Tomorrow morning. Never come back."

"Oh, really?" Anderson said in his best Jack Benny voice. "What about the law?"

Catching Brushman out of the corner of his eye, Anderson noticed his partner crouching for his gun. Bursting out of the closet was Lt. McGrath, his pistol drawn and ready as he strode toward Brushman.

"Now, now, Mr. Brushman," McGrath grabbed the man's arm, twisting it behind his back. "I think you and I should take a little trip to the hoosegow."

"What about the Bat?" Anderson noticed Malvotti rising on his feet. "Or Mr. Malvotti?"

"What about 'im?" McGrath asked. "Malvotti hasn't done anything, and the Black Bat's your pal!"

"My pal?" Stiffening in posture, Anderson strode toward McGrath in indignation. "He is definitely *not* my pal."

"Of course he is. You asked Quinn to intervene," Cuffing Brushman's hands, McGrath wanted to leave as quickly as possible. "And there he is."

"I will have you know that Anthony Quinn is a refined gentleman and an advocate for justice with compassion," Wagging his finger, Anderson lectured the lieutenant. "This masked gentleman is a miscreant! His only concept of justice comes out of the barrel of a gun, and he thinks with his fists rather than his heart. I think you'll see...."

As Anderson gestured toward where the Black Bat stood, all four men stared at a now empty space.

"He's gone," Anderson declared.

"What a master of understatement," Brushman grumbled.

"Where's my money?" Malvotti asked.

"I have better things to do," McGrath complained before pushing Brushman out of the room.

"Wait a minute, it was *Brushman?*" Butch asked, sitting with Carol, Silk, and Tony Quinn in the living room of the Quinn mansion.

It had been a long night thanks to Quinn's plan, his three aides managed to keep an eye on matters. Thankfully, the production had gone off without a hitch, and they were all assembled in the living room in the late hours of the evening.

"Makes sense," Silk countered "Brushman had a vested interest; he wanted to be the big cheese rather than the second banana."

"Plus," Carol countered. "He made Malvotti a perfect patsy. After all, who would believe a gangster who claimed he was set up?"

Sipping his tea, Quinn regarded his three compatriots. "That's why I contacted McGrath when I came across those two thugs. Knockout drops kept them unconscious while I snared Brushman in his own web."

"That was risky...." Silk stated.

"I know," Quinn responded. "But this means that McGrath owes me somewhat. I'm more than willing to have him pay back at a later time…"

"What about Anderson?" Butch asked.

"With your help, Butch," Quinn's voice was tinged with fatigue. "I'll take care of it in the morning."

With that, all three went off and headed to bed. Silk and Carol took their leave, while Butch made his way to a guest bedroom.

"Thank you *so* much for seeing me off, Mr. Quinn," Anderson enthusiastically shook Tony Quinn's hand.

Beside them, a train was boarded by enthusiastic travelers. From a distance, McGrath observed both men, then turned his attention to a sign posted that indicated a train bound for California.

"It's no problem," Quinn removed his free hand as his other gripped a cane. "I only wish I could have done more."

"But it's not you," Anderson observed. "It was...the Black Bat. After learning that Brushy had a contract out on me, facing the Bat's gun, I have decided to make my way west."

Quinn's expression remained impassive, but he silently felt gratitude. In order to maintain his mission, the Black Bat needed to remain somewhat anonymous. If the events of the past few days proved anything, sunlight would have been his greatest nemesis in Randolph Anderson's hands.

"So what will you do now?" Quinn asked as the conductor cried last call.

"I have several ideas," Anderson stated. "Perhaps an adaptation of Kafka's *Metamorphosis.* Or even possibly *Don Quixote.* I *still* need to sign a formal contract, but at this point....it's a done deal."

"Well, if anything...I thank you once again for the opportunity. And I will continue to listen to *Tales from the Dark Cloak.*"

Chuckling, Anderson rubbed his neck. "Sorry, old man, I'm being replaced. The producers feel that my Dark Cloak has run its course. Besides, I will leave nocturnal avenging to the Black Bat."

As Quinn said goodbye to Anderson, McGrath approached both men. Regarding Anderson with suspicion, McGrath politely led Quinn toward the entrance back into Grand Central station.

About to board the train, Anderson heard a newsboy yell, *"Wuxtry! Wuxtry! Black Bat Foils Attempt on Radio Star's Life!"*

Gesturing toward the lad, Anderson withdrew a nickel and handed it to the boy. Taking the newspaper, Anderson entered the train and found his compartment.

With a mighty *whoosh*, the train moved. After allowing the conductor to punch his ticket, Anderson placed it into his front pocket. Opening the newspaper, Randolph Anderson saw a headline in big, bold, black letters:

BLACK BAT RESCUES RADIO HACK
An Editorial by Publisher Charles Foster Gladman

"A motion picture about a newspaper man?" Anderson mumbled to himself. "It *could* work...."

The End

THE AUTEUR
& THE
VIGILANTE

I don't know when my fascination for the work of Orson Welles began – maybe it was those wine commercials I saw when I was a kid. Maybe it was when I watched *Citizen Kane* in high school (for English class) and *The Third Man* in college (again, for English class). There's a soft spot in my heart for the very Welles-like Brain in *Animaniacs*...so in many ways I've respected the burgundy-voiced auteur with a slightly noir sensibility.

So when it came to writing a story for the Black Bat, I wanted to take a hard-and-dirty pulp approach to a more upscale, socially ambitious world. So taking inspiration from a mashup of silent movie footage into a fictional Batman movie (thanks, Chuck Moore of *Comic Related*!), I decided to merge the well-known auteur's theatrical background within a very unconventional format. It was an exciting flash of inspiration: if Orson Welles intended his first feature film about a well-known figure, why *not* a nocturnal vigilante operating in New York?

So after a successful pitch (in which I promised that I wouldn't end with a shootout in a hall of mirrors – Gerard Jones did it much better in an issue of *The Shadow Strikes* for DC Comics), I crafted a tale of a fictional Welles and his immediate group. (If you can figure out which characters are based on real people, and which are fictional....I'll send you a congratulatory e-mail). But this couldn't be just "generic characters with new names" - it meant insuring that the characters felt like their real-life counterparts. (And yes, the actress' last name *is* a riff on a famous voiceover actor).

As I wrote the story, I immersed myself into "research", by which I mean "structured procrastination." It involved watching as many Welles movies and documentaries as humanly possible. (Trust me – watching *The Third Man*, *The Stranger*, and *The Lady From Shanghai* for writing purposes isn't a chore). Listening to *The Many Lives of Harry Lime* (all four volumes are available from RadioArchives.com) to catch the cadences of Welles' speech. Making sure that nothing betrayed the era of the story (date: May, 1940) and of course, finding just the *right* scene in the *right* Shakespeare play (which came completely by accident)

The other challenge was getting the Black Bat and *his* crew dead-on. It wasn't my first effort – I've written a yet-to-be-published story for Excelsior Webcomics – so I had working knowledge of the Bat and his team. So I reread Airship 27's *Black Bat Mystery* anthologies and Altus Press' *Black Bat Omnibus* collections. (Like I've said – you can call it "research"; I call it "structured procrastination") It's relatively easy to write Tony Quinn – he's one of the more compassionate characters in pulp – but I wanted to insure that Silk, Butch, and Carol each had their moment in the spotlight. I believe I got it right.

This has been a *very* fun story to write. I hope you have just as good a time reading it.

Gordon Dymowski spends his day hours freelancing as a marketing consultant for non-profits and small businesses. His writing career began with a short story at eight years old, and has taken him through sojourns as a columnist for the **Loyola Phoenix**; writing for the Prodigy online network; and a short-lived humor column for **The Shrubbery.** When he's not editing for Airship 27, Gordon co-hosts the **Zone** 4 podcast (http://www.zone4podcast.com) and writes for a variety of outlets about a variety of topics, including

I Hear of Sherlock (http://www.ihearofsherlock.com)

Chicago Now (http://www.chicagonow.com/one-cause-at-a-time) and

Blog *This*, Pal (http://blogthispal.blogspot.com)

Gordon made his publication debut with "Out There In the Night" in **Les Vamps,** and has been published in Pro Se's **Tall Pulp** For more information, a variety of links, and/or a quick and easy way to reach Gordon, please visit http://www.gordondymowski.com

A Black Bat Adventure

by
Erik Franklin

Acting on an impulse, Carol Baldwin decided to visit Chinatown early that morning. Even though she knew she was in New York City, Carol could not help but feel that she had been transported to exotic Hong Kong. The streets were cluttered with vendors and patrons, with the hustle and bustle of daily life all around her. The aroma of roasted ducklings hanging in the shop windows mixed with the fragrant spices and herbs from the apothecary shops. Colorful facades, mimicking temples, decorated the shops, restaurants, and apartment buildings. Vibrant colors from the textiles and clothing of the residents intrigued Carol as she strolled along the streets.

The same impulse compelled her to walk towards an antique store. The name "Shang Di Rare Antiquities" was embossed on the wooden plaque above the door. Despite the small size of the building, an aura of regality radiated from the shop. The artifacts displayed in the windows, each more beautiful and ornate than the next, caught her eye.

"Here," she thought, "Anthony will never expect this!"

As Carol stepped towards Shang Di's shop, she was seized by the wrist! Turning around, Carol came face-to-face with an older Chinese man. His hair was snow white, his face and body plump from years of good eating. This man was the vegetable vendor that she had passed moments earlier, but the expression on his face... Carol would never forget it. It was of absolute horror. The longer he stared at her, the tighter his grip became.

"You're hurting me!" protested Carol.

"Please, do not go in there! Do not go in!" the man said.

"Why not?" Carol said, wrenching her wrist from his grasp.

The vendor stopped for a moment, his mouth struggling to form the words. He looked from the shop to her, and back again. Finally, he stammered:

"He is a thief! It is all junk! Don't trust him!" he whispered to her.

It did not make sense to Carol. It was understandable that a local would warn a customer about a disreputable store, but the fear in his eyes did not match his story. The vendor was *afraid* of the shop. As he glanced back again, his eyes grew even larger and his manner more jittery. Carol looked over as well, curious.

Standing in the doorway was a man in a long silk gown, elaborately embroidered with a golden tiger. His jet black hair was tied in a ponytail, and his face, though he would be considered strikingly handsome by most, possessed a severity to it that had a subtly frightening effect. He looked at the vendor with piercing eyes, and the man ran away from Carol. He then fixed his eyes on her, and his expression softened.

"You must excuse Lao. His brother owns another antique shop in this district. He does what he can to drive business away from me."

"Oh, I see," said Carol suspiciously.

"I am Shang Di, and this is my store, if you would care to step inside?" he enquired, making a graceful gesture towards his establishment.

"I would, thank you." Carol said, stepping past him.

It was like entering a museum. Bronze tigers, dragons, snakes, soldiers, generals, and other statues filled the shelves. Historical blue and white porcelain vases, scrolls, and paintings lined the walls. The pleasant smell of incense greeted Carol.

"It is all very beautiful, Mr. Di," Carol said, admiring the jade statues and jewelry in a glass case by the door.

"Thank you," Shang said, closing the door behind him. He stepped behind the counter and turned to Carol with a smile. "Are you interested in anything in particular?"

"Well, I'm here to buy a present for my...." Carol paused. It was Anthony Quinn's birthday today, and thinking of the best way to describe their relationship amused her. She was his secretary and they were in love. Yet he was not her husband or her boyfriend, he was the Black Bat, and in order to protect her, Quinn insisted they remain apart.

"I'm here to buy a present for my friend, today is his birthday."

"Some last minute shopping then?" Shang smiled.

"Well, it's not that. My friend is so very clever. The last few times I tried to surprise him, well… it just didn't work out. I decided to go to Chinatown to find something completely unexpected!"

"I see. So your friend, what does he do?"

"Oh, he's a lawyer. He has his own practice."

"I see. Perhaps one of my beautiful paintings to decorate his office?" Shang said, sweeping his arm over to a collection of framed work.

"Actually, I need to find a special gift that a blind person can enjoy."

"So, we need a gift for a truly clever man… one who is blind… a lawyer…" Shang tapped his fingers gently on the counter with a ponderous look, but then his expression brightened. "I believe I have something for you!"

Ducking under the counter, Shang produced a small wooden box. Though it was beautiful, the top had a disjointed and strange carved pattern. "I admit that it is not an antique, but it is fascinating nonetheless. It is a puzzle box. When one slides the tiles around, they are reenacting the escape of General Cao Cao through the Huarong Pass which happened during the Han dynasty. Once the pattern is complete, you will find a treasure inside."

"What's the treasure?"

"I recommend giving it to your friend intact. Why ruin the surprise?"

"But as I said, my friend is blind, how could he see the…?" Carol began to protest, but Shang took her finger and placed it on the box.

"Now close your eyes and feel the pattern," he ran her fingers along the carving, and at once a smile came to Carol's face. The tiles certainly felt different from one another, and it was clear to her that a blind person could have a reasonable chance at solving this puzzle.

"I think this may keep him busy for some time," Carol said, taking her hand back and opening up her purse. "How much is it?"

"The puzzle box is seventy-five dollars," Shang said firmly.

"But that seems a bit…" Carol began to protest.

"With the intricacies and craftsmanship put into this puzzle box, I'm afraid I cannot…"

"Well, if you're not willing to budge…" Carol started, not at all pleased. She turned on her heel and started heading towards the door. Carol had her hand on the handle when "Fifty!" stopped her.

Carol turned to face Shang again, a satisfied expression on her face.

"He's worth it." Carol said, feeling better about the purchase. She also felt better to see Shang's smug visage showing signs of frustration and anger that, try as he might, he could not conceal.

As Carol dug into her wallet, Shang began moving pieces around on the box. She saw him and grew suspicious.

"What are you doing?"

"I'm resetting the puzzle for your friend. It is bad luck to begin a puzzle that has already been started," Shang said matter-of-factly. He glanced over at the money in Carol's hand.

"Is there anything else your friend would like? Or maybe something for you, perhaps? I have a fine collection of rare beads and carved jade from ancient China," Shang began, motioning towards a case of jewelry.

"No thank you, I'll take this with me now. No need to wrap it."

"Would you like a receipt, miss?"

"No, I'm sure that he'll love it."

"Very well," said Shang. He handed her the box and she gave him the money. After they exchanged parting words, his friendly smile dropped. It was soon replaced by another smile, a dark, evil smile. He watched Carol walk up the street, and gave a satisfied sigh.

Carol went back to her apartment. Inevitably, Silk would be coming by any minute with his present for Quinn. Despite being a skilled ex-con, and handy with a knife, he had no talent for doing anything intricate like wrapping a present or tying a bow. She would be meeting up with Butch later; he at least had the sense to have his presents wrapped at the store.

Sitting back for a moment, Carol admired the beautiful box. It was black lacquer with a bronze dragon on the front. She wondered what treasure was inside, and decided to test her skills. After all, she was just as clever as Quinn, and it might be an amusing way to pass the time. Gently moving the pieces around, Carol eventually found the correct pattern and heard the box open.

Click!

Then she decided against looking inside. After all, it was supposed to be a surprise for Quinn, and it would be more fun if they could enjoy it together.

Setting the box on her desk, Carol went to the closet to get wrapping paper. The puzzle box slowly started to emit a green vapor. It snaked across the room silently, engulfing the apartment as it inched towards Carol. A rotting odor permeated the air. Carol turned around and screamed! Her apartment was filled with poison gas!

A tall man in a chauffer's uniform sauntered down the hall to Carol's apartment door with a clumsily wrapped package underneath his arm and a cake box in his hand. Silk Kirby was too far away to hear the scream, so nothing seemed unusual to him. Arriving at her door, he knocked several times, but got no answer.

"Hey, Carol. It's me, Silk. I... uh... I need your help with the present, like you did for me at Christmas." Before he continued the odor reached Silk's nose as well.

It was then that he heard the sound of a window breaking! Ready for action, Silk dropped what he was carrying and forced his shoulder against the door. It loosened, but did not budge. Stepping backwards, Silk raised his leg and gave a mighty kick.

That did it! The door went crashing to the floor. Silk was greeted with a horrible sight. Carol was lying on the ground, face down. Her skin was pale and she was shaking uncontrollably. Not allowing himself to be overcome with shock, Silk pulled Carol out into the hallway. There he got a good look at her. Her lips had turned a shade of blue and her eyes were dilating rapidly. She tried to speak to Silk but passed out in his arms.

Several other neighbors had opened their doors to investigate. Silk hollered at them:

"Call an ambulance, quick!"

Anthony Quinn found himself looking at the floor of the hospital waiting room, unable to focus on anything. They were not allowing anyone near Carol, save for the doctors working on her. All he wanted to do was see her; he wanted to know what happened, and what he could do to help her. He kept replaying Silk's phone call in his head. It was agonizing not to jump in a car and drive to the hospital. His disguise as a blind man forced him to take a taxi, and Quinn cursed his double-life for costing him precious moments away from Carol.

"Is there anything I can get you?" the nurse asked Quinn politely, interrupting his thoughts. He shook his head and she walked away, almost bumping into Silk as he sat down in the chair next to Quinn.

"It's no good, Mr. Quinn, I tried to get in, but no dice."

"Did you see anything?"

"I didn't see Carol, but I did spot one interesting thing, though."

"What's that?" Quinn said, grasping for anything to keep his mind off of Carol's suffering.

"Get this, there are two flatfoots outside her door. I mean, why all the special treatment?"

Silk was right: this was worth investigating. Had Carol seen or witnessed something that she should not have? Was she concealing something that caused her to end up like this? Was she trying to protect the Black Bat?

At that moment, two men stormed into the waiting room. Police commissioner Jerome Warner, a gray haired man with a stern expression, strode purposefully through the doors. Behind him was the large figure of Butch O'Leary, his boxer's build evident even through his boxy suit. He followed after Warner like a dog begging for scraps.

"But you gotta tell me something!" Butch pleaded, "Carol's like my kid sister and I have a right to know what's going on here!"

"All that I can say is…" at that moment, Warner spotted Quinn and Silk listening to them. "Oh, it's you two, might as well tell you all at once."

Butch helped Quinn out of the chair and they gathered around him, while Warner puffed out his chest, as if he were ready to give a statement to the press. "All I can say is that we are keeping Carol Baldwin under police protection. Because of her unique symptoms she has now become involved in a case that is under investigation. Needless to say we are cooperating with the hospital staff and have high hopes of Carol making a complete recovery."

"Thanks for clearing up nothing," Silk said under his breath.

"That's all I'm going to say, I'm sorry," said Warner as he brushed them off. He showed his credentials to the guards who let him pass without question.

Butch joined the other two as he sat in a nearby chair, drumming his fingers nervously.

"Carol didn't have a… she didn't have a… like a condition, did she?" Butch asked, already knowing the answer. When both shook their heads, he sank back down.

They sat in frustrated silence. However, silence was golden to Anthony Quinn, for he possessed a gift that neither Butch nor Silk had: a near super-human ability to hear. A few years ago, before having the operation that restored his eyes, his other senses had naturally compensated for his lack of sight. Therefore, he could clearly hear the door at the end of the long corridor close, with two sets of footsteps walking out. Their heated conversation was clear as a bell.

"What do you mean that you have no idea?" Warner demanded of the other man, most likely a doctor.

"I meant what I said. She's like the others, collapsed in her home with this mysterious poison in her lungs. The only difference between them and her is that she's still alive… but just barely," the doctor said defensively, not pleased with the police commissioner's manner in the least.

"You don't seem to understand, Doctor Jameson, I've got city hall breathing down my neck with these unsolved murders! I need something to give them!" Warner demanded of the doctor.

"I can't give you anything to go on! We're trying to isolate the chemicals in the poison, but when this particular kind mingles with blood, it is near impossible to trace. As soon as I know more, you'll be informed." Doctor Jameson stated determinedly, doing his best to put an end to the conversation.

"See that I am," said Warner as he walked down the hallway towards the waiting room. Quinn had to know more, but he had to plan his moves carefully. Doctor Jameson was the man to see, but getting to him was going to be a challenge.

"There is more to this case, and I need to get to a Doctor Jameson,

Carol's doctor, to learn more." Quinn said in a hushed tone, leaning over to Butch and Silk. "Based on what we heard from Warner, the doctor's off limits, and the police are trying to keep everything hush-hush."

"I could always try to sweet-talk my way in," Silk offered doubtfully "but the cops at Carol's door don't appear to be too keen on conversation."

"Where is he now, Mr. Quinn?" Butch asked.

Quinn listened closely again, and was able to pick up Doctor Jameson's distinctive footfalls as he headed further into the building. "I can't hear him anymore, we need to find his office."

"There's a directory hanging next to the elevator, I'll be right back!" A moment later with an eager smile on his face, Silk returned with the information.

"I got it!" Silk said with quiet excitement. "You need a diversion!" He explained his plan. It was crude and simple, but time was of the essence. The first step in the plan involved Butch walking into the nearby restroom and waiting for his cue.

A few moments later, Anthony Quinn, cane in hand, walked towards the room that held Carol. He tried to enter, and predictably, the police outside the room prevented him. They gently held him back as he struggled towards the door.

"But please, I need to be with her!" Quinn protested.

"Sir, you are not authorized to be here. I suggest that you turn around and…" the police officer began; his tone was becoming more severe. This was exactly what the plan hinged on. A sideways glance into the waiting room showed that some curious onlookers were watching the drama unfold. Now for one more push.

Quinn, acting more frantic, pretended to fumble for the door knob. That tore it for the police officer, who forcibly put Anthony Quinn in a restraining hold, knocking his cane to the ground. As the witnesses in the waiting room gasped, Butch came out of the bathroom on cue, playing his part.

"Hey! What do you think you're doing!" Butch yelled in righteous indignation. "What are ya' doin' roughing up a crippled man? I'd like to see you palookas try that on me!" he shouted at the police officers as he advanced on them. The onlookers were stunned, but all were clearly impressed by Butch's "heroic" gesture. The police officer not holding Quinn approached Butch and put his hand on Butch's chest.

"Sir, you need to leave, or I'll make you leave!"

"Is that a fact?"

Butch grabbed the police officer and hurled him into the waiting room! The other police officer dropped Quinn and attempted to put a similar choke-hold on Butch. That was a terrible mistake. Butch lifted him over his head and threw him into the waiting room, nailing the police officer who had just shakily regained his footing. Earlier, Silk insisted that Butch not use his fists when confronting the police officers.

"After all, they're not bad guys and they're just doing their job," he reasoned with Butch.

Butch stood in the center of the doorway, arms outstretched, ready for a fight. This wide pose diverted all eyes from Quinn, so he had a chance to sneak away while the police officers dealt with Butch. Grabbing his cane, he snuck down the corridor.

Quinn walked briskly down the hallway, until he came across the name Jameson written on the door. "The doctor better be in," Quinn thought, otherwise they got themselves into a bucket-full of trouble for no reason.

Quinn breathed a sigh of relief as he saw Doctor Jameson at his desk consulting a file. The man was of average height, balding, with a calm face that showed signs of exhaustion. Of course, Anthony Quinn supposedly saw none of this, so he asked aloud.

"Excuse me, is anyone in this room?"

"Well… yes, I am. Are you lost?" Jameson said standing up.

"I'm looking for Doctor Jameson. I need to talk with him about his patient, Carol Baldwin. You see, I am her lawyer…"

"I'm not supposed to discuss this case with anyone other than the commissioner or the police. Now if you'll excuse me…" Jameson said, evidently tired of dealing with questions. Quinn had no choice; he put his cane across the door to prevent the man from leaving. Ordinarily, interrogations with him were a much different matter. As a lawyer he had police support and the right to grill witnesses for testimony. As the Black Bat he could use his fists to get what he needed. This was different; Anthony Quinn had to connect with this man on a human level.

"You must understand, Doctor Jameson, that Carol Baldwin is the woman I love. Without her, I am half a man. I need to know what is happening to her, can you at least tell me that?"

Quinn was not lying, nor did he feel that he was exaggerating in any way. Without Carol's donation of her dead father's eyes, the Black Bat would not be able to see in the dark. He would not exist. Who knows how many criminals would still be preying on the innocent, and what would Anthony Quinn have been without her?

"You're not supposed to be here…" Jameson said nervously, his eyes darting around for hospital security.

"I'm a lawyer, and I know exactly how many laws I am breaking. That should make it clear to you how important this is to me."

"Close the door behind you," Jameson said after a moment's hesitation.

After the door shut, Jameson looked at Anthony Quinn and nodded to himself. "I shouldn't be doing this, but…"

"Thank you."

"This is not the first time something like this happened. Rather, she's the first whose made it this far, but, to be frank, without knowing what this thing is, there's not much reason for hope." Jameson said, looking at his files.

"I understand. Who were the other victims, were they like Carol? Female, blonde, attractive?" Quinn ventured a guess.

"No. Other than living in parts of New York City, the victims had nothing in common…" Jameson consulted his list. "The first was a Chinese man, a bookseller, living in Chinatown. Found dead in his shop after hours. The next, a tourist, Caucasian male, from St. Louis, who died in his hotel… You get the picture."

"And the cause of death?"

"We know that each victim was poisoned, and based on the autopsies, we know that the poison came from a gas, and is absorbed through the nostrils…but we can't identify the substance," Jameson turned the page on his notes. "According to the coroner, each victim died within minutes of ingesting a substantial amount of the poison. This young lady was very lucky."

"So if you discover the chemical composition, you can create an antidote?"

"Conceivably, yes. The fact is that we have never seen a poison like this. We simply do not know where to begin."

"I see…" Quinn said, disappointed.

"I am truly sorry, sir," said Jameson, opening the door for him. "I'll walk you back to the waiting room."

As they approached the waiting room, they saw four police officers attempting to restrain Butch. Warner, in militaristic fashion, was ordering Butch to stand down. Silk, hiding safely behind the crowd, pretended to be an innocent observer. Eyeing Quinn walking towards him with Jameson, Butch gave him a wink and slowly gave up his struggle. Warner looked over in shock.

"I shouldn't be doing this, but..."

"Jameson! What is the meaning of this?" he began to yell.

"It's like this, sir…" Silk began, "Mr. Quinn wanted to be near to Carol, leave a note by her table or something, and the cop here, who I thought was using way too much force, decided to attack him! Now Butch here, he's the excitable type, especially with Carol being in the hospital, so he sees these men attacking Mr. Quinn and tries to defend him!"

"And I got lost in the fray and…" Quinn started to lie.

"That must be when I found you and escorted you back here," said Jameson, looking at Warner. "He was lost."

Flustered, Warner was ready to question their version of events, but the onlookers in the waiting room voiced their support for Silk's story. Frustrated, Warner looked from Silk to Butch to Quinn and back again. He threw his hands up in the air and then pointed at the three of them. "It's not worth my time to investigate this matter, but if I catch any of you around here again…!"

"Oh no, sir, we're leaving…" Silk said as he guided Quinn out of the waiting room.

"By the way, Mr. Quinn, Lt. McGrath wants you to meet him at Carol's apartment. Says he feels you may offer him some assistance. You did know her best, after all." Warner ordered Quinn.

The trio made their way to the parking lot while Quinn relayed the information from Doctor Jameson. Silk nodded, and patted Butch on the back.

"You did good, kid!" Silk said to him proudly. Butch glared.

"So how come your harebrained ideas always put me in the thick of it?"

"Because I have all the confidence in the world you'll come out on top, champ!" Silk said with a smile.

"Butch, do me a favor…" Quinn began, cutting into Silk's conversation, "I need you to go to the office and close it up for today. Then meet us back at the estate."

"Sure thing, Mr. Quinn."

Quinn understood that Silk's way of dealing with hard times was with humor, but he could not join in. All he could think about was visiting the crime scene at Carol's apartment.

Hours after the smoke had cleared, the police were on the scene. Lt. McGrath, holding a handkerchief to his nose (the odor was still pungent)

inspected the broken window at Carol's apartment. He turned to Anthony Quinn, who was standing inside the doorway.

"You see this broken window, Mr. Quinn?" McGrath said.

"You know I can't, and now is not the time for games." Normally, Quinn enjoyed this cat-and-mouse game he and McGrath played. McGrath continually attempted to trip up Quinn, proving that he *could* see and thereby implicating him as the Black Bat, but the attack on Carol nullified his sense of humor.

"Well, anyway, I'll humor you this time, Quinn, and say there is a broken window here. It was broken from the inside, as if somebody threw something through it. It probably helped the gas dissipate faster." McGrath approached Quinn, allowing his gruff demeanor to fade a little. Quinn was visibly shaken up and McGrath decided to ease up.

"You know, a few more minutes in here with that gas and Carol would be…"

"Yes, I know."

"How's she doing, Anthony? Any improvement?"

"Not that I know of, the police are keeping a tight lid on this, and it is driving me crazy!" Quinn turned and slowly headed down the hallway towards the elevator, using his cane to help him.

"Where are you going?" McGrath asked, following after him.

"Whatever Carol tossed through the window is likely to still be in the alley. I was going to attempt to find it."

"Aren't you going to need somebody to help you, Anthony?" McGrath said, keeping pace with him.

"I was hoping you'd come with me," Quinn lied. It was true that he'd hoped to find whatever was thrown down there, but he did not want McGrath to see it before him and take it off to the police lab for analysis. Quinn could experiment at his own secret lab and, without the police backlog of cases, could arrive at the truth much faster.

When they reached the elevator, McGrath pressed the button for the ground floor.

"So, why do you suppose somebody wanted to kill her?" he pressed Quinn.

"There could be any number of reasons. Criminals wanting revenge on me, perhaps?" This theory was the most logical, but the most upsetting for Quinn. He had become the Black Bat and held Carol at arm's length for her safety, but to think that someone was using her to get to Anthony Quinn… that was truly disturbing to him.

"But why use gas? I can understand somebody using a knife or a gun, but it takes a strange kind of criminal to use poison gas."

"Have any of the other tenants been affected?"

"No, apparently it was a small, but concentrated dose."

Quinn set his jaw. "Then not only are we dealing with, as you say, a strange kind of criminal, but he is also a diabolical genius. Imagine the mind that can create and control a gas that targets one specific victim!"

"I hadn't thought of that. Sounds like we got an assassin on our hands!" McGrath surmised.

As they stepped into the alley outside, McGrath barked at some of the police officers who were loitering nearby.

"Hey, there might be evidence in the alley! I don't need you knuckleheads trampling over something that will solve this case!"

While McGrath ordered his men about, Quinn gently walked down the alley, deliberately using his cane for assistance. Truthfully, he could see better in the shadows than any of the men. He immediately spotted the object surrounded by shards of glass. Of course, he had to wander in that direction and then "bump into" the object accidentally with his cane. He kept an ear out as McGrath gave more orders to the other men. Quinn had precious few seconds to work.

The object, a small black lacquered box, was in pieces. There was also bronze carving and some tiles scattered about. He felt the wood splinters. Anthony Quinn's ultra-sensitive touch immediately told him that this was a hardwood. It was a solid, sturdy variety, easily able to shatter a window if thrown hard enough. Quinn pictured Carol throwing the box with all her might. He also noticed that the lacquer was only recently applied because it was slightly sticky, not set into the wood yet. The aging on the bronze was artificially achieved with paint, and a few deliberately placed nicks and scratches were present. In short, this was a recently constructed piece, obviously handmade.

There were metal parts that he could not account for: gears and other specialized pieces that had no business being in a Chinese puzzle box. Pulling out a tissue, he collected the other piece of evidence that did not fit: a strange blobby substance, resembling melted glass. Quickly, putting the tissue back in his pocket, it was time for McGrath to look at the evidence.

"Lieutenant!" Quinn called out, "I tapped this with my cane, is it important?"

"With your cane, huh?" said McGrath doubtfully as he walked over and bent down to inspect the broken box.

"What is this thing?" McGrath said, angling his body for a closer look.

"Can you describe it to me?" Quinn asked.

"It's black, wooden, and has some kinda dragon on it. There are a bunch of little square pieces scattered all over the place."

"It sounds like you are describing a Chinese puzzle box, Lieutenant."

"What would Carol Baldwin be doing with a Chinese puzzle box?" McGrath said as he straightened up, looking to Quinn, who could not help but shrug.

"I don't know. It's not the type of thing she normally goes for… Oh god…" Quinn stopped himself, his face turning white.

"What?" McGrath said, suddenly alert.

"Carol would never buy anything like this for herself, Lieutenant!" Quinn said, shouting to McGrath.

"Something wrong, Anthony?"

"Today is my birthday! Lieutenant, she bought me that box for my birthday! Don't you get it? The gas was released from the Chinese puzzle box somehow! It's all my…" Again, Quinn could not finish his sentence, and felt McGrath put an arm around him.

"Listen, Anthony, you can't blame yourself. Besides, Carol is a fighter, she'll pull through."

"She will, but I'll see to it that the ones who did this to her won't!" Quinn felt along the wall and walked down the alley and towards the lobby of the apartment building.

"Where are you going now?" McGrath said, catching up with Quinn. He grabbed Quinn by the shoulder.

"Listen, I know you're upset, but when people are all worked up, they can make some serious mistakes and get themselves into a lot of trouble. You just sit back and let us do our job. When we find whoever did this to Carol, you can throw the book at them!"

"Maybe you are right, Lieutenant. Could somebody find my chauffer? I need to get home."

If the situation were different, Quinn would have laughed at McGrath's speech: "Sit back and let us do our job…" Yes, that is all that Anthony Quinn could do. The Black Bat on the other hand…

A short time later, Silk was driving Quinn home to his secret laboratory to analyze the sample he had taken from the scene. The two rode in silence, Quinn cursing every red light that stopped them. "Mr. Quinn, I know what you must be feeling, but you got to stop beating yourself up! You got to figure out a way to help Carol, and if you can't think straight, then it's not gonna happen!" Silk broke the silence.

"I know that you are right, Silk. If you had not been there… Thank you. I owe you one."

"Keep it. Chinese puzzle box, huh?"

"Yes. McGrath is studying it now."

"Well, if the Black Bat can put the creep who did this in his own box, then I'll call it payment enough for me."

"It can be arranged." Quinn responded darkly.

"What do you need from me?" Silk asked, mentally preparing himself for the mission.

"I want you and Butch to head to Chinatown. In the meantime I'll analyze this sample and follow up on some theories of my own. I want you and Butch to see what you can find there, possibly stir up some trouble."

"Between my smooth talking and Butch's pleasant demeanor, we'll be like ghosts." Silk replied with a sardonic smile.

Entering the lab, Quinn worked faster than he ever had before. He did not know how long Carol could keep fighting, and if there was any possibility of him discovering a cure, then he had to take it. As he studied his sample, Quinn realized that the substance was initially a glass vial, but had melted, not shattered.

As he consulted his reference journals on the subject, Quinn quickly came to the conclusion that the gas alone was not responsible for the deformation of the glass vial. There was clearly a chemical reaction; the glass was merely the vessel. The gears! Of course! Something in the puzzle box was responsible for starting the chemical reaction that dissolved the glass and released the vapor! Most likely, it was connected with the puzzle itself, each piece shifting the gears.

Anthony Quinn had exhausted his usefulness, now it was time for the Black Bat to enter the equation. As Quinn donned his costume, he began to contemplate what he knew of his new opponent. This villain was based in Chinatown, and was a master of mechanical and chemical sciences.

What type of gas he used, Quinn did not know. If there was a cure, Quinn vowed that the Black Bat would mercilessly beat it out of this villain if necessary...

...and for Carol's sake, he would make it necessary.

Dusk fell over the city; various factory and office lights came on, illuminating the smokestacks and towers of the New York Chemical Supply Company. The workday had drawn to a close, and groups of workers left the building, gossiping and chattering as they headed home. Keenly watching them from a strategic vantage point, the Black Bat was patiently waiting to make his move. This was the closest chemical supply warehouse to Chinatown, and if he was right, the criminals had most likely stolen materials from this building in order to make their weapon. As much as he wanted to leap into action and pummel the villain behind this, curing Carol was his highest priority. His plan was to wait for the majority of the work force to leave, and then, sneaking past security, he would check the inventory records. Undoubtedly, the accounting office would record any missing supplies.

Just as he was preparing to make his way inside the building, something else caught his attention. He paused, and watched as a car stopped behind the security fence. They were clever, hiding themselves in complete darkness, but the Black Bat was able to observe everything. He saw three men stealthily exiting from the black vehicle. Though he could not distinguish their facial features, based on the garb they wore and the wide swords they were carrying, the Black Bat assumed they were Chinese. He watched as they silently climbed the fence to the building.

The three Chinese henchmen had stacked themselves, standing on each other's shoulders, until they reached a second story window. The top man removed a small vial from his jacket pocket, slowly and steadily pouring the chemical contents across the top edge of the window. In a matter of seconds, the window melted, in the exact same manner that the glass vial in the puzzle box had. Climbing in, the top man lowered a rope from around his belt so that his other cohorts could climb up and join him. If he had not witnessed this ingenious break-in for himself, the Black Bat would have never believed it!

Unwittingly, they had also given the Black Bat a way in too.

Climbing down from his vantage point and entering through the open window, the Black Bat was able to hear their whispers. They were speaking Chinese, but certain words were clearly in English. Based on the henchman's difficulty with the more complex words, one man was reciting a list of chemicals aloud to the other henchmen. The Black Bat must get his hands on that list! As he followed them, he noticed the henchmen's confidence grow as they detected only minimal security in the building. The sinister trio began to walk on the metal catwalk, their relaxed shoulders revealing their carelessness. The Black Bat allowed them to pass underneath him, and then he made his move!

THUD! The Black Bat leapt and landed forcefully behind the three on the catwalk, shaking the structure and frightening the henchmen! The leader, who had the list in his hand, drew a small pistol and aimed for the Black Bat, but his draw was far too slow. With lighting quick reflexes the Black Bat had fired his .45 automatic and the henchman dropped instantly, the list still clutched in his hand.

No sooner had the .45 found its target when the other two henchmen, swords drawn, rushed him. He aimed his pistol at the henchman nearest him, but a sword strike landed on his .45, knocking it out of his hand! Another strike came, and the Black Bat had milliseconds to dodge.

Jumping back, the Black Bat bobbed and weaved as the two swordsmen launched into a furious assault. Their timing was masterful; they left him no opportunity to counterattack. As soon as one finished his strike, the other swung his sword. The Black Bat felt as if he were a piece of meat on a chopping block in a butcher shop. He had no time to draw his other pistol, and knew that his only chance was to out-think them. Their swords glanced off metal railings, the blows sending sparks like fireworks raining down on the chemical containers. Suddenly, the Black Bat heard steam rushing in a pipe overhead. It was a gamble, and a false move could mean death, but it was all he had!

Even though their attacks had appeared chaotic and random, the two fell into a pattern of assault. Their strikes were too swift to interrupt, but the pattern was exposed. If the Black Bat jumped to the side after a diagonal sword slash came at him, invariably the henchman would bring his sword downwards, as if to cleave him in half. The Black Bat was relying on this predictability.

Biding his time, the Black Bat ducked and dodged, waiting until he saw the diagonal cut he was hoping for. He listened until the sound of rushing steam overhead was close enough. Quickly he hopped to the side, and the henchman, in his predictable routine, swung his sword over his head and then downwards. Instantly, a geyser of hot steam erupted from the impact of the sword. The henchman screamed as the force of the blast struck and scalded him. The other henchman jumped away in time, but this gap was enough for the Black Bat to get away and plan a new strategy. He realized that he needed to capture him, not kill him. The Black Bat's priority was finding a cure for Carol, and he decided he'd let the police interrogate this one.

Spotting the last henchman, the Black Bat bounded for him! The henchman immediately responded with his sword, but that's what he was expecting. He caught the man's wrist and bent it outwards, leaving the rest of his body open to attack. With a hardened, practiced punch, the Black Bat threw all he had straight into the henchman's gut. With the wind knocked out of him, the henchman dropped to his knees, gasping for air. Slamming his knee into the man's face, the Black Bat flattened him. He may not have killed him, but whistling was going to be tough.

Running back to the first henchman, the Black Bat removed the list from his dead hand and proceeded to glance over it. It was indeed a list of chemicals that his boss had evidently asked him to replenish. Just the information he needed!

Finding a phone in one of the offices, the Black Bat called the hospital.

"This is Doctor Jameson," said the man over the phone. A great fatigue in his voice indicated that he was working around the clock on Carol's case.

"Doctor, I have a list of chemicals that may be related to the poisonous gas," the Black Bat said, disguising his voice.

"Who is this?" Jameson said, suddenly becoming suspicious.

"I am the Black Bat, and you need to hurry! Grab a pen and paper," he commanded.

"Ready!"

The Black Bat read the list to the doctor, and hoped against hope that it would make sense to the man. Jameson was silent for a moment and then sighed.

"While this list is a good starting point… I'm afraid it won't do much good by itself. Without knowing the proper proportions of the chemicals, I could not begin to guess what type of poison could be made with them, or even if all the chemicals are necessary," Jameson said with a great weariness in his voice.

"How is the woman?"

"She's fighting it, though I fear that she's beginning to succumb to the poison, as with the other cases. I don't know why you're doing this, but you need to know that she has only a few hours left to live."

"I'll call again."

Hanging up, the Black Bat made another call, this time to McGrath.

"McGrath here," he said in his usual irritable voice.

"I have some new evidence for you in the Carol Baldwin case," the Black Bat said, disguising his voice.

"Oh yeah? I get a hundred calls like this a day. What makes yours the real deal?"

At that moment, the Black Bat heard footsteps rapidly approaching. He turned to see the henchman with the burned face running at him with his sword overhead, cursing and screaming at him in Chinese. His rage blinded him from any common sense, and the Black Bat used this to his advantage. Grabbing a paperweight from the desk, the Black Bat hurled it at the man, knocking him senseless.

"Head to the New York Chemical Supply Company. There are three men here. Two unconscious, one dead. Look for my mark."

The Black Bat hung up the phone and stood over his newly checked-out henchman. He pressed his bat emblem into the man's seared forehead.

Dusk was slowly turning to night, and the neon signs of Chinatown flickered to life. Chinese symbols blazed against the night sky as daytime vendors began packing up their wares and counting their money. Silk and Butch had been pounding the pavement for the better portion of the day. Armed with a picture of Carol, they (along with some of McGrath's men) had been canvasing Chinatown street by street, asking virtually everyone if they had seen or heard of the woman. The duo asked every person they encountered where they could buy a puzzle box, but they received no answer. Yet every single person's eyes betrayed their fear.

Butch threw up his hands in frustration.

"I don't get it," he complained to Silk. "Why does nobody here know anything? You and I have been asking all over town if anybody's seen her. Apparently nobody saw anybody that day!"

"I don't know, Butch. Maybe your aftershave is bothering them," Silk shrugged as they walked down the street.

"I'm not sure about my aftershave, but something's stinking awful bad around here," Butch said as he began to sniff the air. He turned his head and saw a vegetable cart nearby. He examined the produce, taking a whiff of the cabbages and carrots, but could not locate that dreadful smell. "I don't get it. I thought it was maybe rotting food or something, but…"

Before he could say anything else, Lao, the old vegetable vendor, ran back to his cart from the corner teashop. With great annoyance he shouted "Why did you move my cart over that stinking sewer hole!?" Silk and Butch said they didn't. Lao waved his hand in anger and blamed it on the neighborhood children. Composing himself, he smiled at the men.

"Hello, my name is Lao. Can I persuade you…" he began.

"We're not looking for any greens, thanks," said Silk as he produced the photograph of Carol. "What we are looking for is any information about this girl here. Know anything about her?"

Lao's eyes locked onto the photo, his face showed recognition. He quickly tried to disguise it and smiled politely at the men. Anticipating his answer, Butch stepped forward, crossing his arms to appear even more imposing.

"I saw your face. I know you know something. If I were you, pal, I wouldn't make this more difficult than it needs to be," Butch said to the vendor, who cast his head down. Resigning himself, Lao spoke to the men.

"Yes, I saw her earlier today. She went into that shop," he said pointing to Shang Di's Rare Antiquities, "and came out with a small puzzle box. I tried to talk her out of it!"

"Why is that?" said Silk, resting against the vegetable stand.

"You wouldn't understand."

"Well, you may be right if you're speakin' about Butch here, but lay it on me," Silk said casually, ignoring Butch's angry glance.

"I… I… I lied to the lady. I told her that the antiques in that shop were junk. She would be buying junk! Maybe then she would not go in, but it was no use. His sorcery pulled her in," Lao said with bitterness and regret in his voice. Butch and Silk looked at each other, confused.

"Sorcery?" Butch pressed.

"I thought if I told her something that would make sense to her… maybe she would understand. Please listen to me, the man in there, Shang Di… is a sorcerer!" Lao pointed at the antique shop with his outstretched hand shaking, his pleading eyes filled with fear.

"Listen, I don't want to sound rude, pal, but… are you feeling all right?" Silk said, attempting to be tactful.

Butch cut in, "Well, at least we know that she was in this shop. That's something. Thanks, pal," Butch said brusquely as he brushed past Lao. Lao desperately grabbed onto Butch's arm, forcing him to step back.

"Tell me, did anyone in Chinatown tell you anything today?" Lao said forcefully, fearing that the two were not heeding his warning. Butch pushed Lao's hand away, and shook his head.

"She went into that shop…"

"No one spoke to you, I know I am right! It is because Shang Di is a dark magician! He holds this town in a fist of darkness! He never leaves his shop. Like a fierce tiger, he hides to ambush his victims who unknowingly come to him! If you cross him, he will send poison gas to kill you." Lao insisted, trembling as he spoke.

"Then why are you talkin' to us? Butch asked, "Aren't you afraid of him?"

"Yes, I am. But when good men do nothing, that is evil enough," Lao said defiantly.

"You are a brave man talkin' to us, but don't worry, my dukes here… these are real. They'll beat magic tricks any day!" Butch said, rolling up his sleeves, in eager anticipation of the upcoming battle.

"Please, do not do that! I beg you! Shang Di is a great fighter. He is one of the deadliest men in all of China. I see that you have great strength, but you will not survive!" Lao begged.

Butch waved off Lao's warning, and motioned for Silk to follow him into the antique shop, but they did not have to walk far. For at that moment, Shang Di stepped outside the door and studied the two men.

"Are you Mr. Shang Di?" asked Silk, his hand slowly moving towards his pistol.

"Indeed I am. And thanks to Mr. Lao, you know all there is to know about me." Lao shivered as Shang Di stepped dramatically into the center of the street. A small crowd had started to gather, but they kept their distance. There was a charge in the air, an electricity that signaled to everyone that something big was about to happen. Butch felt it, and was ready for battle. Silk was ready to pull the trigger, and Shang Di, the cause of this disturbance, was enjoying every moment of it.

"Indeed, you *all* know me," he said, motioning to the crowd. "I am Shang Di! And perhaps I have grown complacent! A man has insulted me this day, outside of my shop. While I appreciate him glorifying my reputation, Lao would no doubt attempt to lead these Americans, these outsiders, to me in hopes of apprehending me through falsifications, placing me in their hypocritical justice system, and seeing me hanged." Shang Di addressed the crowd as he spoke, a born showman. They all trembled and shook at his every word; anyone he made eye contact with immediately averted their eyes. Butch, for one, had had enough.

"For all your fancy talkin', you're nothing but a bully, pal. And I know exactly what to do with bullies like you," Butch said as he took off his jacket. "Why'd you have to hurt Carol like that anyhow? She did nothing to you!" Butch bellowed.

"Carol? Oh, the American woman. I did not like her, and those that I dislike, I remove. I am really, a very happy man because of this," Shang said, smiling. He knew that this bit of psychological warfare would cause this brute of a man to start swinging. The attack would be impressive, but ultimately imperfect, and that would aid him in battle.

As Shang expected, Butch threw a wild haymaker. Shang ducked and spun around, his foot connecting with Butch's face. The tremendous blow caught the boxer off-guard, and Butch found himself spinning through the air, landing hard on the cobblestone street.

"Did you see that?" Butch said amazed as Silk slowly helped him up.

"Hey, I just blinked and you were flat on your back," confessed Silk. "I'm here to back you up with my rod, but don't be a fool, Butch! We need to keep this guy in one piece to save Carol!"

"I fought guys with fancy footwork before in the ring, he's nothing I can't handle," Butch assured Silk as he stepped back into the fight.

Butch put up his fists, studying his opponent for the first time. He saw that Shang had an unusual fighting style, at least one Butch had never seen. Shang Di was crouched down low, his legs spread apart. His arms were poised, catlike, and his fingers curled, as if he were imitating claws. Shang's every muscle was coiled, like a cobra ready to strike. Ignoring the exotic movements, Butch was looking for a weak spot. He was an ex-boxer who could take apart just about any man who crossed his path, and Butch was never one to back down from a fight. Ever.

Butch charged in swinging, hurling jabs left and right, but he was outmatched from the very beginning. Shang used his legs unlike any opponent that Butch had fought. They moved like whips, impossible to see, but with pinpoint accuracy. His clawed hands scratched and tore at Butch's arms whenever they got close.

Silk, enraged that Shang had turned his friend into a punching bag, pointed his pistol at the dark magician. Then something incredible happened! Shang Di thrust his outstretched arm towards Silk, and suddenly, Silk dropped his gun. A feeling of paralysis crept up from his fingers to his shoulder.

"I… I can't move my arm…" Silk said in amazement. "He never even touched me!"

Butch crawled away from Shang Di, who looked at his defeated opponents with a smug satisfaction.

Shang Di yelled, "Behold the consequences for all those who oppose the mighty dark magician that is Shang Di!" His armd mimicked a miniature whirlwind, then he thrust a rigid arm towards the vegetable stand. The stand burst into an inferno! People in the crowd screamed as the dark magician rounded on them, backlit by the fire.

"Who will be next? You? You? Perhaps you?" he pointed to the crowd with his long, bejeweled finger. The crowd dispersed in fear. They all ran to hide, and no doubt, the next day many tributes would be offered to Shang Di for his mercy. Of course, he would accept some and reject others. It was good to have people afraid of you at all times. He rounded on Silk and Butch.

"You Americans sicken me. Get out; you do not belong in my domain," Shang said as he walked dramatically back to his shop.

Silk and Butch helped each other make their way to Silk's car.

"I've never fought anyone like him before," Butch said with a mixture of awe and humiliation.

"You were doing well until the fight started," Silk said as he pressed his handkerchief against Butch's bloody forehead.

"Yeah, whatever. I just wonder how the Black Bat has a chance if I don't," Butch said, "but hey, didn't he confess to us that he's the one who poisoned Carol? Let's just call McGrath!"

"The man just set a cart on fire and paralyzed my arm with his bare hands. I think he's probably got some deadlier magic in store for the cops," Silk countered. "No, the Black Bat's the only one who has a chance. C'mon, we have to report back to him with all of this."

Silk drove towards Quinn's estate, preoccupied with thoughts of Carol and the inevitable showdown with Shang Di.

Butch relayed his story of the fight with Shang Di, all the while Anthony Quinn listened intently. From the description of his movements and fighting stance, Quinn surmised that the villain, Shang Di, was a master of the tiger style of kung fu. Although Quinn was capable with his fists, and he wanted nothing more than to tear Shang Di apart for harming Carol, he knew that rushing headlong at his opponent, like Butch did, would be a risky strategy and ultimately a fatal mistake.

Then it was Silk's turn to tell his story. When Quinn heard about the feats of magic Shang Di performed, he could not help but doubt the credibility of the tale. Silk grew annoyed.

"I swear to you, he flicked his hand at me and my arm went numb! Then he set the stand on fire with his other arm! It was like magic!" Silk snapped at Quinn.

"He calls himself the dark magician... Maybe you're in over your head, boss," Butch cautioned.

Quinn walked over to Silk and studied his injured arm. "If you'll permit me," Quinn said looking at Silk. Silk nodded. He placed his hands around either side of Silk's uniform, starting at the sleeve, and slowly felt his way up.

Silk held still, not enjoying the process. Suddenly, Quinn stopped, "Aha!" he said, as he stepped back. "Silk, please remove your jacket and shirt."

"Certainly," Silk obliged, handing Quinn the clothes. Taking them and draping them across his arm, Quinn began to examine the back of Silk's arm. There was a tiny mark, easily mistaken for an imperfection of the skin, except for a minute protrusion. Carefully, deftly, he removed the object and discovered it to be a dart. It was transparent, imperceptible to one who did not possess the powers of the Black Bat.

"This explains your paralysis," Quinn said, examining the dart. "While you drew your pistol on Shang Di, possibly one of his henchmen snuck around behind you and shot this into your arm, most likely by means of a blow-dart. I'll analyze the poison on the tip."

"That's all well and good, but what about that cart?" Silk protested. "I didn't see any henchman setting fire to that! Plus, he had most of Chinatown watching him. How could he fake that?"

"That, I confess..." Quinn said, continuing his examination of Silk's jacket. He was about to admit that he had no idea, until he felt something strange on the other arm. It was a viscous substance, leaving a stain in the shape of a dollar bill on the upper sleeve of the jacket. "Silk, where did you get this stain?"

Silk looked at the stain, and was confused as to where it came from, "It sure wasn't there this morning," he remarked. Retracing his steps mentally, the only sensible conclusion he came to was that he must have picked up the stain when he leaned against the vegetable stand.

"That explains the shape of the stain..." Quinn smelled it and suddenly it all made sense. "This, gentlemen, is kerosene. The cart was rigged to burn."

"But how did..." Butch began. "Wait a minute...I remember griping about that awful smell...that was because Lao said some of the neighborhood kids must have moved the vegetable stand over the sewer grate! One of Shang Di's men must have..."

"Exactly!" Quinn agreed. "While Shang Di distracted the audience with his theatrics, one of his men climbed up through the sewer and took a match to Lao's stand! It fits with everything I've learned about him. Shang Di is a technological and biological mastermind, who also possesses keen psychological insight and the know-how to manipulate others. Also, as Butch unfortunately proved, he is a deadly opponent with his fists... But Carol comes first! I have recovered a list of chemicals that Shang uses, and after I analyze what is left on this dart tip, we can cross those chemicals off the list. The remaining chemicals should lead to what poisoned Carol! If the doctors know this, they can administer the right antidote!"

Quinn worked feverishly on the analysis. Eventually, when every compound in the poison was discovered, and each ingredient was cross referenced and sourced, he finally revealed the poison Shang Di used on Carol and the other victims. The poison gas came from an ancient recipe originating near the Karakoram Mountain range in China. A secretive, renegade sect of holy monks created the poison as a means of assassination to gain power. It was a deadly and potent weapon, seldom used today, but modern medical science is equipped to combat it. Quinn flew to the phone and relayed the information to the hospital.

"If what you're saying is true, then you have saved her life!" Doctor Jameson told Quinn. "And you're not pulling my leg? You are the Black Bat from the newspapers?"

"I am," Quinn responded.

"The police are wrong about you. You're a hero for helping this woman. Thank you." The doctor hung up.

As Quinn changed into his Black Bat suit, Silk and Butch stood by anxiously wanting to help him.

"Both of you have been seen by too many people. They'll know that you are with me, and if I fail tonight, I do not want Shang Di to use that information against you." He was insistent.

"But boss, you can't go in there alone! He'll shred you to pieces!" Butch protested loudly.

As the Black Bat loaded his .45 pistols, he turned to Silk and Butch. "I have a special job for you two, and I need McGrath and his men. The only chance for this scheme to work is if we all work together."

"But you're going in blind! And what if McGrath catches you this time?" Silk countered.

"Now that Carol's out of danger, Shang Di is the only priority now, not the safety of Anthony Quinn. Just follow my instructions," the Black Bat said, readying for the final showdown.

When Anthony Quinn became the Black Bat, he had vowed that he would use the same methods the criminals used in order to catch them. He did not wear a badge, he made his own rules. That is perhaps why, in the middle of the night, the Black Bat was breaking and entering. He positioned Silk and Butch in the car across the street, lights off and well hidden. They kept an eye out as he worked, waiting for his signal. Using a lock pick with masterful skill, he silently opened the door to Shang Di's antique store. Unlike the typical cat burglar, who would have to use a torch to see, the Black Bat was able to hunt with complete stealth. His eyes saw clearly in the dark, and right now, he was looking for a secret passage. With the knowledge that Shang Di rarely, if ever, left the store, logic dictated that he must live inside the building. Since this was a ground-level structure, all signs indicated that Shang Di's lair must be underground.

Searching the shop, Black Bat caught sight of something that made him pause. It was a box, very similar to the one that Shang had given Carol. He snatched it and hid it in one of his belt pouches, to be used as evidence later against the dark magician. However, the secret passage way remained elusive. As he investigated, a creaking door, accompanied by a sudden burst of light, came from the corner of the room, causing him to retreat to the shadows. He watched as one of Shang Di's henchmen lifted a trap door (a chair had cleverly been nailed on top of the entrance) and ascended a ladder from the dark hole. He heard Chinese voices calling after him, and the henchman stopped and responded, as if trying to shut them up.

The henchman closed the door and cautiously made his way to the cash register, feeling for familiar shapes in the dark. It was then that the Black Bat seized the opportunity! Trained fighter or not, the man was ill prepared for the force of the Black Bat's punch, which spun his head around and knocked him to the floor. Finding some rope behind the counter, Black Bat hogtied the unconscious henchman and began to rifle through his pockets, looking for anything that might give him an advantage. He found a few keys and pocketed them. He was certain that they would serve him well soon enough.

Putting his ear to the trapdoor, the Black Bat listened intently. Not only could he hear henchmen talking, but could also distinguish a rapid series of clicking noises. It came to him that the guards were playing a game of mahjongg as they talked. He also detected the aroma of alcohol and fried food. It was perfect: the guards were lax in their duties tonight, and he could take them by surprise. That creaking trapdoor would be a problem though, they would look over the moment they heard the noise. He began to make his way to the rafters overhead.

True, his plan was to signal to Butch to get McGrath when he was sure this was the place, but with this being the only entrance, he did not wish to risk the lives of the police officers. They would be caught in a bottle-neck while Shang Di's men shot them coming in.

When he reached the very top of the rafters, he positioned himself over the trapdoor. Clenching his body tightly, he leapt in the air and came crashing through the secret hatch like a human cannonball! The Black Bat had only seconds to press his advantage! With a forward shoulder roll, he headed towards the mahjongg table as the henchmen started to yell and reach for their weapons. He flipped over the table, sending game pieces flying in all directions. He had knocked over one man with his table flip, and he saw three others in the room, all in various stages of shocked surprise. He went for the man closest to him.

The Black Bat saw that the henchman was reaching for his sword, but he swiftly closed his hand around the man's wrist. He had seen enough swordplay for one night. With his free hand, the Black Bat grabbed the back of the henchman's collar and hurled him into one of the men, knocking both of them to the floor. The man underneath the table had crawled out and was about to join the fight, but a swift kick to the face from the Black Bat ended that thought.

The fourth man, who the table had missed, decided to go for his pistol rather than a sword. Seeing this, the Black Bat dove behind the other two men lying prostrate on the floor. This caused the armed henchmen to hesitate, and those few seconds bought the Black Bat enough time. Reaching for a knife from the belt of one of the downed henchman, the Black Bat hurled it with deadly accuracy, targeting the chest of the gunman. The force of the impact was so great; the henchman was knocked off his feet, his gun clattering to the ground. Grabbing the table again, the Black Bat hurled it with great force at the two henchmen on the floor, knocking them out for a very long time. A few moments later, the downed men had the mark of the Black Bat on their foreheads.

Now it was time to call in McGrath. The Black Bat had taken care of the welcoming party, and while the police were storming the underground lair, he could… then the Black Bat stopped. In all the chaos he did not pay much attention to his surroundings, but now that he had time to focus, he saw that he was in not so much a basement area, but a large underground network. Every surface was cold, poured concrete. The flickering lights above the large space indicated that this area was logically meant for storage. Shang Di had obviously used it for more sinister purposes. There were three red metal doors. Behind the door to the left, he thought he heard the sound of a man moaning in great agony. Backup or not, the Black Bat had to help him.

Using a key that he had lifted from the fallen henchman, the Black Bat opened the door to reveal a horrific sight. He saw Lao chained to a torture device. The man was bloody, frail, and suffering. A quick glance around the room confirmed that this was Shang Di's personal interrogation and punishment chamber. No doubt, the evil genius had built these hideous machines himself. Some of the devices the Black Bat recognized as historic, others were of Shang Di's own twisted invention. The device that Lao was chained to was of a particularly diabolical nature.

An iron bucket, precariously suspended from the ceiling, radiated an intense heat that could only come from molten material churning inside. It seemed that if Lao moved a fraction of an inch in any direction, it would set off a chain reaction that would dump the contents on the poor man! The Black Bat noticed whip and bruise marks covering Lao's exposed flesh. Shang Di had forced Lao to remain motionless below the iron bucket while he savagely beat him.

"Do not be alarmed; I will not hurt you," he assured Lao as he pulled out his twin .45s and aimed for the chains holding Lao. Firing four expertly placed shots, the bullets cut through the chains, but Lao was unable to move, the iron bucket still a threat. The Black Bat studied the rigging and with great care and lightning quick calculations, shot away at the chains that would tip the molten material away from Lao and himself.

His idea worked, and the bucket spewed its contents over the empty torture machines, burning them to cinders. The Black Bat carried Lao out of the torture chamber and into the hallway. Lao was impressed when he saw the four unmoving henchmen.

"You must be a great fighter!" he exclaimed weakly.

"I need your help," the Black Bat said, producing the puzzle box he confiscated from Shang Di's store. Lao instantly recognized it and a bead of sweat appeared on his forehead. "Relax, Mr. Lao, I figured out how these work. Shang Di has created a mechanism that releases a deadly gas, but he has a failsafe: a specific method of moving the pieces to solve the puzzle. Any other way is murder, and that is what his sick mind is counting on. Take this to the police to use as evidence against him; there should be several squad cars arriving soon."

Shaking, Lao took the box with great care, understanding the importance of his task. The Black Bat looked to the other rooms, and then turned back to Lao.

"Do you know what is behind these doors?" he enquired.

"That room is where he tests his illusions and magic, and the other room is where his workshop is. It's where he makes terrible things like this box!"

Thanking him, the Black Bat started towards the room of illusion, but Lao stopped him.

"Wait, in there I heard a ferocious growling! Be careful, for I fear he keeps a live animal there."

Before the Black Bat could say anything else to Lao, the door to the workshop opened, and Shang Di stepped out! The Black Bat locked eyes with the dark magician for the first time, and though he wanted to leap at him, he knew (thanks to Butch) that this strategy was suicide. Shang Di, at first startled by the Black Bat's appearance, regained his calm.

"Get out of here!" the Black Bat ordered Lao, who began to hurriedly ascend the ladder. The Black Bat rounded back on Shang Di. "I've sent him to turn over your poisoned boxes as evidence. The police will now know how those people died."

"I have disappeared before, I shall do so again. Who are you?" Shang Di demanded of the Black Bat. A lesser man would have cowered before the dark magician's intensity, but the Black Bat remained unmoved.

"I am the Black Bat."

"Oh yes, I have heard of you, of course. So you are the man responsible for disrupting my chemical supply line," Shang Di said coolly. "I know you by reputation of course, and I have heard about the infamous mark that you have branded my loyal servants with." Shang Di said, tapping his forehead.

"I know you by reputation as well. You are Shang Di, a charlatan and a madman. You make devices of evil and kill innocent people for pleasure! Your "loyal servants" are nothing but a bunch of thugs that enjoy spreading fear among decent citizens. It ends tonight," the Black Bat said, taking steps closer to Shang Di. He observed the man for any sign that he was about to fight, but so far there were no visible giveaways.

"My motive was to test my devices, and as you can see, they've been very successful. Not to mention that I enjoy the tributes that the neighborhood gives me so that I may spare them," Shang Di said calmly. "You and I both know that fear is an effective motivator, and if some tourists or other fools wander into my shop, it gives me the opportunity to test my devices." The

"You must be a great fighter."

Black Bat began to advance. Shang Di tensed his muscles, his control so precise that it went unnoticed. Though the Black Bat could not see it, the dark magician was like a coiled snake, waiting for its chance.

Trying to flank him, the Black Bat jumped to the side, but Shang Di was too fast. Whipping his leg around in a roundhouse kick, he clobbered the Black Bat on the side of his head. He immediately followed this up with a backward kick that caught the Black Bat square in the chest. Had the Black Bat not tensed and released his muscles with perfect timing, it would have been curtains for him, his broken, jagged ribs impaling his heart!

Working through his pain, the Black Bat threw a left cross into Shang Di's face. Though not as stylish as the dark magician's attacks, it did the job. The fight could have easily continued, but the punch sent Shang Di running.

"Cowards always run," thought the Black Bat.

The Black Bat knew that he was being lead into a trap, and knowing the technical genius that this villain possessed, it would result in certain death. But he had to take that chance, Shang Di could not escape!

The Black Bat chased after Shang Di. He saw the dark magician run into the room of illusion and slam the door behind him. Using his momentum, the Black Bat shoulder rushed and smashed down the door. No sooner did he do that, then he stopped dead in his tracks. His every muscle froze as he stared at the new danger standing in front of him: the Black Bat was face-to-face with a tiger!

As it snarled at him, the Black Bat weighed his options. Should he try to pacify or frighten away this ferocious beast? Without warning, he felt a strange sensation in his left leg. Then his right! He realized that he was being struck with the same paralyzing darts as Silk had been. He felt a sting in his left arm. The Black Bat had just enough energy and feeling left in his legs to throw himself to his right side, shielding his right arm from a dart. Though he felt tremendous pain landing on the concrete floor, at least he could still use his right hand. Pulling out his .45, he realized his only chance of surviving the encounter was to shoot at the tiger to frighten it away. As he looked up at the jungle cat, the Black Bat saw that his perspective was distorted. The animal, which had appeared incredibly real moments before, was only a moving picture projected onto a well-hidden screen. Behind the screen was a phonograph, emitting the ear-piercing sounds of the dreaded tiger.

"Thank you for testing my latest illusion! You were standing at exactly the right place at the right moment! The Technicolor film was expensive, but your reaction was priceless! Even the mighty Black Bat cowers before the magic of Shang Di!"

He heard Shang Di's laugh. A deep, hearty laugh born out of malice and madness. He stood over the Black Bat, gloating. His position was such that the Black Bat, despite his best efforts, could not reach around to use his gun. Shang Di watched him struggle and swiftly kicked the gun out of his hand.

"The weapon of a weak man," Shang Di admonished, "in America, the gun is the great equalizer. You do not have to be a warrior to kill."

"Interesting sentiment coming from a man who shoots poisoned darts at his opponent," the Black Bat countered. His limbs were still paralyzed, but if he could keep Shang talking, he might have a chance.

"You have dispatched my best men, and I have come to regard you as a worthy opponent, Black Bat. Your death will make this city tremble at the mere mention of my name, and for that I thank you." Shang said as he started to slip a glove over his hand. They were black leather gloves, but each finger had a razor-like curved nail fitted to the tip. Clearly when he fought Butch it was all a show of might meant for the spectators. Now, in his private chambers with no witnesses, Shang Di was preparing for the kill! The Black Bat had to act fast, and with his limbs still numb, could only strike at one target: the dark magician's ego.

"Shang Di, you are a brilliant man! Your poison box, your fire demonstration, your projection, they were the products of a man with infinite possibilities... Why turn to evil?" the Black Bat said desperately, hoping that this would buy him more time. Already he was starting to feel his fingers and toes.

"What started out as simple acts of fooling people soon became my obsession. I now had power over people, so I used it. It grew and grew, my name feared throughout China. My father, a lowly gangster, taught me the tiger style of kung fu." Shang Di related the story with great pride. It was working...the Black Bat could move his hands and feet again, just a minute more...

"Now that I think of it, Shang Di, maybe you're not a genius after all," the Black Bat said. It was a desperate gamble. If Shang had been like some other hoods the Black Bat fought, he would have killed him on the spot. He was counting on a combination of Shang's vanity and scientific curiosity.

"Explain yourself!" Shang demanded, his face contorting with rage. It worked!

"To begin with, your illusions and schemes are clever, yet I figured them all out from the comfort of my home, seeing through your sleight-of-hand. Your poison box was ineffective and failed to kill its target. Had you not cheated, using darts, the American would have shot you dead tonight during your fight, and your last trick fell flat the moment I moved. You have glimpses of glory, but they all fall short," the Black Bat said. He had enough strength now, and rose up to face Shang Di, "and lastly, you have made an enemy of me... not a genius move."

Shang Di did not waste another word and launched into a violent onslaught! Listening closely to Butch's description of his fight, the Black Bat had a good idea of how Shang Di would fight. Shang started with a flying kick aimed at the Black Bat's head, but he sidestepped, caught the dark magician by the robe, and hurled him through the screen that projected the image of the tiger.

Recovering quickly, Shang Di changed his tactics and switched to his claw hands. He slashed and swiped at the Black Bat, targeting vulnerable areas. The poison, though mostly neutralized, did slow the Black Bat down a bit. He was able to block and occasionally counter attack, but the vicious swipes and slashes from Shang Di were taking their toll. Blood was flowing from the tears in his costume.

Under normal circumstances, the Black Bat would have been able to stand his ground against Shang Di, even with the claws, but this was not to be. Shang Di was moving faster, and he knew the layout of the whole area. Suddenly, an idea came to the Black Bat, and he seized the opportunity.

Interrupting one of Shang's kicking combinations, the Black Bat reached around the back of Shang's head and grasped his queue. With all his might, the Black Bat pulled and threw Shang Di over his shoulder. Shang went crashing against the opposite wall while the Black Bat had time to recover his pistol lying nearby. Drawing on Shang Di, the two faced each other.

"You think you can come to my domain and defeat me? I will tear you apart and all that oppose me! My legend will live on!" Shang screamed.

The Black Bat suddenly realized: "I can't kill him, I have to expose him for the fraud that he is. The people of Chinatown need to see him, the great Shang Di, humiliated," he thought as he adjusted his aim away from the dark magician's heart.

He fired. Shang Di avoided the Black Bat's bullet by diving behind a row of crates.

This particular chamber resembled a warehouse with crates stacked high everywhere, and Shang Di could be anywhere! The Black Bat was weak from losing blood, and he needed to capture Shang Di fast. The secret to Shang Di's success was his ability to dazzle and fool the eye. That was his whole life. But what if he could not see?

With expert precision, the Black Bat blasted away at the various light sources in the room until it was plunged into complete darkness. He had run out of bullets, but knew with this advantage, victory could still be achieved. Shang Di stumbled around in the shadows. He was lost and confused. The Black Bat easily snuck up behind him and growled.

"Welcome to *my* domain, Shang Di!"

He side-stepped as Shang Di pounced. Then the Black Bat struck hard! Each attack met its mark with the strength summoned by pure rage! His body became a whirlwind of fists, feet, knees, and elbows, slamming into Shang Di. The mighty magician was reduced to a beaten down thug. Shang Di would feebly attempt to counter attack, but the Black Bat repelled each effort. With each successive blow, he thought of Carol, picturing his life without her. The thought was unbearable, and he needed Shang Di to feel the same pain.

The red lights of police cars competed with the neon lights of Chinatown. A squad of police officers waited outside Shang Di's shop. McGrath paced outside as a young police officer ran up to him with a report.

"Well?" demanded McGrath.

"The two that Black Bat left in the chemical supply house aren't talking. They refuse to say anything!" the officer said.

"Sounds like the Black Bat was stealing from the depot, and those poor workers tried to stop him," McGrath said, as he attempted to distort facts to fit his theory. "Then he called us and says he was attacked in order to throw us off the scent!"

"But the men weren't identified as workers and they were carrying swords!" the confused officer replied.

"Listen kid, I've been on the force since you were a baby! The Black Bat will do anything to get away! I know how he thinks, and tonight, I'll be the one to catch him…" McGrath said eyeing the antique store.

Silk and Butch watched from a distance in the getaway car. Silk kept the engine running, and with each passing second, grew more nervous.

"How do you think the boss is holding up in there?" Silk asked, his eyes unmoving from the antique store door.

"He'd be doing better with me there. Some bodyguard I am," Butch said, downcast.

"Look!" Silk pointed.

The Black Bat emerged, bloody and weak, but victorious. All guns were cocked and ready. He held Shang Di in front of him by the scruff of his neck. Chinatown's citizens cautiously trickled out to the street, amazed that Shang Di could be touched, let alone defeated.

"I am turning Shang Di, the 'dark magician' over to the police. You have nothing to fear anymore, he will be going to prison for a very long time and cannot harm you anymore!" The Black Bat spoke to the crowd. They eagerly looked at each other, could it be true?

Shang Di, clearly the loser of the fight, murmured feebly, "Officers, this... this madman attacked me in my store and accused me of terrible things! I sell antiques, I have done nothing wrong!" Even when all was lost, he was still fighting. McGrath could only see red where the Black Bat was concerned. The police marched towards them, guns raised. The Black Bat was trapped!

"Wait!" a voice called. Everyone turned to see Lao staggering towards Shang Di. In his hands he held the puzzle box that the Black Bat had given him. McGrath, curious to see how this would play out, held up his hand, stopping his men.

Handing the box to Shang Di, Lao then pointed to it.

"I am sure that you can explain away what goes on in your filthy lair, but if you are truly innocent of the puzzle box murders, then you should solve this one and no harm will come to you," Lao said with keen determination in his eyes.

"You must be joking. I can barely stand!" Shang Di protested.

"But you are such a clever man; this should be child's play for you. If no poison is released, consider yourself innocent," Lao demanded, looking at the gathering crowd and police officers.

"We don't have time for..." McGrath said, his annoyance growing.

"Wait!" Shang Di held up a hand, stopping McGrath's advance. The Black Bat released his grip as the dark magician stared down at his deadly invention. "I will accept this fool's challenge and solve this simple puzzle."

Despite his condition, Shang Di masterfully moved the pieces around the box. He finished in a few moments, and held up the box for all to see.

Click!

Lao grabbed the Black Bat out of harm's way, forcing him to run with him as a concentrated blast of the green vapor engulfed Shang Di! It was certain death, as the thick poison invaded his lungs. McGrath watched in horror as the dark magician shook violently, his skin turning a pasty white, his lips blue. The crowd gasped in disbelief.

The deadly vapor covered the escape of the Black Bat perfectly, since all eyes were focused on Shang Di. Lao assisted him to the getaway car, Butch had run ahead and put the Black Bat's arm over his shoulder.

The Black Bat stared quizzically, "How...Shang Di easily solved the puzzle. Why did it kill him?"

"You know of course, it is bad luck to solve a puzzle that has already been started! I moved a few pieces around beforehand, so the puzzle was not at its starting point." Lao said proudly.

"You may be the clever magician here, Lao," the Black Bat said, smiling weakly.

Thanking Lao, Silk drove the Black Bat off into the night. For the first time, the Black Bat felt the enormity of the evening. His every muscle ached, and he had lost plenty of blood. Despite his fatigue, he knew that he must be ever vigilant… the fight for justice never ends.

"I've brought you some clothes to change into," Butch said, handing him a wrapped parcel. "But we gotta fix you up, Mr. Quinn. You got to get some rest, heaven knows I do!"

The Black Bat changed back to Anthony Quinn as he saw the dawn cresting over the horizon. He watched as Chinatown, freed from the evil grip of Shang Di, begin a new day.

"There's a stop we need to make first," Quinn said.

The first thing that she heard was the sound of her boss talking to another man.

"If the Black Bat hadn't called us, this would be a different story," the other voice said.

"Will she be all right?" her boss asked.

"I'd give her a few days of rest and relaxation, then she should be able to return to her normal life."

"Doctor, the Black Bat may have helped, but you were the one who created the antidote to save her," Quinn said modestly.

"It looks like she is coming to, I'll leave you now," the doctor said, exiting the room.

Carol's eyes opened, and for a few moments her surroundings were a blur.

The last thing she remembered was a horrible green vapor overwhelming her, but now she saw that she was in a much different location. She lay in a hospital bed, and as she focused, Carol saw the sunlight streaming in on the faces of the three men standing over her.

Silk Kirby, with his cap in his hands, a smile forming on his worried face.

Butch O'Leary, leaning over her, a look of relief washing over him.

And Anthony Quinn, who despite his reserved manner, was beaming.

He stared at Carol. There were so many things he wished to tell her. Most of all, Quinn desired to tell her that she never looked more beautiful to him than at that moment… but he could not. Even in a moment of joy such as this, he had to remain on guard, because Anthony Quinn was blind to the rest of the world. Despite not being able to say this, he knew that Carol understood everything he felt.

"Hello…Butch…Silk… Thank you for saving my life," Carol said; the first words she'd spoken since the attack.

"Actually, you saved yourself when you threw that box out the window. I suppose you'll need a new window now," Silk said shyly with a modest shrug.

"We all knew you'd pull through, Carol. You're as tough as me!" Butch chimed in, puffing out his chest.

"Butch, you look like you need to trade places with me! I'm glad I woke up, because clearly I can't leave the three of you alone!" Carol said as she started to sit up. She found the effort surprisingly taxing. She slowly reclined back onto her pillow.

"We managed to do all right by ourselves. I thought it might make you feel better to know that the Black Bat dealt with the man who poisoned you," Quinn said stepping forward.

"Oh yes… that awful man. I suppose he's in jail now?" she asked.

"No, he's where he belongs. A little vegetable vendor named Lao saw to that," Quinn said with a sardonic smile.

"Tony!" Carol said with a start. The other three immediately went on alert.

"I don't have a present for your birthday!" Carol exclaimed.

The End

WRITING PULPS

What I like most about pulps is the fact that the heroes are dark and mysterious. There was a genuine edge to these heroes, but it was not forced like it is with today's comic book heroes. Companies attach the words "dark" and "gritty" to try to drum up interest in their characters. Pulp heroes did not need to do this; it simply went without saying that these stories would feature ruthless heroes. Yet despite this, the stories still had more genuine adventure to them than many current comic books, which, in my opinion, are heavy with atmosphere and light on action. Adventure was the keyword I locked onto when I began to give serious thought to writing pulps... I wanted to be taken on a journey, fight an exotic villain, and have a fun time along the way (while looking like a dark, brooding tough guy).

I had never written a Black Bat story, or any pulp for that matter. Looking at the various characters to write for, there was something about the Black Bat that appealed to me. Of course, inevitably one compares him to Batman, so I thought about the differences between the two characters. I decided, if I was going to be successful, that I had to get to know Anthony Quinn. They say that character is revealed under pressure, so the first thing I thought of was putting someone that Quinn loved in danger, and of course Carol was the logical choice.

Their relationship had fascinated me when I read about them. Though she seemed understanding of the situation, I put myself in Quinn's place. When I began to think of what he goes through, the burden of his secret identity, how limiting his life is, I felt that I had to touch upon that. Quinn needs the Black Bat to save Carol, yet he is unable to express himself because of his dual identity. I felt the dilemma was an interesting one, considering that Carol felt the same way about him. Of course, with Carol on the edge of death, *all* of Quinn's emotions would come to the forefront. This showdown would have to be epic, but in order for that to happen, I needed a villain...

Enter Shang Di, a bad guy I hope you all wanted dead. I wanted him to suggest the supernatural without being mystical himself. When I was a child, I watched a few magic shows with famous magicians on television and somehow that memory came to the forefront and influenced my creation of this man. I wanted him to have a massive intellect, but also be physically able, thus the inclusion of tiger style kung fu. Dragons seemed too cliched to me, but I needed to keep this character somewhat grounded in reality. I decided that a tiger would be a fitting motif for him. I suppose that if I had to describe what my aim was with this character, he would be Fu Manchu meets Dracula.

Of course we know that the Black Bat will save Carol and defeat the dark magician, but the story needed more. With Chinatown under his evil power, I felt the only way for Shang Di to be vanquished once and for all was by the community itself rising up against him. Yes, the Black Bat needed to pummel him into submission, but I did not want to portray an entire community as helpless. Lao, a throwaway character that was only meant to provide some exposition earlier in the story, kept popping up. Not only had I frightened him, but I had set his cart on fire and tortured him!

Feeling guilty, I thought, "Well...the Black Bat can give him the evidence to give to McGrath..." But let's be honest, Lao needed a revenge of his own, the poor man suffered enough! Considering that I wanted to showcase Shang Di and the Black Bat's intelligence in this story, I thought it would be amusing to have the dark magician defeated not only by his own gadget, but by a simple trick.

Silk and Butch were a fun duo to write, and I tried to replicate the clever, fast-talk that was batted back and forth through gangster dramas (where everybody seemed much wittier than they are today). However, since the stakes were incredibly high, I did not want to push the comedy, but rather give the audience a slight break from time to time.

Overall, this story was a delightful challenge to write. I wanted to keep the writing style dated, but have the whole story exciting no matter in what era it is read. That is, I think, why the pulp heroes have survived. They are still thrilling!

ERIK FRANKLIN - is a writer/actor/filmmaker based in Seattle. Recently graduating with honors from the Art Institute of Seattle in film production, he is the co-President of Franklin-Husser Entertainment LLC. He is working on two upcoming feature films for his company: A dinosaur action film "Revenge of the Lost" and the martial arts comedy "3 Morons Fighting Ninja". You can give the company page a "Like" at: https://www.facebook.com/pages/Franklin-Husser-Entertainment-LLC/290795021042906.

Drawn to pulp fiction through his love of history, literature, and Americana, he is grateful for Airship 27 Productions giving him the opportunity to write his first story. He looks forward to writing more adventures!